MW01245737

CANADIAN

DESIRES

CANADIAN DESIRES

TINA HULLER

Copyright © 2005 by Tina Huller.

Library of Congress Number: 2005903150
ISBN :   Softcover   1-4134-9229-0

All rights reserved. No part of this book may be reproduced
or transmitted in any form or by any means, electronic or
mechanical, including photocopying, recording, or by any
information storage and retrieval system, without permission
in writing from the copyright owner.

This is a work of fiction. Names, characters, places and
incidents either are the product of the author's imagination
or are used fictitiously, and any resemblance to any actual
persons, living or dead, events, or locales is entirely
coincidental.

This book was printed in the United States of America.

To order additional copies of this book, contact:
Xlibris Corporation
1-888-795-4274
www.Xlibris.com
Orders@Xlibris.com
26021

Danger beyond the border . . .

Cassie Garrette was running away from one bad relationship when she encountered her new boss. The secretive but seductive charm of the man pushed her into a world of business intrigue. When his father dies unexpectedly, he whisks Cassie across the U.S. border into Canada. In a large town called Canmore, Cassie finds herself pursued by two evils—one, a menacing presence from her past; the other, a dark tunnel of buried treasures.

Kelley McGillis, her charming new boss, hires Cassie for her own protection—from what and why, she doesn't know. Keeping her close, however, proves to be more of a chore than he expected. Once his heart interferes, there is no escape. Through a journey of trials and terror, their attraction will grow and ultimately be tested.

In loving memory of my Aunt Leona,
from whom I learned and enjoyed
a love of books.

A heartfelt thank you to all my friends
who helped me achieve success.
To you, April, Amy, and Janet.

In deep appreciation of my parents, thank
you for supporting me emotionally
and mentally, despite my silliness.

To the people of Banff, I say thank you for
making my vacation an exciting and
educational one.

To the town of Canmore, although I didn't
get to stay long enough to visit, I could
imagine what it would be like to live
there.

PROLOGUE

As the stroke of midnight comes, no one is ever really aware—or understands—the evil forces that are at work. The power to hate, kill, or even to become a pawn in some deadly game of chase can be extremely high. One person's will to live becomes another's fate to die. As destiny comes into play on this particular night, the shadows are everywhere. On the final stroke of midnight, a faint new shadow runs through a dimly lit garden.

The shapely figure is exhausted from running but refuses to give up. In the background, footsteps can be heard coming closer. So intent on escaping certain death, the terrified form runs on, unaware of what's around the next corner. Taking only a few seconds for a backward glance over its shoulder, the figure moves around the next corner but, missing the next step, screams in realization that there is nowhere to step, stopping any further escape. As the body hits the cement below, life is wiped out.

Out of the darkness, the attacker looms over the fallen victim, draws his revolver, fires two shots, and disappears into the dark night. The job is finished.

CHAPTER I

The deceptively simple lines in the evening paper entitled "Tycoon Marries Wealthy Client's Daughter" could only have climaxed a day of humid heat, raging thunderstorms, and foggy gloom. A pair of red-rimmed hazel eyes passes over the news item about the body of a woman discovered at the Clawson Family Conservatory and focuses miserably again on the wedding announcement.

Kent! Her fiancé!

The girl in the snapshot that accompanied the article should have been her, Cassie Garrett, not the voluptuous brunette with the catlike eyes hanging on to Kent's arm. Feeling violated, she tried to remember the times before Kent had come into her life.

Cassie had been brought up in the best schools and was well versed in the importance of social status. Her parents had made sure that she lacked for nothing. Even when the money was tight, nothing would be too good for their only daughter. Her father would work all day in a factory and deliver newspapers at night; her mother was the happy homemaker, as well as the town seamstress and interior decorator. They made sure that every penny saved would ensure their daughter's rise in prominence. Even if they didn't fit in, she would. Although at times Cassie had been rebellious and tried to run away from their rigid standards, she eventually gave up because of their powerful determination, love, and support. By the time Cassie had left for college, she was well aware of the sacrifices they had made for her, because within days after her college graduation, she had landed the only position open at one of the biggest companies in the city. Wallace and Son Investments was one of the hardest places to get a job. If it hadn't been for her perfect school records and her so-called good looks, she probably wouldn't have been accepted.

She had congratulated herself for adhering to her parents' restrictions and focusing on her studies rather than pursuing the newest man on campus. Her primary goal would be her career, and her love life would be nonexistent for a while. The work was challenging but rewarding too. She earned the respect and admiration of her coworkers because of her unwillingness to pawn off her own research onto someone else. In addition, she was more than happy to help anyone else in a tight situation but refused to take any credit for the results. Her self-confidence and self-reliance, not to mention physical beauty, won her the attention of anyone she associated with, including the younger Wallace, Kent Wallace Jr. Within days of his close, scrutinizing stare, Cassie was being ushered into the president's office.

If it hadn't been for him, Cassie wouldn't have succeeded to her present position for a good two or three years—long enough to climb the corporate ladder. After moving into the executive office, it took only a week for Kent Jr. to begin his relentless pursuit of her. Sometimes his obsession with her caused Cassie to be a little uneasy. She could remember clearly how Kent would pick her up in the evening and take her to the most expensive restaurant in town. After dinner, he would take her dancing and then sit in a dimly lit corner of the lounge, holding her hand. He would stare into her eyes with his vivid blue eyes, and she would melt every time. They were like clear summer days without any clouds, which caused Cassie to become lost in the endless depth. When he did finally speak, she had to shake herself back to reality.

With the ash blonde hair, clear skin, firm chin, and medium build, he was no Mr. Muscle, but on the other hand, he wasn't all flab. Cassie would get a kick out of watching him when something didn't work his way. He had a small twitch to his firm mouth that made him look like a small child pouting because his mother wouldn't let him have the cookie. In the end, it was his charm and wit that had attracted her to him.

After six months of being what the tabloids were calling "a romance for the ages," he had finally proposed. They had been sitting in a restaurant when Kent decided to take her for a drive. Within five miles of the restaurant was a park with a beautiful fountain. He pulled off the main drive, stopped the car, and turned to look at her. Taking her hand in his, he smiled charmingly and said, "Darling, I think it's about time we discussed our future. I believe you know how I feel about you, and I believe that feeling is mutual." Taking a deep breath, he continued, "What I am trying to say is . . . well . . . will you marry me?" That was the question she had been waiting for, but one that was never answered. Although she had smiled and kissed him passionately as her answer, within the next few weeks, he had wooed, courted, and married another woman.

Closing her eyes against the pain in her heart, she thought to herself, "If that's the way he wants it, fine. But I will not be here when he gets back from his honeymoon."

Glancing around the room, she checked her watch. "Past dinnertime," she mumbled as she reached for her coat and pulled it on. "Well, I refuse to think about the past any longer. As of this moment, I have to think of my future and myself. I will just take a walk and clear my head," she told herself sharply. "Maybe I will meet some tall, dark, and handsome stranger." Cassie was not one to believe in fairytales, but what else did she have left to dream about?

Just as she was about to leave the apartment, the phone rang. She wondered whether or not to answer it. Kent was on his honeymoon, wasn't he? Well, she was not going to risk it. Without a backward glance, she walked out, closing the door behind her. Outside, in the cool night air, her tension seemed to ease. With each step she sensed a sudden feeling of loneliness. She and Kent had walked together a lot. "Oh . . . quit torturing yourself," she scolded. "If you are going to get over him, you are going to have to find a new pastime."

All at once, her feet changed course, and she found herself standing in front of the Clawson Family Conservatory. It was a long building with windows all the way around. The flowers, vines, and shrubs that lined the walls inside were always cut to perfection, and they smelled so good that all her troubles seemed to fade every time she went inside.

As soon as she walked inside, however, the memories came back. This had been their favorite place to go. She had picked out her wedding bouquet here. God, why couldn't she stop thinking about him? It was bad enough he had married someone else and left her out in the cold, but to keep dwelling on the matter was not going to make her feel any better. Taking a deep breath, she started walking faster. Pacing herself, she came around a corner too fast and ran headlong into someone who was definitely in a hurry himself. She could tell it was a man by the size and the impact he had on her.

With a loud thump, Cassie landed on the floor. Startled beyond belief, she didn't move for a moment. From above her came a deep voice, "You should watch where you are going. You could hurt someone at that rate. You're very lucky I wasn't a small child." That's it! She wasn't taking it anymore . . . not from any man. But she was unprepared for the effect this man would have on her.

As soon as Cassie had jumped to her feet and was prepared to lash out at the stranger, she reeled backward as if her feet were going to give way underneath her. If the strong arm hadn't wrapped itself around her, she would have fallen. "Thank you," she half muttered in haste, "I guess I got more wind knocked out of me than I thought," she spoke as harshly as she could to express her bruised ego. After regaining her composure to stand on her own, Cassie looked up to see not doubt but concern for her falling. Why shouldn't he be concerned? It was his running into her that made her fall.

Even though her tone didn't seem to affect him, his attitude had definitely changed, because his next remark was, "I hope I didn't hurt you. Can you stand on your own now, or shall I carry you out of here?"

Her reply came out a little more quickly than she had wanted. "I'm fine. And yes, I can stand on my own. Get your hand off of my arm!" For a moment, all he did was stare at her. Until she got control of herself, he remained completely still.

He began to smile, which seemed to irritate her even more. Instead of calming her down, she reverberated, "What is so funny? Does not watching where you are going and running into people make you feel better about yourself?"

"Excuse me, but I could have sworn you ran into me," he returned angrily. "Anyway, it doesn't matter now. I only hope that I didn't knock too much wind out of you, because you look way too small as it is."

Cassie was, for a brief moment, unable to speak. She knew she was not big by any means. Being only five feet two inches and only one hundred ten pounds, her looks made up for her size, because very few people had noticed her size before. She was a medium blonde with the oddest hazel eyes that seemed to warrant any man's attention.

When she tried to respond, he stopped her by saying, "Let me apologize by buying you dinner, if you haven't already eaten. After all, it is getting late, and you should not be walking alone at night. It's too dangerous, because there was a murder here recently."

Cassie had lost track of time, and the recollection of reading about the murder caused her to shiver. She knew she should refuse but found herself wanting companionship. Despite her inner feelings, she knew he was right about her walking alone at night. "What the hell!" she thought to herself, "as long as it's a free meal and I won't have to cook." She only hoped he didn't dig too much; she had been hurt enough for one evening. She conceded, "All right, as long as you're buying. I left my wallet at home."

"You certainly don't like being put on the spot, do you? How was I supposed to know you didn't have any money on you? I hope you are famished, because I treat big when I take someone out," he said on a very intense note.

While walking to the restaurant, Cassie could see that her head only came to his chest. God, why did he have to be so tall? She knew she wouldn't be able to outrun him. He looked in too good a shape. She could easily tell that he was well over six feet and must lift weights. Realizing that she had been too quiet and that he was smiling, she said, "I don't believe you mentioned where we are going. Would you be so kind as to tell me where you are kidnapping me? Or is that supposed to be a surprise? Oh, by the way, you did not tell me your name."

"My name is McGillis, Kelley McGillis, and no, the restaurant is not a surprise. If you remember where you are, there is only one restaurant on this block." Struck dumb for a moment, Cassie finally remembered. The restaurant was a very expensive seafood place that was not for casual dress. Deciding she wasn't dressed appropriately, she stopped in her tracks. She was not going to be humiliated in a restaurant where she and Kent used to go. Perfect. Why did she have to think about him at that particular moment? Didn't she want to find some tall, dark, and handsome stranger?

By the time he noticed that she had stopped walking, he was already four steps ahead of her. He turned and eyed her suspiciously and then moved in front of her. He stood where she could take all of him in. Suddenly, she became nauseous and breathless and wished she could retreat. Cassie backed up a step before he caught her arm in a tight hold. "I thought you agreed to have dinner with me. Why all of a sudden are you changing your mind? Is there someone there you don't want to see? Because if there is, I will be glad to take you elsewhere," he told her sarcastically.

"No. There is no one there," she lied. "I just remembered I left something on at home. I don't want to go home to a burned apartment, do I?"

"Of course not. Why don't I drive you home and we can just go to dinner from there?" That was not what she had in mind, but his tone suggested he knew what she's doing. He was not letting her off the hook so easily. For the life of her, Cassie could not figure out why she was so important to him.

When she hesitated with her reply, he moved closer to her. "What are you afraid of? I am not going to attack you, although the thought had occurred to me. You are a very beautiful woman."

Cassie was caught off guard; she couldn't say anything. When she found her voice, she meekly said, "I think once I get home, I should fix something there. There would be no sense in leaving again. Besides, it's getting late, and I have to get an early start tomorrow."

"I'm sorry, but you are not getting out of dinner so easily. You already promised, and that's the way it stays even if I have to carry you out. I don't know why you are so paranoid, but I usually keep my word. I wonder if you take your own word seriously. Do you?"

"Of course I do. It's just that . . ."

"Oh no, you won't come up with any excuse good enough to suit me. So don't even try. Now start walking."

The nerve of him! No one should be able to talk to her that way. In the future she would see that no one would, especially him. Although she thought she would never likely see him again, there seemed to be something disturbing about him. Walking beside him didn't help her startled nerves any—being bruised twice is terrifying. She wondered what else would happen this night. She wouldn't wait to find out.

They walked the rest of the way in silence. When they reached the restaurant, Cassie was determined to find out what he wanted and then get up and leave without giving him any satisfaction. She would excuse herself to use the bathroom and then head out the door instead. What a shock and disappointment that would be to Mr. McGillis. It would serve him right for his forcing her to have dinner with him after she had changed her mind. She knew she could not tell him the real reason she couldn't dine with him.

They entered the restaurant without looking at each other, but once seated, he made sure that he was facing her. Cassie found herself staring into his aquamarine eyes. When she realized she was staring, she quickly averted her eyes to the print on the tablecloth. He was probably already laughing at her from behind those unique green eyes. They were so hypnotic—she could have gotten lost in dreamland looking into them. But she could not think about that now. She knew he would be watching her, so walking out wouldn't work. There had to be a better way.

He was looking at her oddly when he finally spoke. "You are a very quiet person, aren't you?"

Cassie didn't know quite how to respond and could have cursed herself. "I suppose so. I usually spend time at home or with my friends," she said, hoping he got the message.

He didn't. "Well, in time I hope you will consider me a friend."

"I doubt it."

"Don't be too sure of yourself. You may find I am real easy to get along with. Of course you are probably wondering why I invited you here."

The thought had occurred to her, but Cassie was just going to sit back and let him talk which seemed to annoy him. He expected her to answer him.

·ious about what I am going to say, or ·st?" he said as emotionless as possible. ·enough. What was he trying to pull on ·oman did he think she was anyway? This ·1 the tables on him. But before Cassie could say anything at all, the waiter approached the table and asked, "Would you like to order now, or do you need a few more minutes?" As the waiter looked from one to the other, it became apparent to him that he should have given them a little more time. "Would you care to have something from the bar? Our special tonight is a cabaret white wine. I highly recommend it," he said as if to dispel the tense atmosphere.

"Why not," Kelley said with a smile, "after all, I think we could both use it. Don't you agree?"

How could she refuse? Maybe if she made herself drunk, he would be forced to take her home. Besides, the tension was getting to her too. Then again, she didn't want him knowing where she lives. "Sure. And," she looked at the waiter, "bring me a dry martini too."

Both men looked quizzically at her, and then the waiter said, "As you wish." After he left, she turned her attention back to her unexpected companion and his look of disgust. Now, she thought, things could start going her way for a change.

"You do know that mixing drinks is bad for you, don't you? Or are you trying to get drunk? I would advise against it, because it won't help your situation." Noticing the confused look on her face, he continued, "Well, I won't keep you in suspense any longer." It's about time, she thought.

He hesitated, causing her to become agitated, and then threw the newspaper article in front of her. Cassie could have fainted. Of all things to throw at her, it was the article she had read just an hour before. What now? She had to leave before the tears came and before he could find out anything. He had forced her to have dinner with him, and now he expected her to discuss her personal life with him. She was becoming nauseous again. How could he have known, or is he fishing for answers? On the other hand, she felt compelled to stay and find out exactly how much he knew and why it mattered.

As her tear-filled eyes looked into his, she slowly picked up the newspaper and scanned the picture. Steeling herself from the pain, she replied hoarsely, "I'm afraid I don't understand. What does this picture have to do with me?" She felt like throwing the paper into his smug face. Throwing the paper, however, would only cause a scene, and she was sure that he would enjoy her display of discomfiture. With a slow, controlled movement, she returned the paper to the table. She knew she had to stay or risk being exposed as Kent's secret lover.

"For one, I know that you work, or worked, for Mr. Wallace. And two, I intend to make a very important deal with him, and you, Miss Garrett, are my bargaining chip. I know that you were involved with Wallace, until this came out. Don't look so shocked. It was common knowledge around the water cooler. You and Jr. were the hottest topic to hit since the last Wall Street scandal."

He had gone too far. Cassie could feel herself losing it. So what if he knew about the affair, she was sure that he couldn't offer any better. To be used as a bargaining chip was repulsive, even she was not that vindictive. "Mr. McGillis," her voice barely above a whisper, "you have overstepped yourself. I think you owe me an apology. Not only are you assuming that Kent and I had an affair and are continuing to do so, it sounds as if you are asking me to divulge personal as well as confidential information about my former employer. As it happens, I resigned today. I am on my own now, so you are barking up the wrong tree. If you are looking for help, find it elsewhere, because you won't get it from me. Now, I am going home, if you will excuse me."

Standing at the same moment, he held her arm firmly and said, "I don't think you understand, Miss Garrett. I don't intend to take you to bed; I intend to make you a better job offer."

Looking at him in disbelief, she glared at him and replied, "Right! I am supposed to believe someone who picks me up at a conservatory. I don't know who the hell you are, and I don't intend to find out. I have had enough of your insinuations and accusations. Now, get out of my way before I run over you." Moving past him, she turned around briefly and sarcastically finished, "You, sir, couldn't offer better either way!" Then she turned and walked out the door.

His look of disbelief followed her.

CHAPTER II

When Cassie finally made it home and closed her apartment door, she listened for footsteps in the hallway. When she believed he was not behind her, she threw herself down into her recliner. The events of the evening had been too much for her, and she started crying uncontrollably. It seemed like an eternity before the tears stopped. With red eyes and a tear-stained face, Cassie finally pulled herself up off the recliner and headed for the kitchen. She needed a cup of coffee.

Suddenly, Cassie realized what had happened. If he knew so much about her, he might know where she lived and come looking for her. What would she do then? She thought blindly for an answer but found none. Soon, she figured, he would try to talk to her again. She wondered why she was so important to him. The only thing she knew for sure was no matter how much Kent had hurt her, she could never betray him by destroying his career. She still loved him too much to humiliate him.

On the other hand, Cassie couldn't help wondering what kind of offer Mr. McGillis was going to make. It had to be better than spending her afternoons thumbing through the want ads. Of course there be no romantic entanglements, either. He had used an unfair advantage in getting her attention and then asking her to spy on Kent. That was too much to ask. She would have to avoid him in the future, regardless of his offer. If he wanted her to help, he would have to beg for it. Deciding she wasn't hungry, she went to bed.

When morning came, Cassie awoke with a jolt. Sitting up in bed, she pressed her palms against her sweat-soaked cheeks. "Thank God," she sighed, "it's only a nightmare." She could still see the looks on their faces—Kent, his bride, and worst of all, McGillis. They were all mocking her for falling in love. The most painful part was Kent's scorching remark—"You little fool. How could you believe what I told you? I hope you have learned your lesson. You should have known that you were not really worth my time." Putting her hands over her face, Cassie refused to give in to tears over a silly dream.

She hurried in the shower, dressed, and fixed herself a small breakfast of toast, juice, and coffee. As she ate, she realized her food supply was getting low. She needed to find a better job or one with the same pay as the other, because she liked to entertain her friends. As she put her coat on, the phone rang. She knew in her mind who it would be, but should she answer? After considering the fact that he might not leave her alone until she did answer, she picked up the receiver and said, "Hello."

"Good . . . you're up. I thought you might be." His voice was extremely chipper for so early in the morning.

"Yes, I am up and getting ready to leave. So if you don't mind, I need to hang up."

"Wait! Please. I don't want to rehash last night, but I would like to offer you a job. I knew you would not continue to work for Wallace, and I know you are well qualified for the job I am offering. Before you hang up, would you please have lunch with me to discuss the matter?" He sounded as if he were desperate.

After a slight hesitation, Cassie realized that she was being given a job on a silver platter. She hadn't even been interviewed for it. Although she knew deep down that he had ulterior motives, and the thought of working for him made shivers run up and down her spine, she knew she couldn't refuse the job. With regrets, she answered, "All right, Mr. McGillis, I will meet you. I have a few questions of my own."

"Fine," the voice responded less than enthusiastically. Cassie could tell that he had been unprepared for such a quick response. "How about noon? There is a seafood restaurant on Third Street called the Ocean Delights. Would that be satisfactory?" When she complied, he said, "Good. Please be punctual. I am a very busy man, and I don't have time to waste interviewing people." Not waiting for her to reply, he hung up.

Irritated, Cassie thought, "Why did he always have to get the last word in?" After calling and getting the address of the restaurant, Cassie finally found it. By the time she got to the restaurant, her feet were tired and had blisters on them. As she collapsed into her seat, she ordered a drink. She was a half hour early, so she had time to freshen herself a little before he showed up. She was just finishing her drink when he arrived—late. As he approached the table, her drink caught in her throat as she became aware of how good he looked in a suit. The first time they had met, he had been wearing jeans and a brown sweater. Now, he looked every bit the businessman. She couldn't turn her eyes away from him as he approached.

He seemed to notice her looking at him as he sat down because the corner of his mouth turned upward. Glancing at her drink, he inquired how long she had been there. The reply was a bold "Long enough. So, Mr. McGillis, what can I do for you, or should I reverse that?"

"First of all, please call me Kelley. We will be working very closely together. Right now I am going to order a drink. Would you care for another?" His question was answered with a brief nod. "You of all people should know that you couldn't rush an important appointment. Correct?" he asked, noting her nonchalant movement which told him she agreed.

"Before we start, however," she eyed him suspiciously but continued, "I would like to know how you know so much about me. And what made you think that I wouldn't be working there anymore?"

Looking slightly annoyed, but trying to ease the tension, he said calmly, "Relax. All of your questions will be answered in time." He paused long enough for the waiter to set his drink down and take their orders.

Once the waiter left the table, Cassie prompted, "Well?"

He looked straight at her and said, "You certainly don't like wasting time, do you? Well, I suppose the most I know about you came from Kent himself. It would appear that you were a joke to him from the beginning. It's a shame that he didn't look beyond your secretarial talents. I am sure that under that cool exterior lies a real woman. You appear to be a wonderful person, and judging by your talents used by Kent's father, you are an excellent worker. Which, before you jump down my throat," he said, noting the icy stare and red face, "I am in desperate need of help, and a very good friend of yours recommended you."

Trying to remain calm, Cassie couldn't think who would confide in him about her. "Would you mind telling me who this friend is?"

"Of course not." He sounded somewhat jovial as he kept her in suspense. He nodded to the waiter as he placed the steaming plates in front of them before reminding them to call if they needed anything.

Thoughts were whirling around so fast in her mind she nearly missed the name. "I'm sorry, could you repeat that, please?"

"Maggie Ricks," he repeated the name as he watched her. "She said that you two grew up together. She works for my company now and put in a good reference for you. You wouldn't want her efforts to go to waste, would you? Besides, it will give you an ally to back you up if you need it."

"I do remember Maggie, but I haven't spoken to her in years. She moved away after college, so I don't know how she would know so much about my past." Pausing shortly, she added, "That doesn't matter, anyhow. I assume you are looking for a new secretary, and I have decided to accept on one condition," she added with force.

With a cautious look, he asked, "What condition, Miss Garrett?"

Looking him straight in the eyes unwavering, she said, "Don't ask why I am accepting the job, and don't ask any questions about Kent and me. That's an old story and best forgotten. Do you understand?"

"I understand perfectly. But you also have to realize that I am a businessman, and whom I deal with should not be taken personally. Right?" She agreed. "Therefore, if I have to do business with the Wallaces, you will just have to grit your teeth and bear it. So you can make no conditions, Miss Garrett. Either you accept the job as is, or I look elsewhere. I will, however, for the sake of good business, refrain from using you to get under his skin. Do you approve?"

"Thank you." At least he didn't undermine her completely, and it was better than waiting in the unemployment line.

"Then I guess it's settled, or do you have any more questions for me?" he asked as he took a bite of his Lobster Newburg.

"You didn't mention salary, benefits, and such. I got the impression I would be working for free without any outside benefits." She noticed the gleam in his eyes at her last remark. The benefit she would receive would not involve him—she would make sure of that.

"Ah . . . well, your salary will be twice what you were making." Seeing her look of surprise and shock, he countered, "And believe me, you will earn every penny. As for the rest, you will have all the standard perks—401K, paid vacation, etc. I take my business very seriously, and I expect my employees to work out on a limb too. Don't you agree?"

"Yes. But I am curious about your last secretary. What happened to her?"

Smiling, he said, "She didn't travel very well." She missed the absent look in his eyes as he continued, "Does traveling bother you, Miss Garrett? Because I do a lot of it. At first I believed in leaving my assistant here to keep order, but then, I realized just recently that I needed more help. So count yourself lucky. You are the first to travel with me."

"I don't suppose your secretary gets paid for these trips abroad, does she?"

"Yes, she will. At least for now," he replied honestly. "I hope that will be sufficient for you. I can't imagine, if you will forgive me, that you went on any business trips with your former employer?" he inquired.

"You are forgiven this time. But no, I never went along. Mr. Wallace always felt my assets were best used in the office, and I never argued. For the sake of my job." She tried to excuse his actions but knew he wasn't buying it. "Anyway, I think the trips would help me learn the business and how to work with you. Don't you agree?" she inquired.

His smile was disarming, but she maintained an air of coolness. "I am glad you are accepting the job. Because if not, I could make things very difficult for you."

"I know you could. But that has nothing to do with this. I need a job, and you are offering me one. That's my only reason for accepting." He knew that wasn't the only reason but didn't pursue the matter.

Instead, he made a toast to their new arrangement, and Cassie couldn't help wondering what Kent would say about her new employer. Smiling to herself, she didn't notice the light in Kelley's eyes as he noticed her smile. "Am I amusing you?"

"Huh . . . oh no. I was just thinking." She stumbled for words. He had caught her off guard again. "I have a lot on my mind right now, but that won't interfere with my ability to do the job. I promise."

"Um. I can't help but wonder if Mr. Wallace ever saw you smile like that. It's a beautiful smile. You should do it more often. Or were you thinking of him?" he inquired with a raised eyebrow.

Without looking into his eyes, Cassie muttered, "No. What makes you think I was thinking of him?" She tried to sound irritated.

"Just a hunch."

"Well, I suggest you keep your hunches to yourself. Now, if you will excuse me, I need to finish some errands before Monday." She started to get up and noticed him rising too. "Oh, no need to get up. Please finish your meal."

"I intend to. But I believe you will need these." He handed her a piece of paper with directions on it. "In case you are wondering where you work, this is a map to get you there." He was being sarcastic, and she would soon find out why. "Your hours are seven to five; however, you might be needed more often. I entertain a lot and will require your attendance at these social functions. It's good for public relations. So you might want to find suitable attire. I believe that's all. I will see you first thing Monday morning. Don't be late," he said matter-of-factly as he sat back down. Without saying a word but flashing a warning glare, she left.

*   *   *

On Monday morning, she dressed with unusual care. She didn't know why she felt it so important to impress him. She only hoped that she didn't live to regret her decision. He had made it very clear he could totally humiliate her if she refused. But for some reason, Cassie found the prospect of working for him to be exhilarating. He offered her the chance to travel, which Kent had thoroughly refused to do. In which case, he had met his bride. She knew she should have insisted, but at that particular time, she didn't see the need. Looking in the mirror, she sighed, "Maybe this was meant to happen. I guess I will never know."

She ate a quick breakfast. Her parents had always insisted on it being the most important meal of the day. Cassie never argued that point, because some of their meetings seemed to drag on for hours, making her miss lunch. When she finished eating, she rushed out the door, locking it behind her. She was not going to be late. Even when her taxi stalled behind an accident, she kept telling herself that she would make it in time. As she glanced at her watch, she realized she only had ten minutes to get there, and she was at least fifteen minutes away. Paying the taxi driver, she jumped out of the cab. Once on the sidewalk, Cassie began to run, cursing that she hadn't worn her tennis shoes like she normally did. She thought for her first day she would be better off walking in her heels. Now, she regretted her mistake.

So intent on making it to work, Cassie was unaware of the blue sedan that was pacing along beside her. When she suddenly stopped, the car moved on around the corner. Looking around her, she almost reeled from shock. Kelley's building was right across from her old employer. She hadn't looked at the address when he handed it to her, so she didn't understand why he had looked at her so apprehensively. She took one more glance at her watch. Two minutes until seven. Thank God! She had made it. As she walked in, the guard stopped her. "ID, please."

Cassie looked frustrated. She didn't have an ID. She tried to explain, but the guard refused to let her by. Glancing at her watch again, she knew she was late. She appealed to the guard to call Mr. McGillis and tell him Miss Garrett was in the lobby. While she was pleading with him, the elevator doors opened and Kelley walked out. Looking a little disconcerted, he smiled at the guard and said, "I'm sorry, Phil. I hired Miss Garrett yesterday. I forgot to inform her about needing an ID badge." He turned his attention to Cassie and placed his hand on her elbow. He guided her to the elevator. Once inside, he faced her. "I hope you will forgive me. Because if I had given you clearance, you would have been here on time. I saw you running into the building. Why didn't you take a taxi?"

"Believe it or not, I had a cab. There was an accident, so I got out. I wish now that I had left earlier, because I like being early and organized. It won't happen again, trust me." She was rambling, and she could tell that he was amused by the grin on his face. "What?" was all she could ask.

"Nothing. I just wondered if you were always this feisty in the morning or if this is a one-time deal." The amused expression appeared and disappeared briefly, "Never mind. It's getting late, and we've lots of work to do." As he unlocked the office door and led her straight into his office, he asked guardedly, "By the way, why was that car following you?"

"What car?" Cassie was suddenly on edge. She had not noticed the car. "I didn't see any car. The only thing I noticed was the location of your business is right across from Wallace Investments. Why didn't you tell me?" she asked rudely.

"If you had looked at the directions when I gave them to you, you would have known. Anyway, I was under the impression that it wouldn't matter. Was I wrong to assume as much?" he responded coolly.

Her icy glare faded as she realized her mistake. "No. It doesn't matter. But I still don't know anything about the car," she reiterated.

One look into her eyes, and he didn't pursue the argument. "Okay. I have several meetings today, and we need to get your orientation going." Using his intercom, he called in an instructor. "Mrs. Harris will be training you. When you finish your orientation this morning, I will require your services this afternoon. Ah, Mrs. Harris, please come in." He motioned for the elderly lady to sit down. "This is Miss Garrett. Cassie, this is Maude Harris, one of the best secretaries I ever had. You will pick up quite a bit from her. Now, if you two will continue in the other room, I have other matters to tend to." He led both ladies to the office door and then turned toward his desk.

Once they were in the outer office, Cassie removed her coat and hung it up on the hook behind her desk. Glancing around the room, she noticed it was simply furnished with filing cabinets, five chairs, coffee table, and two end tables— one with a coffee pot and accessories and one with a lamp on top. The desk was piled high with file folders. There were three very nice wall hangings and a clock above her chair. Returning her attention to Mrs. Harris, she said politely, "I hope you are ready for this, because I am beginning to feel overwhelmed."

Mrs. Harris smiled warmly at her. "It's rough the first few days, but I know you can do the job. Otherwise, he would have never hired you. Mr. McGillis knows people and expects them to work as hard as he does. But he is also a considerate employer. If it weren't for him, I would most likely be dead now. I had a heart attack a couple of years ago, and God love him, he paid my hospital bill. So you can tell I have a lot of respect for the man. Although at times he can be a hard taskmaster, he means well. So bear with him, dearie." She chuckled a little and stated, "I must say his taste in secretaries is improving. I never understood what happened to Marguerite. She just up and disappeared. No one knows where." Maude gave a small sigh as if mourning someone. "Oh well, let's get you started." The rest of the morning proved very taxing, but Cassie was enjoying the challenge immensely. By the time they finished and Maude had left for lunch, Cassie felt she could handle anything.

At one o'clock, Cassie returned from lunch. She picked up Kelley's mail and the work schedule and proceeded to his door. One glance at the schedule told her that he was booked solid for the next two weeks—including one luncheon and one dinner, which she would surely have to attend. She knocked briefly on the door and waited for his response. After a moment, she heard him grumble, "Come in!"

She opened the door slowly and took in a deep breath. She had been so nervous before that she hadn't noticed the difference in the room decor. It was furnished quite differently than she expected. There was Victorian-style furniture, with a small loveseat, two straight-backed chairs covered in crushed maroon velvet, and a large desk made of mahogany. The walls were lined with bookshelves, and there were two filing cabinets behind his desk. The desk was covered with paperwork, but nothing seemed to overpower the man sitting behind the desk. Focusing her attention on him, she could tell that he was displeased with whatever he was reading. She stood there silently, waiting for him to finish the letter. Infuriated, he threw the letter on the desk and stood up in front of the window, which covered the length of the wall behind his desk. As he ran his hand through his thick black hair, he turned back to Cassie. He looked as if he could see right through her. He finally sat down and relaxed. Clearing his throat, he said, "I'm sorry. Is that today's mail?"

She handed the mail to him and asked if he needed anything else. After he glanced at his mail, he leaned back in his chair and looked at her. He spoke politely, "I won't bite you if you sit down. I am not a slave driver, Miss Garrett, but I do believe in hard work. Eventually, you will learn what to expect and when to leave things alone. At this very minute, however, I could use a cup of coffee, black, and get yourself one too," he ordered.

Meekly obeying, Cassie walked back into her office and over to the little table in the corner of the waiting area. As she poured the coffee, she began to feel more at ease. Maybe this was the solution to her problem. After all, she couldn't continue for Kent's father and pretend nothing happened, nor could she have found a job with as much, if not more, challenges. She knew she was up to the job, but could she handle working for the devil himself? As she carried the mugs of coffee back into the office, she had to smile at how she had managed it.

Her smile had not gone unnoticed, because she sensed he was watching her as she entered the room. A sardonic smile played on the corners of his mouth as he asked, "Would you care to share the joke, Miss Garrett?"

Surprised at his audacity, Cassie was briefly speechless. "There is no joke, Mr. McGillis. I was just thinking how lucky I am to have a job on such short notice—and without references too. I would have preferred honesty to the underhanded way you approached me. But that will be forgotten, as I am ready to get on with my new life and my new job. Thank you for the opportunity."

With a slight twist to his smile, Kelley stood and turned toward the window. He seemed absorbed in a far-off place, before taking a deep breath and turning to face her. One look into her hazel eyes, and he wondered why he had hired her. There would be hell to pay later on, and he knew it. "You're welcome," he responded as casually as possible. Pursuing the matter, he countered, "Although I am wondering if you have an ulterior motive for working with me. Am I mistaken?" he queried.

"I thought we had covered that already." She sounded exasperated, and she didn't feel the need to rehash everything. She couldn't understand why he was so interested in her past. "I was out of a job—by choice—and you offered me one better. Is there anything wrong with that? Because there shouldn't be." After a moment's pause, she added, "I think you understand the rest of the story. You have probably been in similar circumstances. Right?" She raised an inquiring eyebrow.

"As a matter of fact, I have. So I guess that answers all of my other questions. I just hope that you have learned your lesson, because I don't intend to cater to you or your emotions. Do you understand?" He didn't believe he could keep it that way. With her excellent looks and drop-dead attitude, she was a definite challenge to his sensibilities.

With annoyance at his ego and tenseness in her voice, she replied, "Yes . . . perfectly."

Ignoring her tone, he said, "In that case, get me the Rotez file and call the financial consultant for a brief meeting. I want him here in an hour. Don't take no for an answer."

Once she was back in her office, she walked over to the filing cabinet and removed the correct file. She was relieved to find all the files in perfect alphabetical order. As she walked back to her desk, the phone rang. She picked up the receiver and said, "McGillis Enterprises, Miss Garrett speaking. May I help you?" She waited patiently for an answer, but the only response she got was silence. After she repeated her name, she heard the click and a dial tone. "Must be a wrong number." As she removed the contents of the file folder, she didn't give the caller another thought. In a moment she found the consultant's name and sat in stunned silence until the nausea had subsided. "Oh Lord, he could have warned me," she told herself angrily as her finger rested on the finely typed name on the bottom of the page. It said, Kent Wallace Jr., advisor. Then, it suddenly hit her why Kelley hadn't told her. She reminded herself she had told him she didn't want to discuss him anymore. Better let her find out on her own. Well, this was definitely going to be a test of wills. Taking a deep breath, she picked up the phone and dialed the familiar number.

After several rings, a very young voice said, "Wallace and Son Investments, this is Megan. May I help you?"

Speechless for a moment, Cassie gathered her thoughts. "Yes," she faltered, "I am calling for Kelley McGillis of McGillis Enterprises. Mr. McGillis wishes to have a meeting with Mr. Wallace within the next hour to discuss the Rotez account. When shall I tell Mr. McGillis to expect him?"

Sounding a little put out for being rushed into an answer, the new secretary returned sharply, "I'm sorry, but Mr. Wallace is on his honeymoon and will not be back for a few weeks. I can have the temporary consultant working on his cases there in half an hour. That is the only time he will be available today."

In response to her rudeness, Cassie flinched and returned somewhat agitated, "That is fine. I will make sure that Mr. McGillis gets the message. Thank you." Without any further comment, she hung up. If that was Kent's new secretary, she thought, "He could have done better." The nerve of the woman. She should remember what kind of people she works for and be more respectful to the clients. The senior Wallace, she felt sure, would not have put up with her rudeness.

"Is there a problem, Miss Garrett? I expected an answer ten minutes ago." As he walked into the office, he noticed the disgruntled look upon her face and tried guessing what had just happened. Although he was wrong, it hurt just the same. "I take it lover boy didn't like hearing your voice, or was the new secretary a little too impersonal for you?" After he saw the response in her eyes, he stated, "I'm sorry. That was completely uncalled for. Let's just make it through the meeting, and then you can relax. Deal?"

"Okay." She didn't care if he noticed the hatred in her voice at his callousness. She handed him the file folder and replied, "For the umpteenth time, it's none of his business what I do anymore. I told you that. What?"

He looked at her momentarily and then said, "I remember." After another short pause, which made her just a little uneasy, he added, "I need you to type out these letters and memos and have them ready to sign before I leave today." As he finished, he handed her a stack of papers she was sure had been sitting on his desk for ages. There had to be over a dozen letters and memos. She could tell it was going to be a long afternoon.

As the time for the meeting approached, Cassie wondered who was going to be taking Kent's place. She didn't have to wait very long as the elder Wallace walked into the room. Looking straight into her eyes with his cold blue ones, he asked, "Is Mr. McGillis in?"

Catching her breath, Cassie replied, "Yes, he is ready for you. I will tell him you are here." She beeped him on the intercom and, with his "yes," told him Kent Wallace Sr. was here for their meeting. When she had finished informing Kelley, she tried as calmly as she could to ask, "Would you care for some coffee or tea?"

"No. I just want to get this meeting out of the way. I have other more important things to attend." His response was short and sounded as if he had a full agenda. Cassie really doubted he had a full slate, because work had never seemed to stop him from playing around.

As Kelley walked into the room, Cassie went to sit down as a hand landed upon her shoulder. "You too. I always involve my secretary. She keeps my notes." His tone defied argument, and she could have slapped him for putting her in this position. But he didn't leave any time to argue. So with a fake smile that he apparently noticed because of the smile on his face, she entered his office with a tablet and pencil in hand.

The meeting itself seemed to drag on and on. All Cassie could do was answer questions when asked and provide the correct documents. Whenever she did manage to catch Kent Sr.'s eyes, they seemed to look right through her with their icy coolness. What made matters worse was Kelley seemed to be enjoying his little party and amused at her discomfort. When Cassie would look up at him to address a question, she would catch his sardonic smile that played at the corners of his firm mouth. He had placed her in an embarrassing situation, and he knew it. "Well," she thought, "if that's the way he wants it, I will play along." She would answer questions with a smile and play right up to both of them and pray she kept her sanity.

The meeting lasted for three hours. By the time they finished their business and drank their coffee, Cassie was exhausted. Her fingers hurt from all the writing. However, she would soon be rewarded for her efforts, because after seeing Mr. Wallace to the door, she was called into Kelley's office. As she stood in front of his desk, she waited patiently for him to finish his business. When he did finally look up from his paperwork, he looked into her eyes and seemed to lose his train of thought. Suddenly he remembered what he wanted to say. Not forgetting his manners, he offered her a chair. As Cassie sat down on the edge of her chair, he commented, "Please relax, Cassie. You did a fabulous job. I am quite impressed with you. You just proved to me that you could handle anything that is thrown at you and make it work to your advantage. I like that. That means that I don't have to take you by the hand and lead you where I want you to go. You have genuine instinct, and that is a bonus in this business." She hadn't been prepared for the praise, and noticing her surprise at his words, he continued, "I don't believe we need a trial period after all. You are quite capable of doing the job. Consider yourself permanent." Glancing at his watch, he grimaced. "It's getting late. Why don't you knock off for the rest of the day? No doubt you could use it."

"Thank you for the compliment, but no, I believe I will finish out the day. I have plenty of work to do, and I like keeping myself busy. So if you don't mind, I need to finish this report, and then I have to finish the memos, which you will have to sign."

As she stood up, he did too. He came slowly around the desk, which put her in close proximity with him, and she could smell his aftershave, which sent tingling sensations up and down her spine. She inwardly cursed for allowing herself to get so heated by him. He walked behind her all the way to the door, which he closed firmly behind her. Once in the outer office, Cassie sighed at her relief that he didn't follow her. With the first meeting between her and Kent Sr. out of the way, she started to believe things were going to be all right. She sat down at her typewriter, and surprisingly, the work just seemed to flow so easily.

She had all but three memos typed when Kelley's door opened. "Good Lord! Are you still here? It's after six o'clock. You should have left an hour ago." He pretended to be surprised.

Slowly looking up to her employer, it took a moment before she realized what he had said. "Oh! Well, I told you I like being kept busy. I didn't realize it was getting that late. Thank you," she stated as she stood up, stretching. She had sat at the typewriter for so long without moving that she could barely stand. When she started to sway, a strong arm reached out to catch her. He drew her to him, and she was completely entwined by his arm. She could feel his hard body against hers through the thin cotton dress she was wearing. Placing her hand on his chest to steady herself, she became very much aware of how muscular he really was. The fresh scent of soap and aftershave began to have an odd effect on her, because when she raised her head, her eyes, stopping briefly on his grinning mouth, looked into his mesmerizing green ones and sensed an abrupt change in his attitude. His body had grown rigid with the first touch of her body to his own. He had a questioning look in his eyes that didn't match his next statement. "Are you all right?"

"Yes, I have just been sitting here too long," she stated firmly as she moved away from him. "I should have gotten up and moved around more. Thank you for your support." With a shaky smile, she could feel the attraction between them as she moved away and covered her typewriter up. She placed all of her paperwork in a neat little pile on her desk. "I don't suppose you would like to sign these before you go, would you?"

"No. We have had a big day, and the rest can wait. Shall I call you a cab? Or shall I take you home?" He seemed anxious all of a sudden, as if he thought something would happen to her.

"No. I will be fine. Sitting so long, I need to stretch my muscles." Noticing the apprehension on his face, she added, "Is there something wrong?"

"I just thought you might like to have a drink before you go home. We should celebrate your excellent beginning in my employment. Would that be suitable?" He smiled that charismatic smile, but Cassie was exhausted and only wished for a hot bath and bed.

"Maybe another night. I just want to go home now and relax. Can I have a rain check?" She stood directly in front of him, so she could have a full view of him when she spoke.

"That's a promise I intend on keeping." With her nod of approval, he said, "I will ride down the elevator with you. Come on." After locking his door, they left the office and walked to the elevator. He allowed her to enter first, and they rode the elevator down in complete silence. Neither one knew really what to say after the encounter in the office. As the doors opened, the night watchman smiled and waved them out the door.

Outside in the cool air, Cassie shivered slightly. "You should have worn a coat," he gently admonished.

"Actually, I did. But I am afraid I left it on the coat rack in the office. I will be fine."

Without allowing her time to argue, he wrapped his coat around her. "You can return it tomorrow."

"Thank you. Good night." Without another word, Cassie turned and walked away. Even though she could still feel his eyes on her, she continued to walk home. Once out of his sight, Cassie slowed her pace down and just enjoyed the fresh air. It had been a great day, despite the fact that Kent Sr. was her first appointment. Before she reached her building, however, she began to feel a cold chill over her body, as if something was about to hit her. Stopping abruptly, she sensed something behind her. Slowly turning around, a car moved on around the corner of the high-rise apartments, but there was no one behind her. She could have sworn there was someone there a moment ago. She was almost sure she heard footsteps, but maybe she had just imagined it. She gave herself a good shake and walked into her building. Once inside, the doorman asked a strange and unexpected question, "Isn't your friend coming in?"

"What friend are you talking about?" she asked, surprised.

"The man that was behind you," he replied with an inquiring look. If it hadn't been for the doorman, Cassie would have ended up on the floor. "Do you need help? Is there someone I should call?" He sounded so excited; she thought he was going to have a heart attack.

Smiling weakly at him, she consoled him by saying, "I'm fine, Ben. It's just been a long day. Good night."

"Good night, miss. I hope you feel better tomorrow." His worried look followed her to the elevator. Once inside, she leaned against the wall and pondered about who could have been following her. Kelley had asked about the car earlier this morning. As the elevator doors opened on her floor, Cassie dismissed the idea and told herself it was only their imaginations. With a renewed spirit, she unlocked her door and entered. Within one hour, she had eaten, showered, and crawled into bed.

CHAPTER III

Moving through a thick gray veil of fog that hung like a curtain of silk, she thought she heard someone calling her name. Squinting hard, she could feel a chill moving throughout her body as if she were standing in front of a freezer. Turning completely around, she found herself confronting a faceless, shadowy figure. Unable to tell if it was a man or a woman, she reached out to touch the image before her, but the silent form retreated into the murkiness of the fog. She could hear herself screaming, "Who are you? What do you want?" But the deadly silence was broken only by a loud and menacing banging noise. Running into the dense fog, Cassie could hear herself screaming as she tripped over something. Falling fast, she opened her eyes in horror. Sweating and breathing hard, she sat straight up and adjusted her eyes to the darkness in front of her. It took her a few moments to realize that the banging noise she heard was her alarm, which had been running for quite a while.

Dragging herself out of bed, she turned off her alarm, pulled out her clothes, and headed into the bathroom. Standing in the shower, she tried to forget the dream. But it had appeared so real that Cassie could still feel herself shaking from the intense fear. There was nothing compared to the sensation of being watched. The only course of action she could take was to not dwell on the matter. It was just a nightmare, and she would have to will herself to forget it. After getting dressed and eating breakfast, she quickly grabbed his coat and her sweater and headed out the door.

When she opened the office door, she came to a dead stop on the threshold, meeting Kent Sr.'s eyes. The icy blue coolness could have frozen her on the spot, but he maintained a businesslike attitude. "Well, it looks as if you have landed on your feet very well. I honestly didn't think you would walk out like you did. But I guess I misjudged you." He was toying with her. She wondered if Kelley was in yet, or if someone else had let him in. Noticing her glance at his door, the older Kent sneered, "Oh yeah, he's in. I just finished talking to him. I must say, you have really impressed him. I hope he knows how to treat you."

Very slowly, Cassie closed the door behind her, and in a strained but controlled voice, she retorted, "Of all the rude and insensitive things to say. I wasn't the one who proposed and then went and married someone else. Furthermore, I have no intention of making the same mistake twice." As she finished her statement, Cassie brushed past him to unlock her desk.

Grabbing her arm roughly, the older gentleman whispered to her, "It's never going to be over." Just as he finished his threat, the door to Kelley's office opened. Kelley's eyes lingered on the older gentleman's hand on her arm. "I hope I am not interrupting anything. Am I?"

"No. I was just on my way out and giving my compliments to Cassie on her new job. I will be in touch with you, Mr. McGillis. Goodbye, Miss Garrett." He turned and went out the door, shutting it firmly behind him. In the next moment, Cassie was being ushered into Kelley's office.

Cassie stood silently, watching him pace in front of his window, until he stopped and turned to face her. His next words were like a glass of ice water pouring over her head. "Please try to keep your personal affairs off company time. Moreover, I thought you had had enough of the Wallace family, or were you hoping for another go around?" His tone was anything but civil. She actually felt as though he were trying to find fault with her at the encounter with Kent's father. No doubt she was shocked by this sudden outburst, but he had no right to accuse her of anything, especially since she had already told him it was over. It was none of his business.

Taking slowly measured footsteps to the edge of the desk, Cassie glared at him as she blurted out, "You don't own me, and besides, I told you that it was over and done with the minute I left his employment. How can you be so rude as to question my sensibility? I have given you no reason to accuse me of anything. You just walked in at the wrong moment. If you had entered the office a few seconds earlier, you would not be feeling this way." With an audible sigh, she finished, "Please drop it. I don't want to relive the past, and I definitely do not want to argue with you over it."

As he stood there silently, she could tell he was aggravated and on the verge of berating her further but checked himself and ultimately said, "Perhaps you are right. I apologize. But let's get one thing straight right now, okay?" When she nodded, he concluded, "I don't want to see him touching you again. Deal?"

"Deal," she wholeheartedly agreed.

The rest of the day seemed to run by very smoothly. Cassie was able to redo the filing cabinet in a more orderly fashion and still get all of the day's memos and letters done. For lunch, she met up with Maggie Ricks from her old typing pool, and they discussed the latest gossip. The biggest topic she found was Kent's new bride. As it turned out, Kent's new bride had a mind of her own, and not even her darling husband could control her passions. She pretty well had him tied around her little finger. There had even been a rumor that they hadn't actually taken a honeymoon, which gave Cassie a nervous feeling when she recalled the times the phone rang and no one responded. Thanking Maggie for her references to Kelley, she finished her lunch and headed back to work.

By the time she had returned to the office, Cassie had pretty well been caught up on all the comings and goings of the rich and powerful. The only one she was not familiar with was the man she worked for, and that seemed to be a mystery to everyone. He had climbed the ladder of success so quickly and efficiently that no one ever questioned how he had achieved it. The papers had always repeated the same stories about the young man from Canada who seemed to have finesse for drawing in the business. He would buy and sell companies and rebuild companies, but no one seemed to understand his methods. He was a little unorthodox, in that he liked to have things done in his own manner and not in the traditional standards. If there were a rule given for a certain number of employees being fired, he would work around it, finding positions for them. Therefore, instead of being the ogre everyone expected, he turned out to be like Robin Hood in disguise.

In other gossip columns, he was the attractive young bachelor that every woman would die for. It would appear that he had a different companion every week. There was a rush each week to see who was at the top of the list. The woman chosen would be given the best treatment and then sent happily on her way—each one willing to be let off the hook. Yeah, just like fish in a stream. Well, Cassie knew one thing for sure; she was not going to be one of them. She had learned her lesson very well. Stay away from the fire, or you will get burned, and she had already been burned once. No matter how attractive, rich, powerful, or friendly he was, she would just have to say no.

As she was putting the final touches on her filing system, Kelley entered the outer office. As he laid a stack of papers on her desk, he asked, "Are you finished for the day? Because it's after five, and I am starving."

"As a matter of fact, I am finished. I just redid the filing system. You would not believe how bad your previous system was. Your alphabetizing really needed some work." As she walked over to the desk, she caught the end of his statement. "If you're hungry, you should go eat something. I know that I am famished. Nothing sounded good earlier, but I think I know what I am going to have." Standing there grinning at her, Cassie couldn't figure out why. Oblivious to the question, she hadn't realized what he asked.

"I am asking you to join me, Miss Garrett. I am taking you up on that rain check you promised. Anywhere you want to go, I will take you." Cassie became speechless, because she hadn't expected him to take her up on the invitation so quickly.

Feeling between a rock and a hard place, she knew she should refuse the invitation because she didn't want to be another notch on his belt. She could keep refusing, but for some unrealized reason, she didn't want to refuse. "Sure. Why not? I have earned it lately, haven't I?"

"Exactly. You've earned it, and it's my congratulations to you on your new job. Where are we going?" he asked as he held her jacket for her. She gave him a name of a little Italian restaurant a few blocks down the road, and he suggested they walk.

For the first few moments, neither one of them said a word. And then Kelley asked, "Are you enjoying your new job?"

Smiling, she answered, "Yes, I am. You have a lot of interesting clients, and I hope some day you tell me where you found them." She paused briefly, which caused Kelley to look upon her quizzically.

"What?"

"What?" she repeated and then realized he had caught her hesitation. "Oh, I was just wondering about a few things. It's not important."

"Sure it is. Anything you can think of is important. All you have to do is ask. But I can't guarantee you a straight answer; at least, not yet. You are still new to the business." Grinning with anticipation, he prompted her to ask her question.

"Well actually, what I have to ask doesn't really pertain to work. Everyone has a past or his way of making it up the corporate ladder. You are the only one I know that doesn't seem to have any skeletons in his closet. Or am I wrong? I was just wondering but didn't feel it was proper to ask the boss how he got there." She sounded breathless in the cool night air but kept pace with him.

"Ah, I see. Has that been on your mind very long, or did you just now think about it?" he casually prodded her.

"Not long. Actually, this afternoon, I thought about it." She hated being goaded into answering that honestly, but she had no other answer to give him. She did, however, manage to keep her gaze straight ahead.

"Well, I think I can enlighten you just a little. I don't want to give everything away. I must admit, I am no saint, but I do try very hard to keep things aboveboard and honest. Although it doesn't always work, I maintain a high profile at proficiency. Business is my life. Let's eat, and then I will explain myself to you." They had approached the restaurant, and he held the door for her as she entered.

* * *

In a sleazy, run-down motel on the other side of town, unknown to Kelley and Cassie, their assailant was planning the first phase of attack. Photos and information were placed inside a green manila folder, and a cigarette was lit. As the smoke was exhaled slowly, a well-manicured hand closed the folder and picked up the letter next to it. After examining the letter, the stalker placed it inside an envelope, sealed it, and wrote Kelley's name on the front. As the envelope was placed back on the table, the follower moved to the little nightstand by the bed and removed a .45-caliber pistol from its holster and began running long fingers down the side of the gun. "It won't be long now, Kelley. I will have everything I need to finish you. There won't be a second mistake." The malevolent voice turned into a sinister laugh as the gun was returned to its holster. Once the gun was replaced in the nightstand, the stalker picked up the envelope and his jacket and left the room, making sure to lock the door.

*   *   *

After filling themselves up with lasagna and garlic bread and salad, Kelley insisted that she try one of their luscious desserts. He waited patiently for the waiter to pour the wine and serve the coffee before he leaned forward and said, "I guess you have waited long enough. Where would you like me to start? Or shall I make this the quick version?"

"It's still early; I think I can handle the entire story, unless you are too tired or too long winded." The wine had apparently gone to her head, because she was behaving unlike her normal self. The cool, confident woman had suddenly turned into an eager, tantalizing adolescent. But apparently it didn't bother Kelley, because he played right up to her teasing.

"Well, I grew up in Canada, just south of Banff, but on the fringes of Canmore. The Bow River was east of my father's home. As children, my sister, three brothers, and I would do a lot of hunting, hiking, and fishing when the weather permitted. By the time I had graduated from high school, I had already gotten the real estate bug. Any information I could get my hands on about buying and selling property, I would buy it or borrow it. It was like a fever, and my father, sensing the fact that I was not going to give it up, began to indulge me, even encourage me, to further my skills. Working a lot of overtime, he was finally able to enroll me into a vocational college miles from home. My major had been small business management and marketing, with real estate as a side job." As he took a long breath, Kelley gazed into her eyes and wondered if she was as interested as she appeared. "This isn't boring you, is it? Because I can stop right now if it is."

The question didn't register on Cassie until he paused again. "Oh no, I am enjoying this. It's not every day you get to interview your boss. Please keep going," she pleaded.

With a slight grin, he picked up his coffee, took a sip, and replaced the cup. "To continue. After finishing school, I applied to several corporations in the United States, in the hope of getting a better job. You see, most of Canada's jobs pertain to parks and tourists. My education was limited in my hometown, so I sought out my fortune away from home. In the end, I came away a winner, because not one but four different companies offered me a position, but only one appeared worthwhile. I started a midlevel marketing job for a Fortune 500 company here in Indiana, and soon I was the head of the department. Although I was at the head of my game, it wasn't enough. Pretty soon, I started getting clients of my own on the side. I would secretly work nights and weekends to find companies in poor financial straits and put them in touch with more profitable companies and influential bankers, and before I knew it, I was earning a commission. By the time my own company figured out what I was doing, I had already made my fortune and was ready to quit and go out on my own. And that's where I am today." Hesitating briefly, he finished, "It wasn't all flowers and champagne. I stepped on quite a few toes, and there are plenty of people ready to sack my rear for it. But let's forget that right now, shall we? I want to enjoy the company." Along with his charisma and the wine, Cassie was willing to drop the rest of the story.

"That was a very good story. I hope you were telling me the truth, because if you're not, there will be hell to pay later on." She made a little giggle, which told her she had better quit drinking and go home. She was becoming entirely too comfortable with him. "Will you be good enough to stick me in a cab and send me home? I don't think my legs will hold me up long enough to walk. I am afraid I have had a little too much to drink." Her smile was somewhat slanted, but he laughed along with her.

"I see your point. Yes, I will call you a cab. Wait here." While he made the call, Cassie made a quick trip to the ladies' room. As she was returning to her seat, she bumped into someone. Mumbling an apology, she didn't look up as she brushed past the blurred figure. Watching her stumble back to her table, the stranger removed a small notebook from his inside coat pocket. Jotting down several notes, the observer placed the pad back in the pocket and turned to walk out of the restaurant. Kelley placed Cassie's coat over her shoulders and ushered her to the door. While waiting for the cab, Cassie turned to him and said, "Thank you for an enjoyable evening."

Her warm smile made him curse inwardly, "Damn, why did she have to be so beautiful and disarming? It wasn't fair to put her in this position." Then out loud, he replied, "You're welcome. Maybe some day we could do this again." That was a mistake, because after he said it, he realized that she would only be in jeopardy if she were allowed to pursue a personal relationship. But before Cassie could respond to his statement, the cab approached the building. Once he had bundled her into the cab, he turned toward the parking garage down the road.

*   *   *

The next morning, despite an enormous hangover, Cassie was in the office unusually early. She had made it in before Kelley showed up. With fresh coffee brewing, Cassie was already busy going through the day's memos and letters.

She was checking the day's itinerary when he walked through the door. As she looked up with a beaming smile, she greeted him. "Good morning, I hope you slept well. Can I fix you a fresh cup of coffee? Here, this envelope was left under the door for you." She held out the envelope with his name on the back of it.

"Black. Extra strong." That was all he said as he grabbed the envelope from her and disappeared into his office. He closed the door behind him as if to say, "I don't want to be disturbed."

Within a few moments, with coffee in hand, Cassie knocked on the door. When there was no answer, Cassie knocked again. Beginning to worry, she slowly opened the door and poked her head around. She softly called out to him, but when he still didn't answer, she opened the door all the way and walked in. Once inside, she paused. He was standing in front of the window staring out but not really seeing anything. He seemed lost in thought. She quickly glanced at his desk and noticed the envelope was open and there were several pictures scattered around his desk. She didn't want to pry, but she could tell the pictures were bothering him. Attached to one of the pictures was a letter. Cassie, feeling suddenly out of place, decided he needed his privacy, set his coffee on the small coffee table, and retreated back to her desk where the mail had just been deposited.

As she sorted through it, a package on one of the end tables caught her attention. Walking over, she slowly picked it up to examine it. There was no return address and no stamp, and it was in a plain brown wrapper. Her first thought was calling the police, but Kelley might have been expecting something and hadn't informed her yet. Carefully, she placed the package on the edge of her desk and sat down in her chair, wondering whether or not to disturb him. Before she found an answer, the intercom buzzed with his curt "Miss Garrett . . ."

"Yes?"

"Miss Garrett, I need you to bring in a tablet and pencil and my itinerary." Without waiting for her to question him, he cut her off. Grumbling to herself, Cassie picked up the notebook, pencil, schedule, and package and opened the door to his office. He was sitting at his desk making notes in a ledger but looked up as she entered the room. "That was fast. Please sit down, Miss Garrett; I need you to help plan a trip. There are some personal things that I need to clear up, and we can visit some old clients at the same time. Please call all my appointments for the next three weeks; tell them we will be out of the country for a while and will reschedule them upon our return. Have them contact my associates if they have any serious problems. I am sure they can handle them." Pausing briefly, he sat back in his chair before adding, "Make sure you get the earliest flight time. We don't want to be late landing, and make sure you pack plenty of warm clothes; it gets pretty chilly where we are headed. That will be all for now. I will give you further instructions as the day progresses."

Cassie sat frozen, pen poised in hand, as she let his words "where we are headed" sink in. She slowly raised her head and repeated. "We don't want to be late landing." She quickly stood up, dropping everything in her lap, including the unmarked package. "I don't understand. Where are we going? You said it was personal business, so why am I going?"

Eyeing her callously, he responded, "Yes, I have personal business, but we will also be attending several business meetings as well. We are headed for Canmore, my hometown in Alberta, Canada. I will be giving you names of several clients we will be calling on, and you can place all the files you need in a file box to take with you on the flight. We can go over them then. That will be all, Miss Garrett!"

His tone defied argument, so she picked up everything from the floor, turned to leave, and remembered the package. "Oh, before I forget, this came for you. There is no return address, so I thought you would want to take care of it." She set the package on the edge of his desk and quickly left the office, closing the door behind her. A couple of hours later, he called her in again.

From that point on, they spent the next five hours going over all the details of the trip. There would be meetings practically every day, except for the first three. He dictated about twenty-five letters, but the last letter was puzzling to her. He only mentioned he would be home soon, and they would discuss the matter more fully in private, and he conveyed his condolences. All the time she listened to him, he didn't once mention the package or the envelope.

Cassie had just finished packing the files and making the reservations when Kelley opened his door and entered the room. Sitting himself between her and the box of files, he made sure that she looked him in the eye. "I am sorry. I know this rushes you, but I just received the call today. My father died yesterday, and I should have been there. But while I am there, I can check in with a few old friends and family, and forgive the timing, a few business associates." He touched her arm, which caused Cassie's heart to skip a beat. When he talked to her that way, he made her aware of his sensuality.

"I guess there is nothing wrong with my going then. Just as you said, it is sudden. But I thought you were close to him, by the tone of your voice last night," she inquired.

"No, not really. My father and I understood each other, but he believed in taking care of the environment first; his family came second. Even though he made a fortune by pinching every penny and earned the respect of family and friends, his family still felt the resentment—me worst of all. That's probably because of my mother dying so young. She died when my sister was born. He wouldn't budge an inch as far as spending a little of his earnings, and when our mother died, he relied on the insurance money for her burial. Therefore, you might say none of his children really regret him dying, which may sound horrible, but true."

Cassie couldn't believe how cold the man sounded but didn't want to push the conversation too much. She was just an outsider, and it was not her family, so it was none of her business. Changing the subject, she asked, "Will we be coming back here in the morning, or shall I take this box of files home with me?"

"Just leave them here. There may be a few last things to pack, and I will probably bring in some snacks for the trip." He removed his hand from her arm and stood up, bringing himself closer to her. "Why don't you knock off for the rest of the day? Go home and pack and get some rest, because you will have a lot to do once we get there. And make sure you pack a few extra dresses, including one for the funeral."

Without questioning him, Cassie moved around the desk and, replacing everything where it belonged, took her key and locked the desk. She brushed him slightly as she went to the coat rack. Once she had on her coat, she turned to him and said, "I don't understand. How could anyone let their wife die like that?" Her pleading look caused him to draw in a long breath before answering.

"The only way you could understand would be if you had known my father. The only reason he paid my tuition was because my grandfather insisted on it, or he wouldn't. And my father did not want to be outdone by his own father." He smiled weakly with that firm, yet sensual mouth and stated, "Anything else?"

"No. I will see you in the morning at five o'clock sharp." He nodded his head in agreement, so she picked up her purse and left. She knew he stood there watching her, until she got on the elevator. Once on the lift, Cassie began to feel a sense of euphoria. She was going to Canada. She had never been anywhere outside the United States, and this would be her initiation and her test. Would she pass or fail? She would soon find out. "But first," she thought, "I will have to go buy a suitable dress or two." Because the only dinner apparel she had was her usual office clothes. In the back of her mind, Cassie knew that he would not approve of her wardrobe. Therefore, it was obvious what she had to do. Go shopping.

Down the road from work was a pleasant and affordable little dress shop. When she walked in, the matron asked if she could help her, but Cassie replied that she was just looking. She was standing by a rack in the corner of the store when a sudden movement in the mirror in front of her caught her attention. As she tried not to look in the mirror directly, out of the corner of her eye, she saw someone in dark glasses and well-tailored suit appeared to be watching her. Every rack she moved to, she was sure his eyes were moving to follow her. Cassie picked out several elegant dinner dresses and one black ensemble for the funeral. As she approached the counter, she took a moment to turn in the direction of the window, which caused her follower to turn the other direction. She turned back to the shop lady and paid for her purchases. By the time she had turned back around, the stranger had disappeared. Within moments after leaving the store, Cassie made her way home but couldn't get the image of the stalker out of her mind. "Or," she told herself sharply, "you are just really tired and imagining things. You have a busy trip in front of you, so just concentrate on that, and you will be fine." Shaking herself, she spent the rest of the evening packing and double-checking everything. She finally took a shower, put on her nightclothes, and crawled into bed. She had no idea what to anticipate in Canada, nor did she have any idea what waited for her there.

CHAPTER IV

The next morning, Cassie arrived an hour earlier than needed to make sure everything was packed the way it was supposed to be. It had been fairly easy making the arrangements with the airline. All she had to do was contact the airport and reserve Kelley's private plane for departure and arrival times in Calgary, and then she had to have them notify Kelley's personal pilot and crew. Once all those arrangements had been accomplished, all she had to do was pack her belongings and their business files and board the plane when it arrived. Cassie thought to herself, "It must be nice to have a plane ready on a moment's notice."

Entering the office, she stopped just inside the doorway when her eyes met his. Apparently, Kelley was just as anxious about the trip as she was, or so it would appear. He was pouring himself a cup of coffee and stopped in midstream when she opened the door. Neither one said a word for a few moments. Then he said, "I thought you might be in extra early this morning. So I thought I would join you and help you double-check everything for the trip. Besides, I need to cover a few more details about the meetings. The family matters, you will just have to adjust as you go. I will fill you in as best I can when the time comes. But," he looked around, "right now, we need to get started. Would you care for a cup of coffee, or do you just want to start?" He surveyed her appearance with obvious approval. The outfit she wore set off her ivory skin, blonde hair, and hazel eyes. The boot-length burgundy-colored velour skirt and contrasting top enhanced her femininity while looking practical. His smile was warm and appreciative. "You look very provocative today. Is there someone special you are trying to impress?"

Cassie was still trying to collect herself from finding him there so early. She knew he didn't have to be there for another hour, but his company would be welcome. Smiling, she stuttered in surprise, "N . . . no. I just felt like wearing something comfortable." She crossed the room and took the cup he offered her and said, "I didn't have time for a cup before I left the house this morning." Inhaling the strong aroma of the mountain-grown Folgers coffee, she sighed and took a big swallow. "That tastes heavenly. Thank you. All I need to do is review the list of files you gave me and match them with the files in the box. Everything else should be set. I set my suitcases in the lobby with yours, so there is little else we need to do." She did her best to reassure him, but she could tell he wasn't going to let her off so easily. Without another word, she started sorting folders in the file box.

She had been halfway through the list when she noticed a dark green folder without a name on it. Cassie turned around to ask who the client was but found herself alone. He had gone into his own office for some unknown reason, and she wondered if she should follow and ask him. On the other hand, he might not want to be disturbed until they left. Holding the unlabeled folder in her hands, Cassie decided to approach the subject after they were on the airplane. For some reason, she felt as if she shouldn't have the folder at all, and she didn't want to be caught reading something confidential that didn't concern her or their trip. Shaking her head, she stuffed the file back into the box exactly where she found it and continued her review of the rest of the files. Once she finished her task, she replaced the lid on the box and walked over to Kelley's office door. Cautiously, as if she were intruding on his privacy, Cassie peered around the door that was halfway ajar. "All set?"

"Yes, I believe I am. Just let me lock everything up, and we can leave." Kelley made sure everything was put away and drawers were locked. Before he locked his desk drawer, he opened it and removed an envelope. As he held the sealed envelope in his hands, he thought to himself, "This will be the last time, I promise!" In the back of his mind, however, Kelley knew there would be trouble ahead. He just prayed to God that Cassie wasn't around when that time came. Placing the envelope in the inside pocket of his suit coat, he closed the desk drawer and locked it. Taking a last glance around the room, he shut and locked his office door.

"Let's go," he grinned. "We'll get some breakfast at the airport, and I will go over some of the itinerary." He followed her out of the office. Within a few moments, they had vacated the building and were waiting for the luggage to be placed in the limousine trunk. Out of the corner of her eye, Cassie could see someone standing against the building, and she felt as if she and Kelley were being watched. Nonchalantly, she turned her head in the stranger's direction, but whoever it was decided he had seen enough, because as she turned her head, the silent observer started walking down the sidewalk, toward the bus stop. Before Cassie could contemplate asking Kelley who this person might be, she was being ushered into the back of the limousine.

*   *   *

A short period later, Cassie and Kelley were seated in an airport lounge drinking coffee and eating a Danish. While they ate, Kelley informed her how the funeral would commence and who would be attending. "You will not be expected to go, but if you want to, I would appreciate the company."

Cassie gave him a sympathetic glance and said, "I would be honored to be there with you. I know he wasn't my family, but if you need me, I will be there for you."

A little smile played at the corners of his mouth as he responded to her sincerity. "Thank you. But all I really need is someone who can hold his or her own. I wasn't that close to him, as I told you earlier. However, for appearance's sake, I should probably show some remorse or the others will think I have turned into a human monster." He acknowledged the shocked look on Cassie's face at his response, so he placed his hand over hers to calm her and added, "I'm sorry, but I have told you before about my father, and I really can't say that I will miss him. I am not even sure the others will either, which brings me to another matter I should address before you meet my charming siblings." Before he could say another word, they were called for boarding. She was so perplexed by his hand holding hers that Cassie missed hearing the page. He abruptly moved his hand and looked at her. "We're on our way. I will tell you the rest once we are airborne. Come on!"

Cassie stood up and knocked her purse off her chair. When she bent to retrieve it, someone else's hand beat her to it. "Here, let me help you with that." Startled, Cassie looked up to meet the darkest brown eyes she had ever seen; so dark they were almost black. He handed her purse back to her, but in doing so, he began to warn her, "You should be careful whom you confide in. Nothing is what it seems to be." Without another word, the gentleman left her standing there, dangling her purse on her arm. The next thing she remembered hearing was Kelley telling her to get a move on. His pilot believed in punctuality, and so did he.

They were taken by limousine to Kelley's private airstrip where his pilot and personal stewardesses were waiting to greet him. Cassie was introduced to them and was immediately relieved to be in such capable hands. Once the introductions had been made, the pilot suggested they board and get underway, because it would be a long trip and there would be one stopover on the way.

As Cassie entered the plane, she was speechless. The decor was fabulous with its blues and greens and the amount of space that was unoccupied. Cassie had been under the impression that the jet would be small and cramped with all of their supplies. She was thrilled she had been wrong. This was going to be one of the best and most comfortable flights she had ever been on. Come to think of it, this was the only flight she had been on. She seated herself on a pale blue plush rocker that just seemed to relax her the moment she sat down. Kelley watched her intently for a few moments and then sat down directly in front of her on a blue-green printed loveseat. "I take it you like what you see." He placed his suit coat on the back of the couch.

"Like? I love it. I have never flown before, but if this is paradise, I won't want to get off. Are you sure this is business— or pleasure?" Her playful teasing provoked a strangled response from Kelley.

"Business, mostly. But there will be time for me to show you some of the sights before we leave town. Also, I don't believe my family will let me leave until after the festival. There is an annual gathering that my family has always attended, and I don't see why we should miss it. I hope you have enough clothes." He eyed her curiously.

"Well, if I don't, I guess I will just have to go shopping. Would you allow me some free time?" she prodded him.

"Of course." As the stewardesses handed out beverages and snacks, Kelley stood up and picked up his coat. After he deposited it into a small closet, he returned his attention to her. "Before we get started with the itinerary, there are some things you should be made aware of." Interrupting his speech, the pilot announced that they were commencing takeoff and should fasten their seatbelts. He also stated, "The weather is supposed to be bright and sunny, and the winds a mild ten miles per hour—a great day for travel. Liftoff will be in ten minutes."

Kelley, as well as Cassie, got up and moved to one of the other chairs. The rocker was not the best seat for takeoff, especially if she had never flown before. Any trip she took to see her parents or relatives had always been by car. Therefore, she was elated when he mentioned this trip. Not only would she get to fly, but also she would be able to interact with Kelley and his family. She would learn about his past, which somehow frightened and thrilled her. Not knowing what to expect made this trip much more appealing and definitely more dangerous than she realized. As she fastened her seatbelt in the seat next to him, she took a sidelong glance at him. He was busy with his own belt, which gave her a little time to observe him. His lean, hard looks didn't always match his personality, which thoroughly confused her from the start. On the other hand, he could make her take notice of him anytime he wanted, which irritated her. Whenever she thought she was beginning to understand him, he threw her a curve, and she never knew which direction it was going to come from. This trip would give her ample opportunity to observe him in different capacities—son, brother, and employer. She had a feeling she would follow him anywhere.

Cassie could feel the plane leave the runway and gripped her chair. Smiling at her weakness, Kelley soothed her, "You'll be fine. You are in capable hands, and once we are in the air, you won't feel a thing." He very briefly placed his hand over hers again, which caused tiny shivers up her spine. All he had to do was touch her, and her nerves tingled. For some unknown reason, he just seemed to know how to reach her. In this case, though, he was right. Once they had achieved the right altitude and removed their seatbelts, Cassie was fine. Within minutes after takeoff, Cassie was taking files out of her box.

She and Kelley went over the itinerary, and she began putting all her information in the correct order. When she came upon the green folder, she toyed with the idea of opening it and reading the contents; after all, it was in her box. On the other hand, she hadn't put it there, so he must have wanted it. She looked over at him and decided to remind him. When she cleared her throat, he looked up. His eyes immediately dropped to the folder on her lap.

"Where did you get that?" he snapped, as if he hadn't known it was there.

"I thought you placed it in here, so I left it. I guess I should have said something back at the office, but you don't have to snap at me over it. It was a logical mistake. But if you didn't put it here, who did?" she snapped back. It wasn't her fault that he had forgotten.

After a long and careful consideration, his face softened. "I'm sorry. I suppose I had a lot on my mind and simply misplaced it. Here, let me have it." Cassie handed it to him, and he placed it on the bottom of his briefcase. "Now, that will be the end of the matter." Somehow, she wasn't so sure.

By the time Cassie finished all of the work he had given her, they were three hours into their flight. She was getting tired and thirsty. Stifling a yawn, she placed all the folders back into the box and put the lid on. Apparently Kelley had noticed her yawn. "I think we could both use a drink." He got up and summoned the stewardess. When she appeared, he ordered, "Please bring Miss Garrett a glass of white wine and myself a glass of scotch and soda. Thank you." When he finished, he returned to the sofa and relaxed his tense muscles. Cassie watched him as he stretched out. He was long and lean, and the thin material of his Armani shirt did little to hide the muscles underneath. Cassie took a deep breath before she said anything.

"Thank you. I was getting a little thirsty myself." She stood up and stretched her tired muscles as his eyes rolled lazily over her petite figure. "We should almost be there, shouldn't we?" She eyed him wearily.

"Another hour. Which reminds me, I was going to fill you in on some things. Please sit down." He indicated the chair next to him, but Cassie sat back down in the rocker, not wanting to get too close for fear of her attraction showing through. His look of chagrin told her she had annoyed him, but she wasn't going to give in to him. Still looking at her as they accepted their drinks and some unsalted nuts, he commented, "My family is somewhat divided. We have all gone our separate ways, but we still keep in touch. At least some of us do. I have three brothers and one sister. There has been some trouble in the family for many years, but I am hoping to resolve these problems before we leave. Hopefully, I won't have to get you involved. But I will apologize now, if I do. It seems anyone that is close to my family gets hurt somehow. I will try to shield you, I promise." He looked at her earnestly. She didn't understand why he was telling her this, but she willingly accepted his apology.

"Don't worry, I am sure everything will be fine, and as for my interfering, I don't believe it will happen." She tried to sound reassuring but knew he didn't believe her.

"We shall see. I just thought I should warn you before you walked into a hornet's nest. Some of the family stick together more than others, so be careful." She was holding his steady gaze when the pilot's voice broke the silence.

"We are approaching the Calgary airport, Mr. McGillis, and will be landing in approximately thirty minutes. This is your pilot wishing you and Miss Garrett a safe and magical stay in Canmore. Please fasten your seatbelts for landing." Silence filled the aircraft.

Tearing her eyes from his, Cassie stood up and stretched again, dimly aware of his eyes roaming over her. She tried desperately not to pay attention to the look of desire on his face. Willing her legs to move, she returned to the front seat and fastened her seatbelt and waited for Kelley to do the same. When he finally did, Cassie was feeling a little nervous about sitting so close to him. There appeared to have been a chord struck between them that she hadn't expected. She silently prayed that she would control herself before she messed up again.

Kelley leaned over and whispered in her ear, "You are going to love it here. Look out your window." He pointed to the mountains down below. Stunned by his mouth being so close to her cheek, Cassie briefly lost her train of thought. Then getting her bearings, she quickly turned her head and became utterly spellbound at the magnificence of the snow-capped mountains. It seemed strange that these mountains could sustain a wild habitat, but she would learn how much life there actually was on top of those giant time-sculptured cliffs, not to mention what was hiding in the green valleys below. There seemed to be an endless array of color and light, which defied all the author's books and pictures. One had only to look at the Canadian land to see God's grace and magnificence. This had to be heaven, was all Cassie could think.

"It's beautiful, Kelley. I don't know how you could have left it." As they approached the runway into Calgary, she became even more mesmerized by her new surroundings. She really hoped they had plenty of free time for sight-seeing.

Within moments the plane landed perfectly on the runway, and the pilot announced, "Winds are light and comfortable, and the temperature is seventy-two degrees— perfect weather for hiking. Enjoy your stay, and we will see you on the return trip."

As the plane pulled up to the terminal, Kelley warned her, "I hope your evening dresses will be compatible with the weather. Sometimes the nights can be pretty cool up here. Did you bring a warm overcoat or lightweight jacket? I just thought I should ask, because on some occasions, we have an early snow."

"Not to worry, I have everything I need. If not, I will go shopping like I told you before we left." She made a smug face at him, which caused him to laugh. Unable to stop herself, Cassie started laughing too. It seemed to be contagious.

They were escorted out of the plane, and once outside, Cassie deeply inhaled the fresh air. Catching her perfume in the wind, Kelley leaned against the stair railing and reveled in her presence. She turned to look at him and caught a slight gleam in his darkened green eyes. They were almost a sea green—dark and dangerous. Reaching out, he took her by the elbow and escorted her to the terminal. Within an hour, they had made it through customs, the money exchange, and the luggage retrieval and were on their way to his family's home. Driving along Route 1 out of Calgary, Cassie wondered to herself if this trip was going to be a blessing or a curse. She didn't want to know the answer, but she feared she was going to find out. At the moment, though, all she wanted to think about was the man sitting beside her in the driver's seat. Nothing would go wrong as long as she stayed with him. She didn't know how wrong she was.

CHAPTER V

While gazing out of the car window, Cassie smiled to herself. She had never been allowed on a business trip with Kent, let alone leave the country. Sitting inside Kelley's Cutlass Sierra, they began their journey to her employer's family home; she had so many questions and wanted to see so much, but deep down, she felt she shouldn't question him too soon. If she asked too much too soon, she thought he might shut her out completely, and she wanted to know more about this man that had opened so many doors for her. Saying "thank you" just didn't seem to be enough. She concluded that she should at least wait until after the funeral to begin her interview.

Her smile and silence had obviously caught his attention, because he asked, "What's so funny, or can you share the joke?"

Even though she was tired, Cassie seemed more jovial than she felt. "It's nothing, after being left behind at the office so much, I guess I am a little overwhelmed at being here." She flashed a brilliant smile in his direction, which caused him to falter slightly.

"Well, from now on you will have to get used to it. I am glad you are here. It will be educational for you and give us a better chance to get to know each other." He didn't say personally or professionally, so Cassie was left wondering which one he wanted.

She refused to ask which, as she replied, "You're right, it will be educational for me. But I do hope there will be some time off to take some walks and enjoy the surroundings. Or should I ask permission first?" She prompted a smile from him.

"No, you won't have to ask permission to go for a walk on occasion, but I would insist that you take a guide with you. Someone who knows the territory. That way you won't get lost, and he or she can tell you about the environment here. You will find it fascinating." He smiled briefly in her direction and then turned his attention back to the road ahead. He had already informed her it would take a good hour to reach their destination. They had to follow Route 1 from Calgary to Canmore, and his father's house was just beyond Canmore's northern boundary, between Canmore and Banff. "Banff," he told her as they rode along, "is one of the national parks. It's a municipality and has limited residential areas. For that reason, my father set his family comfortably between the two cities. From where we are situated, we have a clear view of the Bow River. It's about five miles from our home, but we can see it from our bedroom windows."

After a little over an hour's drive, Kelley turned between two iron gates. From that point, they were heading west on what appeared to be a paved driveway. All along the drive were tall dark green Douglas fir trees. They seemed to tower over everything, including the car. After recovering from shock from the size of the trees, Cassie could make out a house in the distance through several big bushes. Off to the left of the car, Cassie could make out several large elk grazing in an open meadow. When the car rounded a bend in the drive, Cassie's breath caught in her throat. The sheer size of his childhood home caused her to be awestruck. The house, she believed, was a three-story mansion. The length she couldn't be sure of because most of the front was concealed by hanging vines and shrubs, neatly trimmed against the house, as if they were put there on purpose. In addition, it wasn't made of brick but stone or cement block. Cassie shuddered as if something cold had been placed on her neck. She wondered how anyone could live in such coldness but reconsidered the notion after remembering how Kelley had described his father. "Perhaps," she thought wryly, "the rest of the family won't feel so cold."

As they pulled up to the front steps, a man in a black suit appeared on the porch. He stood there watching as Kelley parked the car and got out. With a huge smile, the man came down the steps and gave Kelley a big hug. Cassie slowly emerged from the car and stood motionless as the two men looked at each other and then looked at her. She could tell by the dark hair and green eyes that he was a relative, but she didn't know how close. Coming around to her side of the car, he introduced himself, "Forgive me, but I haven't seen my brother in ages. I am Roderick. Please call me Rod. Everyone else does. I am the second son, and I have been trying to get Kelley to come home for some time, but I am sorry it had to be this way." Taking a breath, he looked her up and down appreciatively before asking, "And what might your name be, young lady?"

Kelley moved around the car, standing between her and Rod, "Cassie, Rod is known as the family flirt and clown. Rod, this is Miss Cassie Garrett, my secretary. I plan on visiting some people while I am here." Rod briefly shot him a cold glare, and then he turned his smile on Cassie, which looked exactly like Kelley's, and shook her hand.

"Pleasure to meet you, Miss Garrett. I do hope that he doesn't make you work the whole time you are here. If he does, let me know. I will take you around town." He laughed and brushed his brother aside as he took her hand in his and kissed her knuckles. Folding her arm under his, Roderick led her up the steps, leaving Kelley staring behind them. Swiftly, he removed the luggage from the car and helped a waiting butler, who had appeared after their arrival and carried the baggage into the house. Once inside, Kelley deposited them at the bottom of the stairs and gave orders for the butler to get help carrying them up. As soon as they finished, he followed Rod and Cassie into the salon, and as Rod offered her a seat on the small sofa beside him, Kelley asked if anyone wanted a cocktail before dinner. Trying to avoid meeting Rod's inquisitive green eyes, which were darker than Kelley's eyes, she too eagerly replied, "I'd love one. It was such a long flight; I don't think I could eat. If you gentlemen wouldn't mind, I would much rather retire early." She smiled at Kelley, hoping he would catch the hint; he did.

"I think we can both understand how tired you must be," he stated as he handed her a drink. "Don't we, Rod?" He glared at him, as if he expected him to disagree.

Rod's response was equally understanding. "Of course, you should be excused. The flight was long, and every beautiful woman deserves her rest." Taking her hand, he added gaily, "You need not get up early, either. The funeral will be at one thirty p.m., so you will have plenty of time to get ready, if you are going. I am sure that our brothers and sister will not mind you being there. They will probably treat you like one of the family, which I would support wholeheartedly," he squeezed her hand while she smiled weakly, and that made Kelley's eyes burn with a jealous fire.

Cassie placed her glass on the small coffee table in front of her and summoned enough energy to get up and walk toward the door with Kelley a few paces behind. Turning around briefly, she looked at Rod and said, "Good night. It was a pleasure meeting you." She turned to Kelley and asked, "Are you going to show me which room it is or just tell me how to get there?"

"I intended on showing you. After the funeral, I will show you around the grounds, so you won't get lost later on." He looked at his brother as he said, "I will be back, Rod. We have to talk. Now, follow me, Miss Garrett." He headed toward the stairs, and Cassie followed close behind, so close that when he turned around to look at her, they bumped into each other. "Sorry. I guess I am just a little nervous about being here," she apologized.

"Don't be. Everything will be fine." As he gently reassured her, he placed a possessive hand on her elbow and led her up the stairs. At the top of the stairs, Cassie turned slightly to her left and noticed Rod staring blankly at them as they disappeared down the hall. She didn't know why, but a small shiver ran down her spine, as if something sinister lay deep inside this house and she was on the verge of being swallowed alive.

By the time they had reached her room, she had regained her composure and her senses. She didn't want Kelley to sense anything wrong. He opened a door for her and allowed her to enter the room first. Looking around, she was astonished at how modern it looked. Except for a four-poster bed and washbasin in the corner on an antique stand, the room had a more rustic finish. The furniture was either oak or walnut stained, and there were expensive paintings of Western backgrounds and ladies sitting on lounge chairs. There were two chests of drawers and one cedar chest at the foot of the bed with an afghan sitting on top. Off to her right was a vanity with a mirror and the door to her own bathroom beside it. The thing that caught her attention most was the French door leading out to a balcony. She walked over to them and opened them wide enough to step outside and view the river before her.

The view was breathtaking. She had mountains to her left and the Bow River flowing just a few miles away but close enough to catch the beauty of the moon glowing on the surface of the water. She inhaled deeply and held her breath for a few seconds to capture the essence of her surroundings. The steps behind her brought her back to reality. "It's beautiful. I don't understand how anyone could leave this behind. But," she lowered her eyes briefly and then met his, "I know you had your reasons, and you told me part of them. Thank you for bringing me here."

Kelley let his right hand run alongside her left cheek and then whispered, "I am glad you approve. I knew you would appreciate this room. This was my father's room, but it's also the best in the house, and you deserve the best." His face was only inches from hers, and his eyes darkened as they scanned her face and bore into her own hazel ones. She thought for a moment that if he kissed her now, she knew she wouldn't resist. So for her sake, she prayed he wouldn't. As her knees began to weaken under his watchful eyes, he dropped his hand back down and broke the spell by saying, "You had better get some sleep. We have a big day tomorrow. Then we have to start calling people. Good night." Without another word, he left the balcony and walked out of the bedroom door, closing it behind him and leaving her breathless.

Recollecting herself, she left the balcony, closing the doors behind her and locking them. Her bags had been left on the bed. Retrieving the smallest bag, she entered the bathroom, which had decor in black-and-mauve patterns. The carpeting was in mauve, and the shower curtains, towels, and accessories were in black-and-mauve print. There were assorted pictures adorning the walls, besides a clock and several different colognes on the sink top. It was on top of the bathroom vanity that she set her bag and removed her gown, robe, slippers, and other necessities. Within a half hour, she had showered and changed and hung up the towel and washcloth to dry.

She turned off the bathroom light and moved to the light sitting on the bedside table. As she moved to turn the switch, a flash of light outside caught her attention. Slowly, she moved beside the French doors and peeked outside the curtain. She hoped to God that no one was there. But as she peered out the corner of the window, she noticed a dark figure lurking in the bushes below. Whoever it was appeared to be writing something, and it was obviously the silver pen that had caught the moon's reflection. She fought hard against the lump in her throat. Had her stalker followed her, or was this stranger actually looking for her? She couldn't be sure, but she felt she had walked into the middle of something she didn't understand. Should she call for Kelley? Would he even believe her? No. She couldn't tell anyone yet. She had to be sure it was her the stalker wanted, and one way or another she would find out. Peeking out of the window again, she found out the figure was gone. With her hand on her stomach, she staggered to the edge of the bed, and as she sat down, there was a knock on her door.

Cassie jumped to her feet as she said, "Come in."

Kelley entered the room with a .38-caliber gun in his hand as he moved to the window. As he looked out, he whispered, "Did you see anyone outside your window a few moments ago?" He looked at her as if he knew what the answer would be.

She was on the verge of telling him everything, not knowing why she reconsidered. "No. Is something wrong? What's going on, Kelley? You are frightening me, and put that gun away. I hate guns." He noticed the anxious look in her eyes and lowered the gun to the bedside table.

"I'm sorry. I was looking out my window when I saw something silver. I guess it was nothing; sorry I bothered you. But just to be on the safe side, I am leaving the gun in the table drawer. That way, if there is a threat, you will be protected." Suddenly, he realized her state of attire, and his eyes seemed to blaze a green fire as they ran down her figure in the moonlight. She had put on a negligee of sheer pale green material and matching chemise. Slowly, she moved to cover herself with the short filmy robe, but he stopped her. As he held her hands in his firmly, he took a long, lingering look at her figure, as if he could see right through the robe. "Rod doesn't know how right he is. You are a very beautiful woman, Cassie, and I would never do anything to hurt you. I believe you know that." Without another word, he moved closer to her, wrapping his arms around her thin body until one arm enveloped her waist and the other hand slowly crept up behind her neck, allowing his fingers to run through her hair. Before kissing her, he hovered over her lips, anticipating the sweetness beyond them. He could also smell the slight scent of body spray, which made his senses heighten. He knew he couldn't stop now, even if he wanted to.

Cassie was frozen in place, both breathless and confused. His green eyes and fiery passion hypnotized her. The scent of him that close caused her to forget everything, including the danger he had put her in. With her senses reeling from desire, she was powerless as his lips closed over hers. The first touch of his lips was brief and brushed sensually across hers, drawing her passion out further. No longer able to hold herself back, she abandoned reasoning and let the heat of passion move her forward. As she moved closer, he folded his arms more firmly around her, allowing her to feel how hard his passion was for her. But as his lips covered hers again, somewhere in the back of her mind, she knew this was wrong. The timing was bad. Their lives—or her life— were threatened, and she didn't know why or who was behind it. Suddenly, warning bells started going off in Cassie's head, and she began to stiffen, fighting off the wave of desire she was feeling for him. Not willing to accept her refusal, Kelley tried to force her to respond, but when he realized something was wrong, he raised his face within inches of hers. In the moonlight, he thought he saw fear in her eyes and released her. He moved backward and turned toward the window. His voice was hoarse with dying passion. "I'm sorry. I guess I moved a little too quickly for you." He regained his composure long enough to face her, "Don't worry; I will not put you in this position again. It's obvious our minds are on two different wavelengths. Good night." Without allowing her any time to respond, he walked out of the room, closing the door behind him, and closing the door on her heart.

What had just happened? Cassie moved back to the side of the bed to sit down. Her legs were like jelly and couldn't hold her up. For a few brief moments, she had been content to be in his arms, where she felt desirable and safe at the same time. She had never experienced such passion with Kent and doubted she would ever again. As the tears rolled down her cheeks, Cassie curled up on the bed, willing the pain to stop in her heart. Deep down, she knew it couldn't and wouldn't work. But she could still feel his arms around her, and his masculine scent was still in the air. She closed her eyes and prayed for sleep.

CHAPTER VI

The next morning, Cassie woke up with a splitting headache because of all the tears she had cried during the night. It took what seemed to be hours for her mind to black out the events of last evening, but eventually she had managed to concentrate on finding the intruder outside. Somehow she knew she would find some answers, even if Kelley refused to help her. After dressing in her black dress and pumps, she applied fresh makeup and put her hair up in a neat little bun with ringlets along the side of her face. She was always told that was her best hairdo, because it showed off her marvelous facial features: a small oval-shaped face with smooth skin, a pair of wide hazel eyes with long lashes, a small nose, and round full lips. Her mother always told her she would be a man killer, but she would only laugh and say, "I will." By the time she made it downstairs, breakfast had already been served, and the men had just finished eating.

As she entered the room, Rod got up and approached her. "You look stunning, my dear. Would you care for some coffee or juice?"

"Coffee, please." She smiled meekly, showing she was much stronger than she felt. Before she sat down, she caught Kelley's gaze and held it briefly. Nodding her head, she accepted a cup of steaming coffee from Rod.

"Well, I hope you slept well. After all the ruckus last night, I would be glad if anyone had slept." Acknowledging her surprised look, he added, "Yes, I know about the intruder. He or she has been appearing here since before father died. However, we have never been able to get more than a glimpse. No tracks. No clues. One of these days, though," he smiled for Cassie's benefit, "we will know . . . I promise." Taking a drink, he paused, "Now, after breakfast, the rest of the family should be arriving, and you can get acquainted with them also. I am surprised Kelley hasn't told you about them yet. There is Johann and Kirk; they are the younger brothers, and there is Janelle, the baby of the family. I am afraid we spoiled her as a child, so don't be surprised by her attitude." Looking at her, sipping coffee, he offered, "You really should eat something, because it will be a long afternoon, and the services here tend to take longer. I can't explain why, but they do."

"Thank you, but I can't eat." Before she could say anything else, Kelley pushed a Danish in her direction. After giving him an icy glare, Cassie smiled at Rod, "I guess I could eat a little something to tide me over." She picked up her fork and started to cut into the cream cheese Danish. She had only gotten one small bite when the front door opened with a bang. It was obvious who the first to arrive was, but the stunning beauty that walked through the door didn't look a thing like her brothers.

The woman who entered the dining room was a tall thin well-tanned beauty with straight long black hair and the most amazing brown eyes with little specks of green in them. She could not have passed as one of the family, except for her height and exceptional smile. Her smile did not quite reach her eyes as she glanced in Cassie's direction and locked eyes. Just as quickly as she caught her eye, Kelley's sister turned her attention to her brothers, throwing herself into their arms. Cassie was so awestruck by her dark beauty that she almost didn't hear the introductions.

Cassie stood up and shook hands with the stunning woman, whose manners belied her looks. Cassie had expected to be snubbed by this elegant person, but instead, she was greeted with a warm smile and robust "Hello! I'm Janelle. But then, you probably have guessed that already. My brothers and I have remained close despite the distance." She turned to Kelley and apologized, "I am sorry, but Alexander couldn't make it. As usual, business comes first." As Rod held out a chair for her, she fell into it with a heavy sigh. "I hate to say this, but he always seems to feel that he doesn't belong here." Catching the peculiar look on Cassie's face, Janelle explained, "You probably know by now all the problems we had with Father. Well, as much as I loved him, he never returned that love. So I guess you could say there was no love lost. Right?" She glanced from one brother to another, as if expecting them to agree.

But all Rod would say was, "He had his shortcomings, and we just accepted them. Although he never meant to hurt any of us intentionally, his mind was constantly on finances and the environment. Anything else came last. Unfortunately, that meant us and Mom." He faced Cassie as he finished, "I believe that gives us cause not to miss him, doesn't it, Miss Garrett?"

Out of compassion for the dead man, Cassie said, "I am sure that he provided whatever you needed." Catching the raw look in Kelley's eyes, she countered, "But I guess the one thing you needed was love, and he didn't know how to give it."

With a glance of acknowledgment, Kelley offered, "I think everyone has their own opinion, and we should leave it at that. Agreed?" Everyone nodded approval, and he went on to ask, "Janelle, have you talked to the other two this morning? They haven't called."

"Yes. Johann is en route. He will be at the gravesite, and Kirk is not coming. There is a lot of water under that bridge, and I really didn't think he would come, did you?" she queried.

"No. I guess not. But he should learn to bury the hatchet and get on with life." Kelley tried to sound aggravated, but

Cassie thought she saw relief in his eyes. Why he should feel this way was completely lost to her. She figured sometime she would get the chance to ask, but now was not that time.

"It's almost ten thirty. Is there anything that needs to be done before the funeral, because I would like to help?" Cassie tried to change the direction of the conversation, and apparently everyone was willing not to argue.

Rod stood up and poured himself another cup of coffee. "There is not much left to do. The town donates its time, and budget money is put aside for such things, mostly because of where he is to be buried. You will learn, Cassie, that this little town is much more than what it seems, as well as the people in it."

"I don't think Cassie needs to be that concerned at this point." Turning to look at Cassie, Kelley pointedly stated, "Don't listen to him, Cassie. There are some old stories floating around, and they don't concern you, so you are in no danger." His icy stare at Rod made her uneasy, but she didn't pursue that matter, because she didn't want to start a family quarrel. In fact, the look he shot Rod caused him to turn away and pick up the newspaper sitting on the bar.

Tapping her fingers on the table, Janelle muttered, "I know what we can do, Cassie. Come with me." The two men looked at her quizzically, and she continued, "Don't look so paranoid. I just have some things I need to pack up, and Cassie can help me." She took Cassie by the hand and led her into the entryway. Once outside the room, Janelle turned around to make sure they weren't followed, and then she looked at Cassie anxiously and said, "I'm sorry for bustling you out like that, but I thought you could use a break. Sometimes, my brothers can be overbearing, and this will also give me a chance to get to know you better. It's not every day that Kelley brings a woman home, especially a secretary. His mind is usually on business; so I guess you have a special quality he finds appealing." Taking a deep breath, she whispered, "There is something I want to show you, and I didn't want them to know about it, because it was a painful part of our history. Come on." She led Cassie to a door hidden behind the main staircase and quietly opened it.

Before she started down the steps, Janelle looked at Cassie and said, "Unfortunately, the light switch is at the bottom of the steps. That's the way Dad designed the basement. We kids always played tricks on each other by hiding down there. Once, I hid under the stairs, and Kelley came looking for me. When he got halfway down the stairs in pitch blackness, I grabbed his leg; he tripped and landed on his right arm, breaking his collarbone." Smiling at Cassie, she added, "I felt bad afterward, and Dad gave me the spanking of my life afterward, because that was the only time Kelley ever broke a bone. I wouldn't say anything to him, because he would only deny it." Taking her hand and leading her into the darkness, she cautioned Cassie about a couple of loose steps and that she should stay as close to the wall as possible. There was no railing to hang on to.

With each step, Cassie became a little more nauseous. It seemed like they were being swallowed up by a huge black hole from which there was no escape. They descended until Cassie felt as if she were becoming claustrophobic. Forgetting the caution Janelle had given her, she stumbled slightly over the weak steps. "Okay?" The voice sounded muffled in the darkness. Cassie managed to laugh in response to Janelle's concern.

"Fine. I will be better once we reach the end of the stairs. This seems endless." She had no more than got the words out of her mouth when Janelle stopped and flipped on the light. What Cassie saw confounded and amazed her. There were several expensive paintings, obviously by original artists, several racks of aged wine, and furniture of a wide variety. Over along the east wall were three cedar chests sitting side by side. The chests were apparently what Janelle was looking for. They were locked with combination locks, and Janelle soon had one of the chests open.

Cassie stood on the cement floor, looking bewildered at her surroundings. Their father had obviously been a big art enthusiast and an avid wine connoisseur. But the bottles of wine appeared to have never been touched, and Cassie wondered why he hadn't hung the paintings in the house. Upon closer examination, she realized the artist was Kelley's mother. She guessed their father hadn't wanted any reminders of his dead wife in the upstairs part of the house. Cassie reverted her attention to Janelle and the open trunk. Walking up behind her, she had to catch her breath. There could be no match for what Janelle was holding in her hands. There, in the palm of her hand, lay the largest stones she had ever seen in a necklace. The sapphires were inlaid around diamonds and rubies, with more delicately cut tinier emeralds in the center. "Mesmerizing, isn't it? I was afraid Dad had sold it to the highest bidder."

"Whose was it, or whose is it? If you don't mind telling me?" Cassie couldn't stop staring at the brilliant stones. It reflected a rainbow of light along the basement wall when Janelle lifted it up.

"It was a gift to our mother, but no one ever knew for sure who gave it to her. Dad was too much of a tightwad to have bought it, so we could only guess it was a lover. Dad always told me I couldn't have been his because I didn't look like my brothers. There were times I believed him, but my brothers always laughed it off saying I was just like him, too stubborn to quit. But it always came down to coloring. I was a lot darker than anyone in my family, but rather than dig up any dirt, I let it lie." Sighing, she said, "Here, will you hold this for a moment? There is something else in here I need to find." After a few moments, she became frantic. Cassie became uneasy as Janelle started pulling everything out of the trunk.

"What are you looking for? Maybe I can help you." Cassie tried to calm her but was not succeeding.

"No, you can't help. This is only something my father would have understood." Standing up and glancing at the other two trunks, Janelle stated, "Well, it is obviously not here, and I don't have the combination to the other trunks. They belong to my brothers." Replacing the contents of the trunk and retrieving the necklace from Cassie, Janelle closed the lid and locked the trunk. "I will just have to look for it later. We had better go." With an exasperated sigh, Janelle grabbed Cassie's hand and turned out the light. When they appeared at the top of the steps, Kelley was coming out of the study.

"What the hell did you think you were doing taking her down there? You know how risky those steps are." Kelley admonished his sister so harshly that Cassie flinched. Rod seemed to agree because he stood behind his brother and shook his head.

"Kelley is right, Janelle. You should have remembered what happened a long time ago." He didn't finish explaining, which left Cassie wondering what happened but feared asking.

Janelle looked perplexed. "I had a hold of her. Nothing was going to happen, I swear. Anyway, I had to find something, but it wasn't there. It's missing." She sounded distressed.

"What, Janelle? What is missing?" Rod asked.

"Oh, nothing major, I guess." She sounded so vague, as if there had been nothing specific she was looking for. But Cassie knew something was wrong, so why was she lying? "The funny part is whoever broke into the trunk left the necklace that was Momma's, which should be extremely valuable. I would have thought that would be stolen first." Her brothers looked at each other with caution in their eyes.

"Look, Janelle," Kelley soothed, "after the funeral we can sit down and figure out what you are missing, but right now we have to be leaving." He was right, and she knew it. As swiftly as she had become anxious and upset, Janelle became placid and content. Kelley suggested they retrieve their coats and meet downstairs. When they appeared outside, the long black limousine was waiting for them.

CHAPTER VII

By the time the funeral was over, the sky had clouded over and threatened to pour rain onto the mournful people surrounding the gravesite. But the weather did not stop the minister from giving his final prayers for the lost soul to be reborn in heaven. After he finished and had given the family his condolences, he informed the mourners there would be a luncheon at the deceased's family home. They could spend a few more moments by the grave, and then he would be lowered into the ground.

During the brief staying period, Cassie took a few moments to look around. There seemed to be an assortment of people. She was certain all the family members had worn black, but some of the others wore bright colors. There were a few couples with children and several elderly gentlemen; one in particular didn't keep his eyes off of Janelle, and another seemed interested in Cassie. What on earth for, she could not figure. She knew she had never seen him before, or maybe she had. She turned to get a better look, but he had turned and started walking toward the vehicles. Cassie was on the verge of following after him when Kelley placed his hand under her elbow and motioned her to the waiting limousine. "We need to get back before everyone shows up." She followed his lead back to the car and slowly climbed in.

On the way back, knowing it wasn't the time or the place for inquiries, Cassie asked, "Who were most of the people there, because I thought you said he had no family left except for his children?" She caught the caustic look from Janelle but kept her ground as she looked up at Kelley.

"Most of them were members of the Banff town council, and some were loyal friends of Dad's. There were a few there that I don't remember meeting, but I am sure we will meet them at home." After a short pause, he added, "I must admit, however, I never expected such a big turnout. Did you?" he looked at Roderick, as if he would know why.

"Nor did I, but he must have maintained a high profile, despite his family failures. What do you think, Janelle?" Roderick nudged her arm playfully as he addressed her.

"I don't know. I thought once I left home that would be the end of things. Lord knows I hadn't planned on coming back for his burial. If it weren't for my husband's urging, I don't think I would have been here." She looked at her hands in her lap rather than face the fury in both her brothers' eyes.

"You should be ashamed of yourself. Our father treated you the same way he treated the rest of us. Despite our misfortunes, he did provide a roof over our heads!" Kelley sounded bitter as he chided her for her thoughtless attitude.

"Barely, he wouldn't even part with money to help Mother. That makes him a no-good father and husband, doesn't it?" Janelle had made a point, but today was not the day to be passing blame, especially when the one being accused was dead.

At that point when Kelley was on the verge of un-controllable rage, Roderick intervened. "I think we can think of something else to discuss, don't you?" He looked right at Cassie, as if he needed to point out this was a family matter and best discussed behind closed doors. "He is dead and buried. We need to let it go now. Arguing is not going to help the situation. After today, we can figure things out, but we need to show strength in front of his friends, or all respect will be lost. And you know how Momma felt about respect." He cocked his head to one side as he reminded everyone of their mother's belief. Everyone fell silent, and Cassie looked from one to the other, trying to figure out what had just transpired between them.

"I'm sorry, Janelle," Kelley broke the brief silence.

"Me too. This wasn't the right time or place to hash this out." Janelle turned to Cassie and said, "Forgive me. I didn't mean to start a family quarrel in front of you, but my emotions have been really high lately. Will you forgive me?" She smiled childishly.

Cassie looked around at the other two and then grinned, "You don't have to apologize, I understand completely. This day has already taken its toll on everyone. Let's just forget it and get through the luncheon, all right?" She urged everyone to agree. When they all began to laugh, the electricity in the atmosphere seemed to disappear, and they all started sharing childhood memories. Cassie found herself laughing as she was told of several pranks Kelley and his brothers used to play on Janelle, and vice versa. As the cheerful conversations continued, they approached the house, where several cars had already been parked, and the people were waiting to be ushered in.

Once they were all inside the house, Kelley escorted Cassie over to one of the sofas in the salon and then returned to greet the other mourners. After brief handshakes and hugs, the awaiting butler announced the buffet was ready and the guests could eat at their leisure in the family room. Cassie stood up and started to head toward the door when she noticed the stranger that had stared at her during the burial. She locked eyes with him before he swiftly looked away. She was on the verge of following him to the front door as he prepared to leave when Janelle approached her. "I hope you feel like eating. I know I don't, but you are probably in need of nourishment after your long trip yesterday. Am I right?" Janelle had locked arms with her and began leading her in the direction of the family room, which she hadn't seen yet.

She quickly turned her head, just in time to see the gray-haired man walk out the door, missing her chance to find out who he was, and then looked back at Janelle. "No, actually I am not very hungry, but I might try a little something if you will." On impulse, Cassie inquired about the stranger. "You wouldn't by any chance know who that man was who just left, because he seemed to be interested in me? Or maybe it was my imagination. He didn't look like a member of the family. Do you know him?"

"You mean the man who just left here? That was Bernard Callis. He and my father had been rivals for years, but I find it fascinating that he showed up here today. I guess after all of these years, he must have acquired some respect for Father. Any other reason is beyond me, but don't worry. He probably is interested in you because of Kelley. Any woman with Kelley is news around here. You should be flattered." They entered the family room, and Janelle released her. "Well, I should mingle a little while. Make yourself at home." Without another word, she walked over to one of the younger couples and greeted them.

Left on her own, Cassie found herself wandering over to the buffet and found several tasty tidbits. Picking up a plate, she gingerly chose the most appealing appetizers. She was reaching for a glass of ice tea when another hand picked it up for her. She expected to see Kelley beside her, but this was the man who had been watching Janelle. Stunned silent, she waited for him to speak.

"I'm sorry. I didn't mean to startle you." He handed her the glass of tea, which she accepted politely. "My name is Matt Jamison, and I was a friend of the family, especially their mother. Whenever Bethany needed help and Patrick wasn't around, she would depend on my wife and me to lend a hand. You might say that I helped raise those kids. I guess you can tell that I am partial to Janelle. She was so young when her mother died, and she always believed Patrick wasn't her father." With a small grin on his face, he added, "I wouldn't blame her for her beliefs, but I only hope that she doesn't pursue the matter. She might be disappointed." Looking around at the other mourners, he said, "Well, I should be going. It has been a pleasure talking to you, Miss . . ." He realized he hadn't asked her name, so she told him. "Miss Garrett, I hope we can talk again sometime. Goodbye." He left her standing in shock, holding her plate and glass.

Very slowly, Cassie walked over to one of the straight-backed chairs and sat down. As she placed her glass on the floor beside her chair, she casually glanced around the room. It was a charming room filled with family photos. Most of them were missing the father, but the ones including him made it seem like the perfectly happy family. There were many pictures of the boys, but Cassie noticed that Janelle appeared in only six of the twenty-something. She couldn't imagine not having pictures of Janelle. She was a breathtaking young woman, so why wouldn't he show it? He was obviously disappointed in her, but to leave her out of the pictures seemed to Cassie to be cruel and heartless. "Janelle was sent to boarding school."

Cassie jumped, almost knocking over her glass on the floor, as Kelley sat down beside her. "I don't understand. Why would he leave her out of the family portraits? That seems cruel." She almost felt sad for Janelle, and it showed in her tone.

"From the time she was born, Father stayed as far away from her as he could get. There had been constant arguments before she was born. Because Janelle had a dark complexion, Father accused Mother of being unfaithful and vowed that he would not accept her. When Mother died, leaving him to take care of her, he carted her off to a European boarding school instead of taking care of her. And that's where she grew up. All of us kids kept in touch with her, because she was still our little sister, and nothing could change that. When she would come home for the holidays, she would stay here, but out of sight of Father. Whenever their paths did cross, however, they would quickly pass each other silently or turn the other direction. By the time Janelle was a teenager, she had vowed not to let him destroy her, and so far she has won. Does that answer your questions?"

"Yes, it does. But it doesn't excuse him." Remembering her conversation of a moment ago, Cassie asked him, "Have you ever considered that she might be someone else's child?"

Kelley leaned over and removed the plate and glass from her hands and placed them on the coffee table in front of them. His eyes burned into hers before answering, "It was a thought I didn't want to pursue. This family has been through so much, and to start inquiring about her paternity would have jeopardized our family's integrity. So we buried the past with Mother, and now we bury it again. Maybe this time it will stay buried." He sat straight up and stretched his arms out in front of him. "Why do you ask?" he countered.

"I don't know. It just seems like someone doesn't want it buried." She knew she couldn't stop now. She had to tell him about Jamison. Before she could ask, however, a young man approached Kelley. Judging by his height and familiar looks, he had to be another brother, but which one she didn't know.

Kelley stood up and hugged the man before he turned to Cassie. "Cassie, I would like you to meet Johann, my second younger brother. Johann, this is Miss Cassie Garrett. She is my personal assistant . . . and friend." Cassie was flattered by the revelation but didn't let on as she shook hands with the younger brother.

"It's a pleasure to meet you, Johann." She smiled, and he took her hand in his and smiled back.

"Oh no, the pleasure is all mine. I see you are getting better at picking your women, Kelley. I hope you hang on to this one; she's special." The compliment made her blush, and she lowered her eyes. He returned his eyes to Kelley and, after hesitating briefly, said, "I am sorry I didn't make it to the funeral. I would have been here, but duty calls. You know how it is. In this case, though, it was family business. There are some things we need to discuss, dear brother, and you are not going to like what you'll hear." His tone had lost its playfulness, and he seemed genuinely annoyed.

"Not here and not now. I am fully aware of what's been going on, but we can't very well put an end to it until after the guests leave. Where is Kirk?" Kelley asked stiffly.

"I haven't been able to locate him. It would appear he doesn't want to be found, at least not at the moment. I can only assume he got the message, and I am guessing he has come into some more trouble. You know him, always the schemer." Smiling back at Cassie who had been listening and waiting patiently, he excused himself, "I think I will find something to eat and greet our friends. It was a pleasure." He sighed heavily and then walked over to the buffet.

"Charming man. You didn't tell me your family was so nice, or was I just supposed to grin and bear their company." She looked up into his discerning eyes questioningly, but he obviously didn't care to answer her.

"We all had to learn manners. It was Mother's rule, and we never fought her on it." Changing the subject, he reminded her of their previous conversation. "What did you mean that it wouldn't stay buried?"

"Oh, nothing. Someone by the name of Jamison approached me and talked quite a lot about Janelle. Could he know something that you don't?" By the look on Kelley's face, she wished she could have retracted her question.

"Don't ever bring it up, Cassie. Wounds run deep in our family, and in this neighborhood, families are very loyal to one another. Now that Father is dead, the matter is closed. If I were you, I would forget what Jamison told you and not let anyone hear you mention it again," he admonished. Gazing around the room, he concluded, "The people in this room don't need to know about our family problems, okay?"

"I understand. I am sorry. I realize I made a mistake, but I had to ask." Her apology fell on deaf ears as her gaze followed his to the entry hall. On the door's threshold stood a gray-haired man with a mustache and goatee, probably in his midsixties. He was handing the maid his coat and hat and asking her a question, which she answered gaily. As he walked into the room, Kelley's body seemed to stiffen as if he expected to be slapped in the face. Eyeing Kelley, the gentleman walked over to within four feet of him and moved his eyes up and down before he spoke.

"Well, you are looking pretty damn good, Kelley. I wondered how you were faring in the States. I see now that Patrick at least did right by you." For once, Cassie could see Kelley was fuming, and she was completely dumbfounded. Trying to assert himself after the cold meeting, the gentleman glanced over at Cassie and introduced himself. "Hello, my name is Mick Clawson of Canmore Falls. That is the name of my estate. It's just on the other side of Patrick's northern gates. We're neighbors, although we haven't been sociable for a long time."

"And still unlikely to be." At last Kelley had found his voice, and it wasn't very pleasant. "What do you mean by coming here? I thought we had ended our connections a long time ago." He was still seething but, because of the surrounding guests, tried to be civil.

"Why? I should think that would be obvious. I am paying my respects to your father; he was, after all, a pillar of the community and an active environmentalist in Banff. I consider it my civic duty to show my respects even though we never actually got along. But I can see that I am not welcome here, so I will say, 'I'm sorry for your loss,' and be on my way. Please let Janelle know I was here. Good day, miss." With a maleficent grin, he walked out of the room, gathered his coat and hat, and left.

Cassie's eyes followed the man out the door before she asked, "What happened? He said he came to give his respects, so why are you behaving as if he were the devil himself?" She turned on him vehemently.

"Because he is the devil as far as this family is concerned, and don't ever forget it." Walking away from her, he approached his brothers with apprehension in his eyes. Cassie was left staring after him, confounded by the turn of events the day had taken. First, Janelle had put her in harm's way; second, the man at the funeral couldn't keep his eyes off of her; third, another man was genuinely interested in Janelle's future plans; and finally, this unexpected encounter with a man who, for some unknown and controversial reason, was not allowed in their home, not to mention on the grounds. There seemed to be a storm brewing, and Cassie felt as if she were drowning in floodwaters already. She hoped it would all blow over soon, or someone might be in danger. She just didn't know who—yet.

Cassie slowly moved to the outer hall. Once out in the open, she walked over to the stairs and took her first step when a hand came down on hers, stopping her retreat to her room. Anxiously, she raised her eyes to cool green ones, eyes which to her were pleading for forgiveness. "I am sorry for that display of temper. Can you forgive me?" Kelley's eyes stared into hers. "You have no idea what that man has done to this family."

Cassie focused her attention on the hand that rested on hers. His touch was a little overwhelming to her, but she managed to reply, "It's okay, but you're right. I don't understand why, and I don't believe you are going to fill me in either, are you?"

"It's family business." His eyes roamed her face, taking in the tired expression. "But someday I will tell you all you need to know. Right now, I would like you to stay down here with my family and me. We are all grateful you came. You released our tensions and made things easier to handle. My only regret is that you have observed some unfortunate circumstances. I will have to make sure you aren't put through them again." Removing his hand from hers, he stood aside to let her pass, but she had other plans.

"Don't worry about me, I can take care of myself. Thank you for your compliment, but I really haven't done anything. You have a very strong family from what I have seen. As for returning, I am afraid I am still suffering from jetlag. I am extremely tired and would like to lie down if you don't mind." She must have looked totally exhausted, because he sympathized with her.

"Yes, I suppose it has been rather exhausting for you. After all, this is your first trip outside the States, and on a plane too." His hand gently raised her chin, so he could gaze into her eyes, causing her heart to miss a beat. "All right, you rest for a few hours, and I will wake you for tea later." He turned and walked back into the family room, and Cassie weakly climbed the stairs.

By the time Cassie reached her room, her head was spinning. She pulled out a bottle of aspirin from her knapsack and walked into the bathroom to get a cup of water. After swallowing two tablets with water, she returned to the bedroom and lay down on the firm but soft mattress. Within a few short moments, she was sound asleep and oblivious to any noise in the room. Sleep, however, turned into one nightmare after another. Shadows appeared and disappeared, leaving her running breathless, exhausted, and frightened for her life. In one dream, she was being followed down a long corridor with no windows or doors to open to escape the certain doom behind her. She was sweating and panting for air, but when she thought she had found the way out, it was another detour. She could feel a warm hand upon her shoulder. Screaming in horror, she turned and looked at her assailant. Before she could tell whose face she looked upon, she opened her eyes with a jolt and sat straight up in bed. Looking around her, she breathed a sigh of relief, "Just a nightmare, thank God."

Slowly moving out of bed, Cassie stumbled into the bathroom and turned on the cold-water faucet. After she rinsed the sweat from her face and wiped it off with a fresh towel, she looked at her reflection in the mirror. "What made you dream like that, girl? You need to get a grip before you lose all your sanity." Standing straight and shaking herself, she left the bathroom. As she came out, her bedroom door began to creep open.

Scared stiff, Cassie didn't move until the brown-haired maid peered around the corner and smiled. "Sorry to disturb you, Miss Garrett, but Mr. McGillis said I should check on you and make sure you were all right. He said he heard noises in the room. He also suggested that you come down for dinner in an hour. I will leave you to get dressed."

"Thank you, I will be there shortly." Laughing weakly, Cassie confided in her, "For a moment I thought you were someone who was going to harm me." Seeing the worried look on the girl's face, Cassie hurried, "Oh, don't worry. It was just a bad dream. I know you would never hurt anyone. Tell Mr. McGillis that I will freshen up a little and then make my appearance for dinner." Without another word, the maid left, closing the door behind her.

Cassie was turning to pick up her handbag when she noticed that a small object had fallen off the bureau drawers in the corner of the room. She walked over and picked up a small silver box and held it briefly in her hands before she placed it back on the dresser. Cassie couldn't figure out how the box could have ended up on the floor, because she had been sound asleep, and she hadn't touched anything in the room except her bags and the bathroom supplies. Maybe she had just overlooked it when she came into the room the first time. No, she was sure she hadn't. Everything had been in its proper place, so why was the box on the floor now? She didn't want to believe the obvious, that someone had indeed been in the room while she was asleep, but what else could it have been? Kelley had told the maid he heard noises in the room. He didn't say what kind of noises he heard, so Cassie could only imagine an intruder. Picking up the box again, she opened it to find the shock of her life. There in the silver metal box was the necklace that Janelle had shown her earlier, but who could have put it there? She closed the box and placed it back in its place.

Cassie redressed herself in a blue chiffon dinner dress. It fit her to perfection, and she applied just the right amount of makeup to hide the stress of her sleep and the shock of her discovery. After she fastened her Gucci sandals, she retrieved the silver box and headed out the door. Once in the hallway, she ran into Rod, who apparently had missed her leaving earlier. "Ah, I see you have revived yourself, and just in time for dinner too. May I walk you down?" His roving eyes did little to ease her frazzled nerves, but she allowed him to take her arm and lead her down the stairs.

Once downstairs, they entered the dining room, which was just off to their right. Dinner was being served as they entered the room; Kelley looked up and glared at them both until Cassie had been seated directly in front of him. His face was a shade darker, but he attempted to hide his annoyance by picking up his glass and inquiring, "I hope you had a pleasant nap?"

"Let's just say I feel better than I did. I must have been more exhausted than I thought. Thank you for asking." She accepted a glass of wine without looking up to avoid the icy look in his green eyes. She couldn't understand why he was so irritated that she came down with Roderick. After all, they were family. "Besides," she thought, "Rod was just playing the polite host." As she took a sip of her wine, the butler proceeded to set a nice crab salad plate in front of her. She remembered the silver box in her hand and was about to mention it when the front door blew open and a woman appeared in a chic black dress and expensive high heels.

Forgetting the box in her hand, Cassie sat in her chair in awe of the woman who had just appeared as if she owned the entire house. From where she was sitting, Cassie guessed the woman to be in her midthirties and possibly five six or seven, she couldn't be sure, and she was well groomed all the way down to the nail polish on her toes.

"Charisse, what the hell do you mean barging in on such short notice?" Kelley demanded, sounding furious at being surprised by an unexpected guest. Moving around the table, Kelley stood within a couple of inches from her. Taking a bite of her salad to steady her own nerves, she could see Kelley was fuming inwardly.

"Oh, darling, don't be in such an uproar. I was out of town when I got the news about your father, and I just assumed you would need some comfort. So I told myself that I should hightail it back home and be here for you." Eyeing Cassie, however, stopped her short. "But I see you have other arrangements, or am I missing something? Please fill me in, dear." With a puzzled expression, she sat down and accepted a glass of wine from Rod.

Everyone's eyes were on Kelley as he gathered his composure and returned to his seat and, at the same time, answered her inquiries one by one. "Thank you for your consideration," he started, "but we really haven't had time to discuss the matter. It's been a long day, and we are all exhausted, that's all. As for Cassie, Miss Garrett, being here," he paused briefly, "it's business, and anything else is none of yours." That "anything else" was beyond Cassie's comprehension, but the business part was absolutely correct. Looking around at everyone, he refused to be goaded into saying anything by attacking his salad with gusto.

Unperturbed by his statement, the woman responded, "Well, I guess I made a mistake in coming so late. Maybe I should come back tomorrow, if that's okay with the rest of you. I don't want to be an intrusion, especially on such a solemn occasion." Placing her hand briefly over Kelley's, which caused him to stiffen, she added, "I am deeply sorry, Kelley, about your father. I know he wasn't the best father in the world, but he did what he thought was right."

Kelley squeezed her hand before removing it from his, "Thank you, and I am sorry about jumping on you. I think you had better leave, though. It has been a long day." He refused to acknowledge the caustic look in her eyes at being so easily dismissed.

Charisse stood up and looked around at everyone. "Well, this is good night, and I will come back tomorrow." Her eyes rested on Cassie for one brief icy stare, and then she turned to Kelley and lightly kissed him on the cheek, as if to say, "I'm still here for you." Then without another word, she left, leaving everyone in stunned silence.

Finishing her salad, Janelle was the first to respond, "What just happened? I would swear that a cyclone had just blown through, and wearing too much perfume at that." Wrinkling her nose, Janelle looked at Kelley with a huge mocking grin. "I thought you had ended that one when you left home, or does she know that yet?" Eyeing Cassie, she grinned at her, "Oh, I wouldn't worry about it, dear. She's got the money and the looks that kill, but nothing upstairs, if you know what I mean. She's just plain mean when it comes to getting what she wants. All you have to do is play along as long as you're here, and after you're back home, well, don't worry."

Cassie was reeling from shock of the woman's icy glare and from the nausea of the reason behind it. Apparently, the woman, as well as the rest of the family, had misinterpreted her reasons for coming. Kelley had needed her support, sure, but she was officially there on business, and she was sure that Kelley had told the rest of the family. She knew they were reading the situation wrong, but deep down, she knew she was powerless to change their minds. The only thing she could do was remain cautious about any physical signs that might mislead them. At the present moment though, she was dumbfounded and speechless. Thankfully, Kelley defended her.

"That's enough, Janelle! Cassie is here for professional reasons, but that doesn't mean she should be treated any differently. Right?" He scowled at her.

"Absolutely," Roderick interrupted. "Cassie is also a guest in this house, and we mustn't forget our manners." He sat down beside her and pretended to hug her, which caused Kelley's jaw to twitch. Janelle, who had been watching Kelley with amusement at Rod's mock affection, giggled.

"Right," Janelle said as she placed her glass on the table and began to yawn. "As you wish, Kelley. I'm going to turn in. It's been a long day, and we have a lot to do tomorrow. Good night, everyone." She kissed her brothers and shook Cassie's hand. "Good night, Miss Garrett. I hope you find some time to enjoy your stay here." Winking, she turned and walked out of the room and headed up the stairs.

Johann, who had been completely silent until now, stood up and walked over to the brandy decanter. Turning around, he addressed Cassie. "You will have to excuse our sister. Sometimes she lets her opinions get in the way of her logic. Anyone can see that you are a very professional young woman and far too smart to get involved." Replacing the decanter on the counter, he took his drink and headed toward the door. "I am turning in too. Kelley, Rod, I will speak to both of you first thing in the morning. There are some things we need to discuss, and now is not the time. Good night, Miss Garrett." His leaving the room for some unknown reason made Cassie breathe a sigh of relief. Up until now, she had been too shell-shocked by all the events of the day. Her eyes fell on the box in her hand, and after careful consideration, she decided not to broach the subject this night. She would wait until Kelley was alone with her, and then she would explain what happened; only thing was she didn't really know herself how it got into her room, on her dresser.

She folded the box in her hands and lifted her head to meet both gentlemen's stare. "I'm sorry. Did one of you say something?" she asked.

"Yes, I said we should turn in as well. It has been a long day, and I believe you are still getting over our flight." Kelley repeated himself calmly. It appeared he had had enough outbursts for one day. Then he added, "We will be very busy tomorrow, so you had better get your beauty rest. You will want to wear something comfortable for walking, because we will be doing a lot of that. I will take you up." He came around the table and stopped behind her to pull her chair out for her. Keeping the box hidden in her hand, she stood up and allowed him to place his hand on her elbow. As they approached the dining room door, Rod stood up, and as he bid them good night, he went over to the brandy decanter and filled his glass one last time before he too turned in.

Once Cassie and Kelley had reached her bedroom door, Cassie fiddled with the box in her hand before she turned to walk into her room. On the threshold of her door, she suddenly turned and said, "I need to tell you something, but I am not sure how I should approach the subject." Her words had obviously caught his attention, but the look of exhaustion on his face told her she should have waited.

"If you don't mind, I think we should discuss whatever is on your mind tomorrow. I have had enough surprises for one day, and I don't feel prepared for a battle of wits with you. Good night, my . . . confidante." She thought for a brief moment he was going to say something else, but he apparently thought better and changed his mind. After one brief stroke of his hand along the side of her face, he turned and walked down the hall to his own room, closing the door behind him. After he disappeared, Cassie entered her room, numb from where his fingers had just moments ago brushed against her smooth skin; she sat on the edge of her bed feeling bewildered. She had walked into the lives of a very mysterious family but was fast becoming enthralled with the eldest brother, not to mention her boss. Too tired to think anymore, Cassie moved across the room to place the silver box back on the dresser. With one final look, she opened the box to make sure the necklace was still there, and then she retrieved her overnight bag and headed for the bathroom. Once changed, she crawled into bed and, within moments, was sound asleep.

CHAPTER VIII

While the McGillis house slept, there lurked a certain danger just miles away. For in one of the Banff hotels, a stranger awaited orders for the next series of accidents. There would soon be no way out for the McGillis family, and McGillis Enterprises would be destroyed. A sinister smile played on the stranger's lips as his fingers toyed with the gun that was smuggled into the country. Everything was going according to plan, except the interference of the woman, which would soon be taken care of as well. In the back of the stalker's mind, the thought of her being Kelley's undoing was exhilarating, but patience and caution was key, and all the years of humiliation were about to end. Laying the gun on the nightstand, the stranger turned over and nodded off to sleep.

*　　*　　*

After a good night's rest, Cassie awoke to sunshine flooding her room. Glancing at the alarm clock beside her, she read seven o'clock and wondered why no one had woken her up. She picked out her outfit for the day—a peach-colored cotton dress with small pockets in the front and a beaded collar. She laid out her undergarments and white pumps, and pulling out her bathroom accessories, she headed for the bathroom. As the water poured over her smooth skin, she began to come alive for the first time since they had arrived. At least she hadn't had any more nightmares. She was beginning to think she was haunted but couldn't see how anyone would be after her. She didn't have any enemies. Turning off the water, she wrapped a towel around her clean body and returned to the bedroom. Before dressing, she pulled her hair up into a neat little bun with ringlets hanging down the sides of her small face. Looking at her reflection, Cassie was reminded of her mother saying that was her more sophisticated look. Deciding it was time for a change, Cassie pulled the pins out and let her long blonde hair wrap lovingly around her shoulders. It gave her a bright, youthful look. Silently, she hoped Kelley would approve of the change. Shivering slightly, she brought herself back to reality.

After dressing, she applied a light makeup and hooked a strand of fake pearls around her neck. As her fingers ran over the pearls, she thought, "Some day I will have real pearls." With one last glance in the mirror, she sprayed a light mist perfume and headed out to the stairs. Reaching the bottom, she encountered Johann coming out of the study, which was to the left of the stairs. "Good morning!" she vibrated.

"Is it?" he stated in grumbled protest. "I hadn't noticed . . . ," was all he said as he retreated up the stairs, as if to say, "don't bother me." But Cassie was in too good a mood to let his pessimism get to her. Loud voices, however, broke the silence, and Cassie could tell that Kelley was furious. Whoever the visitor was seemed to be agitated as well.

Slowly, she moved toward the study door. Peering around the corner of the door, she could only see Kelley standing directly behind a huge pinewood desk. He looked aggravated and ready to pounce on anyone or anything. Not wanting to interrupt his verbal assault on the unexpected visitor, she was on the verge of leaving when Kelley noticed her.

"Cassie! Come in. I didn't see you there. I would like to introduce you to my youngest brother, Kirk." He motioned to the other side of the room. Cautiously, she entered and scanned the room for the other man. Leaning against one of many bookcases was a tall lean man with the same dark hair and, instead of green, a pair of doe brown eyes met hers. As she faced him, he stood up and eyed her suspiciously; then he turned a charming McGillis grin to his eldest brother.

"Well, I see your taste is improving, big brother, or is she just the latest?" His tone caused Cassie's stomach to turn, and she turned menacing eyes to Kelley.

"Of all the . . ." She didn't have to finish, because he obviously hit a nerve with his brother.

"Damn it, Kirk! That was uncalled for. Cassie, Miss Garrett, is my secretary and a damn good one. You have no right to insult her that way. She is here because we have business meetings." Turning his eyes on her, he said, "You will have to excuse him, Cassie. He has forgotten his manners and should apologize to you. Kirk?" He shot Kirk an insolent glare.

He hadn't missed Kelley's slip of using her first name but, being the proper gentleman, replied sheepishly, "I am sorry, Miss Garrett. My brother is correct, but if you were my girl with those looks, I wouldn't let you out of my sight." Blushing and embarrassed by his compliment, she lowered her eyes to the floor. Kirk turned steady eyes on Kelley and said, "Let's finish this later. I have to be somewhere in an hour . . . Cassie." He bowed his head slightly in her direction and headed out the door.

Cassie's gaze followed him out the door. The sound of Kelley's voice caused her to jump a little. "That boy will never grow up. He still thinks the world belongs to him. Do me a favor and stay out of his way, Cassie, and don't take him too seriously. He will get you into trouble and come out clean on the other side. Believe me; all of us have paid for his gambling and philandering. I don't want to have to bail you out as well. Promise me?" She nodded, and he slowly took in her appearance with male appreciation. "I must say you do look better this morning, and more beautiful." In order to avoid his searching eyes, she turned around to examine the room.

The lamps with the exception of one floor lamp were all Victorian. Someone had obviously loved the smell of pine because most of furniture was made out of the lightwood, the exception being the bookshelves, which were made of oak. There was a huge fireplace on the west wall nestled between two of the shelves, a couple of French-style doors leading out to a veranda, a small sofa in the middle of the room with a coffee table in front, and three straight-backed chairs with one in front of the study door and the other two on the opposite side of the coffee table. There were several tapestries and paintings aligning the walls that were not covered with books, but the painting that caught her attention was the one above the fireplace. There, in a large golden frame, was a portrait of a beautiful French woman.

Cassie hadn't realized she had been staring until Kelley touched her arm. Keeping her gaze on the portrait, she commented, "She's beautiful. Is she your mother?"

"Yes." Kelley couldn't take his eyes off of her, but Cassie assumed he was talking about his mother. "Yes, she is beautiful, and I don't believe there are enough compliments to give her." She turned around and made eye contact with him, which caused her to suddenly go weak in the knees. If his arm had not wrapped around her, she would have ended up on the coffee table. "Are you all right?" His tone had gone from seductive to concerned in a matter of seconds.

It took a moment for Cassie to get her bearings. "I'm fine. I just haven't eaten yet. I was hoping to have breakfast with everyone this morning, but I guess I overslept," she muttered weakly, trying to pry herself from his iron grasp without much success. He seemed to be enjoying holding her close, but it was causing warning bells to go off in her head. She knew she had to move away before she regretted it.

"True, we have already had breakfast, but if you are hungry, I can have the cook fix you something. Or do you think a cup of coffee would suffice?" Letting her go, he briefly glanced over her face before turning toward the desk.

"Coffee would be fine. I hadn't intended sleeping so long, but I guess the jetlag finally set in. It won't happen again, I promise," she tried apologizing for her tardiness, but Kelley's mood had obviously improved, and he refused to be aggravated.

"That's fine. I half expected you to sleep the morning away. But since you're up, we can get started. I will have the maid bring you a cup of coffee, and then we can set our itinerary for the rest of the day. I hope you feel like walking and riding today, because we have a long list of people to visit and errands to run." As he turned back around to face her, he added, "I expect most of the legwork to be done today, but we will have to play it by ear. Now, let me see about your coffee." He brushed against her as he left the room, causing Cassie to grab onto one of the straight-backed chairs for support.

Once he was gone, Cassie took a moment to look around the room and take a long breath of air before she returned her attention to the stack of papers on the desk. She noticed the file box on the floor and the contents of the box on the desk. Several of the files had been opened as if he had been arranging meeting times and making notes on which ones were urgent and which ones could be left until later. Among the files, she noticed an envelope. She was sure that she had not packed it, so it must have been in his briefcase or just mixed up with their work. As she went to move the envelope from among the stack of papers, she heard the sound of footsteps in the hall. When Kelley entered the room, he immediately noticed the envelope in her hand but stammered, "The coffee is on the way." Standing in front of her, he questioned, "Where did you get that envelope?" He seemed anxious, as if she were prying into his personal business.

Faltering at his tone, she answered him, "It was mixed up with your files, so I thought I would match it to the correct file. Is there something wrong?" she asked with childish curiosity.

Kelley grinned at her immature actions as he removed the envelope from her grasp and responded lightheartedly, "No, there is nothing wrong, but you don't need this document. It doesn't concern you and should not have been brought here. Forget about it." He walked around the desk, opened the bottom-left drawer, slid the document inside, and then closed and locked the drawer. "There, it's forgotten. Now, let me give you our daily schedule." As he pulled out a sheet of paper from his briefcase, the maid arrived with their coffee, and for the next three hours they remained in confidential conference mode. The only time he would lighten up was to refill their coffee mugs. By the end of the session, Cassie's fingers felt as if they had been frozen and were about to fall off.

As they were finishing up the last brief, a loud hello rang out from the entry hall as the front door was thrown wide open. She didn't bother to shut the door as she spied Kelley in the study and made her way into the room. Pausing for only a brief cold nod in Cassie's direction, she wrapped her long slim arms around Kelley's muscular frame and planted a passionate kiss on his mouth that would have made anyone blush. Although at the time Cassie thought he was enjoying the interlude, for her benefit he cut the scene short by pulling her slightly away from him. Once at arm's length, he commanded, "You shouldn't do that, Charisse, especially in front of company. I would think by now you would know that, but I guess I have been away too long, haven't I?"

"Yes, dear, you have. But I will wait until we can be alone, which hopefully will be soon." She smiled in Cassie's direction, hoping she would get the hint. Not wanting to be in the way of their "happy reunion," Cassie made up an excuse, and ignoring the protesting grimace on Kelley's face, she left the room.

After she closed the door, she stood there for a moment, flexing her fingers. She couldn't believe she was actually glad to be done working, at least for now. Looking around the great hall, she decided she would do some sight-seeing of her own. Because of the funeral, no one had had a chance to show her the grounds. So while she had the time, she figured no one would mind if she toured the grounds herself. She had noticed a rock path outside the study door and wondered where it led. Now would be the best time to find out. So without another thought, Cassie hurried up the steps to fetch a light sweater. "Mornings in Canada," she decided, "compared to Indiana, are much cooler, mostly due to altitude." But Cassie was not about to let the coolness keep her from her new adventure. Upon entering her room, she felt a cold shiver run up her spine, as if someone had been watching her. Looking behind her, she breathed a sigh of relief. As she reached for her sweater that was lying over the vanity chair, she had an odd feeling something was wrong. She stood up straight with the sweater in hand and took a quick glance around the room. At first, everything appeared normal, but as Cassie went to the door, she caught it out of the side of her eye. Her attention quickly went to the dresser and the silver box, which she had placed there to ask Kelley about it later. The box, however, was now missing. Opening the dresser drawers, Cassie made doubly sure that it was missing before the panic could set in.

"Where is it?" she asked herself in sheer panic. "I know I didn't move it. Maybe the same person put it back." The sickening feeling in her stomach made her dizzy, so she sat down on the edge of her bed to consider what might have happened. Did someone leave it here accidentally or on purpose? Why would they leave it in her room? Did Janelle know that it had been missing? Who would do this and why? The only thing Cassie could do—though she knew it would be hell if she were caught, but she had to be sure—was go down to the basement and make sure it had been returned. She tied her sweater around her slim shoulders and ran out of the room. As she approached the bottom of the stairs, she caught sight of Kelley escorting Charisse out the door. "Damn!" She was too late. If only she had a little more time, or maybe now would be a good time to tell him about it. "Or," another thought hit her, "he didn't know about it to begin with, so why arouse suspicion?" If she checked later on, she would be off the hook. She would just have to make sure she found some time alone. As she watched him close the door and turn and walk toward her, she could tell by the look on his face that he had not been pleased with her desertion.

"Well, that was a short visit. Will she be back?" she asked coyly, trying to hide her nervousness.

"No. At least not today, thanks to you. You knew we had a lot of work to do, and I would have thought you would be eager for a chance to get out for a while." He noticed the sweater on her shoulders. "You look very refreshed and prepared to go out. Did you have something in mind for your escape, or had you planned on being alone?" Without waiting for a reply, he stated, "Never mind answering, I don't want to know. But since you are here now, we might as well load up the car and head out for our first destination." He led her back into the office and picked up his briefcase and a few other notes, and Cassie picked up her steno pad, files, and a few extra pencils.

She followed him outside to a dark blue Cutlass Sierra where he opened the passenger door and deposited all their folders and his briefcase in the backseat, and then he waited for her to get in. After he closed her door, he turned around and headed back up the steps. Cassie could see the butler come out the front door carrying a picnic basket, which meant that he didn't plan on stopping anywhere for lunch. They would be on the run all day. Kelley deposited the basket in the backseat, and then he sat down in the driver's seat and shut his door. "Do you have everything you need, because I don't intend on returning until we have completed all or three-quarters of the list?" he asked impatiently.

Cassie glanced through her list of supplies and notebooks, and after counting all the files they needed, she returned, "Everything appears to be here. If not, I guess we will have to wing it." She tried to sound humorous, but he obviously was not in the mood to be funny, so she lapsed into silence as they drove off.

Once out on the highway heading toward Banff National Park, the silence began to annoy her. Breaking the silence, she asked, "Where is it we are heading? It would be nice if you could tell me a little about my surroundings, because if I have to run an errand, I will need to know where I am going and how to get there."

"You won't have to run any errands by yourself, so don't worry about getting lost." Rethinking his words, he added, "But I guess I am being rude by not telling you a little about the country." He offered her a smile.

"It would be nice. I mean, this is a beautiful country, and I am not likely to be coming back anytime soon. Right?" she prompted, almost teasing him.

"You never know. You may find a reason to return, but let's not worry about that now. I guess I should start when the Canadian Pacific Railway was established. Canmore was mined for coal to run the locomotives. It was just a small mining town in the early 1880s but ballooned up to four hundred fifty people by the year 1888. In 1914, oil was discovered in the southern part of Alberta, and by the end of 1922, the mines were closed. Since then, it has grown from just an industrial town to residential community and tourist attraction. The biggest landmark in this area is the Three Sisters, which are the mountains along the south edge of town. Originally called the Three Nuns, the locals secretly called these peaks Faith, Hope, and Charity. I promise I will give you a better view of them later, but we are too busy today." He paused shortly to turn onto a side road, off of the main highway.

"Later on, in 1988, Canmore hosted the cross-country ski events in the winter Olympic games. The town built the Canmore Nordic Center. Every year now, the town holds the Canmore Folk Festival, and in September, the Highland Games are held with thousands of musicians, Scottish dancers, and visitors. Incidentally, we may still be here for the festival. I am not sure how long the business will take."

Cassie shot him a nervous glance. "I hope not too long. I mean, I would love to see the festival, but I didn't pack enough to stay longer than a few weeks. You may have to let me go shopping and grant me an advance on my paycheck."

"If I need to, I think I can arrange that. But for now, let's just play it by ear. I am hoping the major business will be taken care of within the next few days; if not, we could have a problem." His tone suddenly changed. It was as if a stranger had replaced the man beside her, and she could feel a cold chill run up her spine.

"What do you mean 'we could have a problem'? You didn't sound unsure about this trip earlier. Kelley, is there something you're not telling me, because you know you can tell me anything?" It was a feeble attempt at invading his thoughts, which he didn't mind, by the smile on his face.

"No. There is no problem. But if it matters, I would confide in you. I just don't think you should be in the middle of everything, especially when things could get ugly. I will try to warn you ahead of time. For now, though, I think we should concentrate on the clients at hand. Okay?" He flashed her a smile that always seemed to melt whatever fears she had. Deep down, however, she had a gut feeling he was hiding something.

Abandoning logic, she appealed to him. "I still don't like the sound of what you just said. I think I should know a little more about these dealings. After all, how am I supposed to answer any question the client has if I don't have the correct information? You owe me a little more than that." As she stiffened up in her seat, he could tell she wasn't about to give up the fight.

"You will have the right answers when you need them. You are just going to have to trust me, and that's the end of the argument!" He was beginning to sound irritated, but Cassie was still uneasy.

As she sat back in the seat, her response came out a little more contentedly than she actually felt. "I guess I can't fight the boss, can I? But I still don't like the sound of this situation. I don't understand how these follow-up meetings could go wrong. I had the understanding that you were just checking up on some old clients and their progress. Am I wrong, or did I miss something, because I am beginning to feel there is more going on than you are allowing me to know. If it's business, I wish you would let me help." Her pleading didn't get the desired response.

"You know enough for the time being. You will pick things as we go along, but until then, let's drop this discussion. Do you have the first client's folder handy?" He was determined to change the subject, but sooner or later, Cassie was going to have her answers, as sure as the sun sets in the west. Although in the end those answers might come at a considerable cost to someone.

"Yes, I have it right here. It is Mr. Jergen. You last spoke to him six months ago about a land acquisition. There is no indication that land was bought or sold, which leads me to believe the deal never went through or was on hold for some legal reason. No one finished the paperwork." She looked up inquiringly as he turned onto a side road with no street sign. After a few moments, a huge brownstone building came into view. "This doesn't look like a very big business. In fact, it looks very much like someone's personal property. Are you sure this is where we need to be, because I don't have this address anywhere in the file?" Cassie was beginning to feel a little nervous, and she could tell it was showing.

"Yes, this is where we are meeting. I never allowed this address to be printed. You will just have to trust me and not question why we are here. There are reasons why Mr. Jergen allows me here, and you are about to find out. Consider yourself privileged, because you are the first employee to be allowed here. Pay attention, and I will explain everything later, okay?" As he parked the car in an empty space, he shot Cassie a warning glance that irritated her but also prevented her from arguing.

Once the car was parked, Kelley turned off the ignition and motioned toward the opening front door. A small gray-haired man came out of the door and began walking toward them. Both Cassie and Kelley emerged from the car and waited for the gentleman to approach them. Upon his arrival, the man anxiously looked at Cassie and immediately turned his attention to Kelley. "What is she doing here? You know I told you no one else should be here."

"Relax, Orville. I trust Cassie completely, and besides, I can't do all this by myself anymore. We need as much help as we can get. Now, let's go inside and see if we can figure out a plan of attack. After you, sir." Grumbling a little, the man led her and Kelley into the humble dwelling. The modest decor inside the home was anything but fancy. However, Cassie could feel herself begin to relax as if she were coming home. They were led into a small sitting room where they were instructed to sit down and wait a few moments.

While they waited, Cassie was compelled to ask, "What is this place?" Looking around, she saw what appeared to be medical and geological journals. "Is this man dying?" Before Kelley could answer, the old man returned with a binder in his hand and passed it directly to Kelley.

"You might be interested in this one. We just finished the investigation, and this is the final profile we came up with. If he succeeds in his plans, we could all be in danger or out of our homes. This is not good, Kelley. A lot of people are counting on you for support. Question is, are we going to get it?" The man sat down on a cushioned rocker made in the old-English fashion.

As Kelley thumbed through the report, Cassie could tell he was not happy with the results, whatever they were. She was becoming more and more confused about their business, but she was caught between asking what the hell was going on and obeying her boss's orders. There was very little in her file to suggest a major land dispute, but there had to be a good reason why Kelley had left it out. Maybe both men feared the file would fall into the wrong hands. That would explain Kelley's sudden mood change, and it would explain why the old man had been nervous about her being there. But it did little to explain the problem to her. The longer they sat there, she could tell Kelley was becoming increasingly agitated. Suddenly he threw the file on the small antique coffee table in front of them and ran his long tanned fingers through his thick black hair.

Rubbing his chin, he asked, "Who did the investigation and who took the photos? I want to meet both of them immediately. Also, we need to have everyone involved meet at the same time. The land he is trying to acquire is definitely unstable and will cause massive rockslides, putting people's lives at risk. We can't allow that. Get a hold of everyone and meet us at my residence tonight, seven o'clock sharp." Kelley looked at Cassie and said, "We will need to set up for a small meeting tonight. There should be about fifteen to twenty people coming. I want you to do some research for me and type up some information that I will give you. Let's go. See you tonight, Orville. We will show ourselves out." Taking Cassie by the elbow, he led her out the door and back to the car. Once he had seated himself in the car, he turned to her and very intensely said, "I hadn't planned on this so soon. Cassie, we may have a court battle on our hands, but if I can,

I am going to try and avoid it. Everyone on our list is involved in this case, and I can't allow one man to destroy this town."

"I don't know what you are talking about, but back at his house. you talked about people being hurt. Who would want so much land and put so many lives at risk? It's absurd." Cassie was stunned at the growing magnitude of the problem. If it affected so many people, how and why would anyone take such a risk?

"When it comes to mineral rights and land mass, some people would risk anything. Especially if you're someone like Mick Clawson. That man has no heart, except where Janelle's concerned, when it comes to buying people out. Prepare yourself, dear, because this is going to be an uphill battle all the way." Peeling out of the driveway, Cassie wasn't sure if she liked his tone. Mr. Clawson had seemed a respectable person the day of the funeral, but Kelley had treated him like dirt then too. So this man must hide behind a well-worn mask until someone crosses his path, and if Kelley's words were correct, she would soon be in the middle of land disputes involving an entire town. In the end, Cassie knew there would be a price to pay.

CHAPTER IX

As they drove back to the house in silence, Cassie was forming all kinds of questions in the back of her mind but refused to voice them. Kelley had already informed her she would understand the situation the more they talked to the clients. However, he hadn't prepared her for the prospect of going to court over land. It was becoming more apparent that quite a number of people were involved, and Cassie wondered why they were all laying it upon Kelley's shoulders to take care of them. It didn't seem fair to her, but Kelley was obviously unaffected by the obligation. In fact, he seemed to be thriving on the circumstances, whatever they were.

"Confused?" his soft voice startled her thoughts.

"No, not really confused. I was just wondering what you had to do with all these people. This problem seems to be a little more personal than professional, and I don't think I am going to be of any help to you by being here." Shaking her head, Cassie sounded deflated, "What purpose would Mick Clawson have for destroying a town, let alone you with it? He seemed a perfect gentleman at the funeral reception. After all, he is your neighbor."

"'Seemed' is the correct word. Mick is a very dangerous man, Cassie. There have been several accidents surrounding his association with some of my clients, whom he was trying to buy land from. When they refused, there were accidental fires set, which authorities called arson, but blamed the tenants. All the evidence pointed to them. So they were fined, and Clawson was off the hook. No one has ever been able to prove his guilt."

"So why you? Can't they hire someone to investigate him?" Cassie sounded a little nervous. Kelley was obviously putting himself in the hot seat for these people, and they seemed to be using him. But he loved it. God only knew why. "This makes me wonder if there isn't a personal reason for your involvement in all of this. Is there? I know this is none of my business, but if I am going to help you, I need to know." Cassie was not about to be put on hold, and he could tell by her demeanor.

He took one hand off the steering wheel to run through his thick hair before he stammered, "I guess you sensed the tension at the house, but Cassie, my family has been battling him for years over where our property ended and where his started. It isn't anything new, and I grew up with the people in this town. Some of them have been lifelong friends. They don't deserve what Clawson is attempting to do. And I don't believe the Canadian government will allow him to take the land either. You see, our land was inherited long before the government started running things, and we have been arguing with the politicians over land rights as well. If Clawson succeeded in running us out, he could succeed in taking over the town too. Canada owns the town of Banff because it's a national park, but our land runs pretty close to its border, so the government is trying to gain control of that four-acre area, which is the same section that Clawson wants. Are you beginning to understand now?" He glanced briefly at her and returned his attention to the road. "I have an idea. Why don't we head up to the Three Sisters for lunch? They have some nice trails up there, and we can enjoy the scenery."

"That sounds like a marvelous idea. I need some fresh air, and so do you." She smiled broadly and started to relax as they turned the car in the direction of the mountains. Within an hour, they had made their way over the interstate and up the tourist entrance to the bottom range of the mountains. After parking the car and taking the picnic basket out, they proceeded to walk up one of the many trails aligning the side of Faith Mountain. As they came to a secluded spot along the trail, there were a couple of picnic tables placed carefully away from the side of the cliff. Placing their basket on the table, Cassie started to unpack the cold chicken sandwiches, fruit salad, and wine.

After eating a few sandwiches, Cassie picked up her wineglass and held it up to her lips without tasting it. Suddenly, she commented, "This is so overwhelming. What is so valuable about the land that Clawson and the government could want it?" She lowered her glass instead of taking a sip and looked into Kelley's face.

"The land contains minerals that would be worth millions if mined. But because the town sits on most of the land needed for the mines, Clawson is at a dead end. People are not willing to sell out everything they have for the sake of big business, but Clawson is a stubborn man and determined to win no matter what the cost." Taking a deep breath, he added, "On top of that, ten acres of our northern property at home is under fire. The government is saying that the land belongs to the Banff National Park; our ancestors said it belonged to them. My family was given the land long before Canmore even became a city, and it is stated in writing because of the mining rights to it. Now, we are fighting to keep it, and Clawson has been backing the government in the hopes of acquiring the land for himself. He thinks once the government owns the land, they will be willing to sell. But I know that won't happen because of how valuable that land is. So now, do you understand? I know it's a lot to understand." He took a long, slow drink of the wine and raised himself up off the seat, walking over to the edge of the cliff.

"Yes, I guess I do. It sounds like a terrible position to be in. Can't there be a compromise reached somehow? I mean, if people are getting hurt over this, shouldn't there be some sort of mediator involved?" she countered nervously.

Turning to face her, he sounded weary, "Yes, it is precarious, but I have no choice. My father is the one who sold most of the land to those people, and I am not going to see them thrown out or destroyed without a fight. Because when it comes to the land, it's as priceless around here as a man's family, and it can't be replaced, not even by money. I told you this might get ugly. The less you know, the better, because we are on the verge of catching Clawson off guard, but if he decided to use you as leverage, it could turn everything in his favor. Promise me that you will not let him influence you, Cassie? He can be very charming and conniving at the same time, and if you get hurt, well . . . I can't let that happen. Promise?" he pleaded.

"You know that I promised to help you. You could have told me about this earlier. That way I could have been prepared for this situation." Standing up, she slowly walked over beside him, gazing out at the Bow River and the town. Quietly, she persisted, "Why didn't you tell me?"

"I had reason to believe you were being followed, but I didn't want to alarm you. If you are still being followed, I would like to catch this person in the act and find out why. You have nothing valuable as far as knowledge of this situation, and if they think they can use you to gain information, you could end up in danger. From now on, I want you to tell someone where you are going, and how long you expect to be gone, and please do not accept help from any strangers. If you need assistance, call a member of my family and one of us will come and get you or provide assistance somehow. It's just a precaution," he warned her. "Because no one can be too careful right now. There has been enough bloodshed over this already. You have no idea how dangerous a game this is, and I couldn't bear to lose you like . . . someone else."

"Someone else? Who? Please don't leave me in the dark." Her startled eyes pleaded with his. "I want to know."

Placing both hands on her arms, he looked deep into her eyes. Searching her face for understanding, he confided, "Her name was Marguerite Snow. She was my assistant before you, and a damn good one too. She had been with me since I started the business, and she knew all about the land disputes and the danger involved, but she would never back down. I kept warning her not to dig too much, because I was never sure how Clawson was going to respond. The day before I met you, I received disturbing news. Along with photographs, I received a letter telling me certain people were going to be in harm's way if I proceeded to help the town. The next day, Marguerite didn't show up for work." He paused briefly, as if he were trying to read her thoughts. "After trying to reach her at home, the phone rang. Upon answering, I was informed where to find her and to read the morning paper. Hanging up, I grabbed the paper and began browsing through it. I needn't look further than the first page, because under the main story about your beloved Kent, there was a story about a body found at the conservatory. A woman had apparently lost her footing and stumbled to her death. But what puzzled the authorities were the two bullet holes in the back of her head. A .45-caliber gun had been fired, as if making sure she was dead, but the police had nothing else to go on. Thus, I decided to see if I could find anything. Arriving late, I hoped to be alone, but no such luck. I found a teary-eyed young woman who needed company." Smiling at her, he added, "And I decided to play the hero and then return later, which I did after you went home." He looked at her incredulous face and let it all sink in.

"Did you find anything?" she demanded in horror, still trying to comprehend all he told her.

"Yes, I did. But I can't tell you what it is, because that would put you in the line of fire, and I am not losing you. You mean too much to me." His fingers came up under her chin, and if he had decided to kiss her, she had a distinct feeling she wouldn't rebel. But he gazed into her eyes and then turned away, leaving her with a sense of regret and relief at the same time. "As much as I would love to stay here and keep you all to myself, we really should get going. There is so much to do." He helped her repack the basket, and they walked hand in hand back down the mountainside and to the car.

Once they were on their way home, Kelley told her, "What we need to do is make an agenda of what we will discuss tonight. Then we can plan our course of action. I need to make some phone calls while you unpack the files in the study." As they drove home, they remained in silent communion, each one thinking of the other.

After arriving at the house, Kelley hurried up the stairs to make the phone calls while Cassie first carried the picnic basket into the kitchen and then returned to the car to get the files. In the study, she began to arrange the files in order of importance. Once that was done, there wasn't much left to do except wait on Kelley. As she sat there, she wondered if he would be very long, because she hadn't taken that walk yet. If he were going to be awhile, she could take her walk and still be back in time to finish their business.

She slipped out the French doors and walked along the cobblestone path. She began to relax and enjoy her surroundings. The different shades of green and the many different colors and fragrances of the flowers made Cassie's mind clear, so she could begin to comprehend everything that had been relayed to her. "This walk was a necessity," she told herself sharply. It was a shame that Kelley couldn't share this time with her, but she had a gut feeling they wouldn't have any spare time to do any sight-seeing. "Although it was his fault," she told herself, "he could have filled me in a long time ago. I might have been able to help him." Thinking back, however, he had told her about his secretary, Marguerite. "Still," she frowned, "she was new and couldn't see any reason why she would be in any danger from Clawson.

What did he think she knew?" Then rounding a bend where the evergreen foliage met up with multicolored flowers, Cassie slowed her feet down, almost to a stop. Voices. There were voices coming from somewhere close.

Before Cassie could announce her presence, she heard footsteps coming in her direction. Without thinking, she ducked into the green foliage, hoping it would camouflage her being discovered out there all by herself. Within a few moments, the unwanted visitors were standing in front of her hiding place. Crouching down, she could hear the anger in their voices and hoped they would leave soon. Listening intently, she could make out one of the voices, Janelle's. The other voice was familiar but remained elusive.

"Please, I need an answer. I have to know, and only you can help me." She could tell that Janelle was on the verge of hysterics. But why?

"You know I can't tell you. It would break the promise I gave your parents a long time ago," the tenor voice responded. Cassie wished she could make out voices, but to look would expose her, and she didn't want to be caught in the middle. As she continued to listen, she began to wish she were safely in the house working with Kelley, because Janelle was obviously not finished and beyond furious.

"You know who my real father is, and you're hiding it. My parents are dead; you needn't keep your promise to them now. I guess I will just have to let your wife know how much you really are loved around here. I don't think she will be very happy with the news, do you?" A threat. That didn't sound like the Janelle she had met a few days ago. In fact, it was turning into blackmail, and Cassie was hearing it all. Cautious and unmoving, she listened again as the man countered.

"That wouldn't benefit you. My wife has known about the other women for a long time, and we are on the verge of separation. I applaud your tactics though. You have learned a lot since you have grown up. Let me know if you find anything." Without another word, the footsteps headed further into the garden. Whoever it was obviously knew the grounds well and must live within walking distance, because there were no other cars in front of the house. Still, Janelle hadn't moved. Cassie could hear her moving around. Then footsteps moved in the direction of the house.

Cassie stayed in the shrubbery for another few moments, making sure both parties had disappeared completely before she emerged. Once she was back on the rock path, she headed back toward the house. As soon as she hit the edge of the veranda, Kelley was out the door walking toward her.

Judging by the look on his face, he was not pleased with her disappearing on him. "Where the hell have you been?" His mood had certainly gone downhill.

Cassie raised her face up to look him in the eyes, and with the guiltiness of a child caught in the cookie jar, she apologized, "I'm sorry, but I thought you would be tied up for a while, so I took a short walk, and if I had more time, I would go for another walk. Seeing how you haven't even shown me around here yet." She drove her point home, because his face softened, and there appeared a sheepish grin on his face.

"I deserved that. You're right; I haven't been a very good host. Let's get through the meeting tonight, and first thing tomorrow we can explore the grounds. Will that be satisfactory?" The seductive look in his eyes as they stared into hers caused a shiver of excitement to flow up and down her spine.

"I guess."

"Good. Let's get busy."

Cassie looked briefly toward the walkway and wondered where Janelle had gone. There were two walkways, but she had been on the same one Cassie had followed. She only hoped that Kelley had not run into her before Cassie returned, or Janelle would be suspicious. That was something Cassie didn't want to have to explain. Taking a deep breath and praying silently, she followed him into the house.

CHAPTER X

Several grueling hours went by before Kelley allowed a break. He seemed intent on making sure no one involved was left out of the conference. Letter upon letter was dictated and expected to be ready by the end of the day. After he dictated the last letter and listened to her read it back to him, he told her to take a five-minute coffee break and then type them up for mailing tomorrow morning.

Flexing her fingers, Cassie walked over and picked up a coffee pot that had been placed on the hot pad by the maid. As she poured the coffee, she took a sideways glance in his direction and asked, "Would you like a cup?"

He looked up with a blank stare and then shook himself, "Yes, thanks." Closing the file he had been reviewing, he walked over to receive the cup she held out for him. "I'm sorry. I don't mean to push you so hard, but if we don't move fast enough, Clawson will intimidate everyone into submission. He already has a huge lead on us."

"Couldn't you find a way to compromise somehow? I mean, there has to be a way of working things out to where everyone is benefited." Her words agitated him further.

"No. Clawson isn't the type to compromise. He is somewhat like my father. If it's not his way, it's no way. If we can find proof that he had something to do with these mysterious accidents, then we could have him arrested, but until then, I am afraid we'll have to watch our backs." He relaxed when he noticed the scared look in her eyes.

Brushing his fingers lightly across her cheek and lower lip, he reassured her, "We will beat him. I promise I am not going to let anyone get hurt, if I can help it."

Caught between fear and a physical need to be close to him, Cassie didn't move away when his mouth lowered to hers. With a small whimper, she submitted to the sensual pleasure of his mouth over hers. To her astonishment, however, he didn't prolong the passion any further. She stepped back slightly as he looked into her eyes, looking for something, but what she wasn't sure. Instead, he said, "We should get busy." Then it was over as quickly as it had started.

Stunned for a moment, Cassie fought for control of herself and her desire for him. With a forced effort, she turned her attention to the letters on the desk. She walked around the desk and sat down in front of the typewriter. As she began pulling out paper to type on, Kelley told her he would be back in a couple of hours. When she didn't respond, he looked over at her, but she was keeping her eyes on her work, avoiding him. With a shrewd expression on his face, he stormed out of the room. Once he was gone, she sat back in the chair and breathed a sigh of relief. Because she realized if he had pursued the kiss any further, she would not have fought him. That realization brought tears to her eyes, because she had sworn she would never get involved with anyone again, especially her boss. She had been burned once; she wasn't going to be burned again. Brushing the tears aside, she concentrated on finishing her task.

After sheet upon sheet of mistakes, Cassie breathed a sigh of relief when she inserted the paper for the last letter. What normally took her only a half hour to do turned into two solid hours of mishaps. In the back of her mind, she blamed Kelley for knocking her off balance. "He should never have started something he was not willing to finish," she told herself sharply and regretted her reaction to him. "He deserved everything he got," she thought helplessly. She pounded the keys on the typewriter, taking out all of her frustrations on her work. As she proceeded with the document, she allowed herself to relax a little and, in doing so, made fewer mistakes. By the time she pulled the paper out of the typewriter, she felt more at ease. With her tension gone, she proofread the document, failing to hear the study door open.

Looking up, she was startled to see Janelle's curious expression. "Do you have a minute? I think we need to talk." As she closed the door behind her, Cassie became apprehensive. She had a distinct feeling where this was going to lead but believed she had been safely hidden.

Cautiously, she stammered, "Yes, I have a moment, but you will have to make it quick. I have to get all these ready for mailing, and then I have to arrange for a meeting tonight."

Janelle responded, "Oh, this won't take long. I promise."

Cassie watched nervously as Janelle walked over to the small floral-printed sofa. Sitting down on the soft cushions, she looked Cassie straight in her anxious hazel eyes. "I think we both know where this is going, don't you? I know you were outside awhile ago, because you have a very distinctive perfume." Without waiting for a response, she inquired smugly, "How long were you there, and how much did you hear?"

Cassie stood up uneasily and began arranging the pile of letters in front of her. "You know, it is none of my business who you talk to and what about. So why don't you just forget the matter?" Cassie hoped Janelle would drop it, because she didn't want to get between Janelle and her brothers. It was a family matter and should be left that way. God knows she wasn't a part of the family and not likely to be. For this reason, she felt she had to deter Janelle from making a big mistake, but Janelle had other ideas, and she wasn't about to let her off the hook.

"I just want to know what you heard and make sure that you are not going to talk to Kelley about it. What Mick and I talked about is no one else's business but ours. Understand?"

Cassie was so dumbstruck she missed the question. Could she have heard right? Mick Clawson was the voice she had heard. True, his identity was shadowed by the shrubbery, but she should have recognized the coolness of his tenor. In light of this revelation, Cassie could only warn her.

"Janelle, I think you should be careful who you confide in. You may find that certain people are not as congenial as they appear. Anyway, I didn't hear enough to do any damage." With a vacant look in her eyes, Cassie added calmly, "I do think, however, that if you want to find your real father, you should check county records or talk to other people who knew your mother and father. Maybe you could come up with a better lead. Using Clawson like this is dangerous. He could expect something big in return, something which he knows you really can't deliver."

Exasperated, Janelle countered, "That's my point, no one wants to talk about it. Everyone thinks I should leave it alone. But, Cassie, until I find out I am going to feel incomplete. I need to know, and I'm willing to do anything to get what I need, including talking to the devil himself."

Cassie didn't have time to answer because the door opened and Rod walked in. "I'm sorry, was I interrupting something?" With a brief nod to Cassie and a brief "think about it," Janelle stood up and walked out the veranda doors.

After she had gone, Cassie took a deep breath and turned her attention back to Rod. "No, you weren't interrupting anything. What can I do for you?" She stacked the letters in a neat pile and placed a rubber band around them before she looked up at him.

"Well, I just ran into Kelley, and he had to go meet someone in town." He registered the disappointed look in her eyes but continued, "So I volunteered to run you into the post office and run some other errands at the same time. Does that sound satisfactory? It's not very often I get to escort a beautiful woman around town, you know. Business is my life." His smile was so convincing that Cassie had to laugh.

"That would be great," she agreed. "I could use some fresh air and some company. Give me a few minutes to get everything together, and we can leave." With a slight gait to his stride, Rod left the room, whistling like he had just won first prize in a race.

Within just a few moments, Cassie had initialed the last of the documents that needed it and rounded up her list of supplies for the meeting later that night. She picked up the stack of letters and rushed out the study door. Before she could get any further, Rod appeared in the doorway with Kirk right behind him. "I hope you don't mind if Kirk comes along for the ride. He has some business to take care of, but he will not be returning with us. Is this okay with you?" How could she say no? This was his brother, and she certainly had no problems with him, at least none that she was aware of.

"No, that's fine. But we need to hurry, because everything needs to be done before the meeting tonight." Kirk looked a little anxious but said nothing as Rod agreed with her.

Rod held the door of his white Cadillac open for her as she crawled into the passenger seat. Kirk was seated directly behind her. As Rod seated himself in the driver's seat, Cassie turned the sun visor down to check her makeup in the little mirror on the back. As she did so, she became aware of Kirk's eyes on her. She couldn't understand why when he watched her that her stomach should suddenly convulse. Busying herself with her lipstick, she tried to avoid looking directly at him, wondering what he found so fascinating about her to stare. With her lipstick repaired, she raised her visor and watched out the window at the magnificent mountains. They just seemed to rise up into infinity. Some were snow capped, and some were just jagged rocks jutting out at precarious angles. Cassie wondered how many of these magnificent mountains had been climbed by professionals. It seemed an impossible feat to her, but then, millions of people thrived on the rush or excitement of a good challenge.

"Beautiful, aren't they?" Rod seemed to read her thoughts perfectly.

"Yes, they are. I hope I can see more of them before we head back to the States." Cassie decided to probe a little bit, even though she knew it would probably be futile. "Tell me a little about your family, Rod. Kelley has never actually confided to me much about you. So I kind of feel out of place." She braced herself for a refusal, but instead of Rod answering her, the solitary form in the backseat spoke up.

"Our family is really quite boring. You know, the typical family squabbles. You wouldn't be interested." His statement was made with a disgusted undertone, which made Cassie shiver. He obviously thought she was just being nosey, or maybe he was just trying to distract her, but she was not about to be thrown off course now.

"On the contrary, Kirk, I think our family is quite unique, in its own way." Rod was ecstatic about informing her about his family's past. "You see, Miss Garrett—Cassie—may I call you that? Well, our family has been in this area for decades. We came here as miners and eventually became enveloped in the marketing industry, mostly land and personal properties. Our father, on the other hand, believed in preservation of the land rather than selling it. That is where our family becomes dysfunctional, because he thought we should be conserving our natural resources, not selling land to people who needed homes. He was continually thwarting our plans for residential areas being built, but we succeeded more often than he wanted us to. As I think back now, he was furious about our dealings with Clawson."

"Clawson? Where does he fit into your history?" Cassie had become enthralled with his family's trials.

"I have to laugh about it now, but there for a while, Father was afraid we were going to sell part of his land to Clawson. There had been a distant family rumor that Dad had a verbal agreement with Clawson when he first acquired the land from our grandfather who allowed Clawson to assume control of the northernmost section of our property. There was said to be two hundred acres sold, and supposedly, money exchanged hands, but no one ever saw the money. Clawson accused Father of taking the money and reneging on his word. Father denied there had ever been an exchange of any kind. Therefore, the feud had been building for many years."

"Wow! No one had ever found proof. But what does Janelle's real father have to do with Clawson?" she queried.

"You had better leave that one alone. That is a family problem, and besides, Janelle has been questioning her heritage for a long time, and there is no reason for it. She is our sister, and that's where it ends!" Kirk sat with his arms folded across his chest, challenging her to continue.

"I'm sorry if I offended you. It's just that I see her struggling with questions, and no one seems to be answering them. I only hope that she doesn't look for answers in the wrong places." Ignoring her apology, Kirk looked out the window, but Rod seemed more willing to talk.

"You have not offended anyone." Rod shot his brother a cross look in the rearview mirror. "It's just you being an outsider to the family makes it difficult to talk about. But I don't see any reason why you shouldn't understand where she is coming from. Janelle was born four years after Kirk. It was an unexpected pregnancy and a difficult one. Our mother became ill and died soon after Janelle was born. He was disappointed she was a girl and always called her his little Indian girl, because she was so dark. However, she was just like Father with her stubbornness and single-mindedness. Once she had her mind set on something, she would proceed with her ideas until they were completed. I must say, though, there were times she appeared to have someone else's facial features. Because if you look at her from a certain angle, she doesn't look at all like our father. But we have never questioned it, and we try over and over again to convince her not to question it either." Glancing over at Cassie's astonished face, he smiled, "I am afraid that she has been working on you. Tell me, Cassie, has she confided in you?"

"Not really. I mean," she tried to sound convincing, "she has asked me what I would do in her shoes."

"And I suppose you told her," Kirk snapped.

"No. Yes. I just told her to be careful what she said and who she talked to. People can get the wrong ideas real quick," she lied, but she was obviously successful.

"Thank you. A woman with some brains. I like that. Hey, bro, there's my stop." Kirk was pointing to a small trailer park. Rod pulled the car onto a side street that led directly to the entrance to the park. As he pulled up outside the entrance to let his youngest brother out, he said, "Be home early, because we have our meeting tonight." Kirk shot him a disgusted look before nodding his farewell to Cassie. Once he was gone, Rod turned the car around and headed for the shopping district where the post office was also located.

"I guess I should apologize for my questions," she said, hoping to ease the tension that had suddenly filled the air.

"Nonsense. Kelley should have been a little more considerate of your feelings before he brought you here." He was smiling brightly, which eased her conscience and caused her to smile in return. He looked so much like his younger brother Johann when he smiled that it would have been easy to call them twins, but Rod was a few years older.

"He really didn't have enough time to fill me in because of the workload, and the arrangements for the flight had to be made. So I can forgive him this time. There is, however, something I don't understand, and maybe you could help me clear it up." She was playing detective, but Rod was willing to talk, and it seemed the perfect time to ask. "Did Kelley tell you about his secretary, Marguerite? About her death?"

"Yes, he did. It was a tragedy. She was a good woman but prone to asking too many questions. She apparently went overboard when she found something incriminating against someone, but no one knows whom. She died before she could tell anyone. Her last words were recorded on Kelley's office machine, but by the time he found her, it was too late." He sighed heavily but kept his attention on the traffic.

A thought struck Cassie so hard she almost choked on her next question. "Do you know what she found?"

"Actually, no. Kelley wouldn't say exactly what he saw, but I gathered there was something about him in the documents. What it entailed, I have no idea." Rod pulled up outside a small square building with glass doors and said, "Here we are. This is the post office. It's not very big, but it serves its purpose most efficiently. Take as long as you need, I will wait."

Cassie smiled brightly and left the car. As she reached for the door, a larger hand with long dark fingers opened it for her. Smiling, she raised her head to thank the gentleman. With one glance, her smile faded, however, as Mr. Mick Clawson stood in the doorway with her. He was smiling too.

"Hello. It's Miss Garrett, isn't it?"

"Uh, yes, it is. This is a surprise. Thank you for opening the door as you can see I have an armful." She tried to sound businesslike, but his charming persona seemed to lessen her hatred for the man. The man, who had done almost everything in his power to destroy Kelley and his family, was not finished yet.

"Yes, I can see that. I take it you are not here for pleasure then." As they entered the building, he continued to interrogate her. "Are you Kelley's new secretary? If you are, his taste is obviously improving after the last one. I must admit, however, that I would have offered to whisk you away to an island paradise, not hire you for work. You must be the professional type, who concentrates only on work. Am I right?" His compliment had worked perfectly. She couldn't help but laugh at his portrait of her.

"Partially, Mr. Clawson. I do believe in having some fun in life. But when I am at work, I try to remain the efficient type. As Kelley could tell you, if you were on speaking terms." She was playing cat and mouse, but she was enjoying the sparring with him.

"I suppose Kelley could tell me." He smiled at her use of Kelley's name, but it was lost on her why he smiled. "Tell me, Miss Garrett, have you found everything satisfactory in his employment, or are you finding yourself overwhelmed by his business affairs?" His interest, she knew, was more than platonic, but she willfully answered him.

"I find it very satisfactory. In fact, Mr. Clawson, I am learning new things every minute. Now, if you will excuse me," she dropped the letters in the outgoing-mail slot and turned her back to him, "someone is waiting for me. It was a pleasure running into you."

"The pleasure was all mine. Maybe some day we could have lunch together, if that's possible?" His grin was sardonic, causing her stomach to quiver.

"Oh no. I don't think that would be proper. After all, I work for your rival, and I am staying with his family. That would not look very professional." She hoped he would accept her refusal graciously, and he did.

"That's a shame. We could have lots to talk about. But I suppose you are right. It would not look kosher, as you put it." Taking her hand and kissing it tenderly, he murmured, "Until we meet again then. And I am sure that we will." Without another word, he opened the door and allowed her to leave.

Frowning slightly, she returned to the car and noticed the strange look on Rod's face as she climbed in. "Don't start. I didn't invite the man in. It's a public place, and he seemed quite the gentleman. What was I supposed to do?"

"I don't think I should answer that, and if I were you, I would not tell Kelley you ran into him." Concentrating on the traffic, he pulled away from the curb and headed back toward the shopping district. They both remained silent until he reached the intersection where the grocery store was located.

"What are we doing here?" Cassie asked quietly.

"Kelley wanted me to pick up a few things for tonight. Whenever we have guests in the house for meetings, we serve finger foods instead of having the cook fix a complete dinner. It saves time—and money—actually. Come on, I will show you." Within minutes after parking, Rod was guiding her through the store and had her marveling at his shrewdness when it came to picking out and paying for all their items. By the time they returned home, they had enough food to last a week. But Rod assured her, "There won't be much left, I guarantee it."

Cassie, smiling, helped him carry the groceries in but was brought up short by Kelley standing just inside the study door. "Where the hell have you been? We have business to finish, and our guests will be arriving soon." His manner had deteriorated drastically since the morning, but she wasn't going to be downgraded, just because he was upset.

"Rod took me in to mail the correspondence, and we went to get the hors d'oeuvre for tonight. Any more stupid questions?" she added sorely.

Her coyness had Kelley rethinking his comment. He ran his left hand over his eyes and responded, "None. I'm sorry. I guess things are just a little uneasy today. This problem keeps getting worse. Come on, let's finish some things before the clients arrive and pray we accomplish something." He took her hand and led her into the study. Before he sat down, he turned and said, "I am glad you haven't run into Clawson yet. He apparently got to Janelle earlier. I don't know what he would expect you to know, but I would be worried if you were alone with him for any length of time. Let's get going."

Cassie remained quiet. She knew she couldn't tell him about her run-in at the post office. He probably wouldn't let her out of the house anymore without him, and she wasn't going to have that. She didn't believe she was in any real danger, because she didn't know anything. She was no threat to anyone, so there wasn't any point in worrying about it. No, for now it would just be hers and Rod's secret.

CHAPTER XI

Cassie had just finished putting the final touches on her makeup when a knock at the door startled her. As the door opened, Kelley's head peered around the door, and he smiled at her. Without waiting, he entered the room and closed the door behind him. His eyes drifted lazily over her neat hair pulled back by combs with ringlets hanging loose over her soft cheeks, on down past the pale pink lip gloss and the necklace dangling around a small neckline, and down the length of her blue chiffon dress with just enough cleavage to leave a man tempted to explore its depths. The blue pumps on her feet were a perfect match. Finishing his appraisal of her, he walked over to her and asked, "Are you ready?"

Nervously, she answered, "I think so. I hope everything has been arranged perfectly, or I have a feeling you will tell me about it. Is the entire family involved tonight?"

"No. Roderick and I are the main brokers on the project. I believe Janelle is out for the evening, and Kirk had some last-minute business. Johann left earlier for England. His wife has become ill, and he needs to care for the children while she is down. Shall we go?" He opened his arm for her to entwine hers through it, and together they walked down the stairs. For some inexplicable reason, Cassie felt comfortable and excited walking beside him arm in arm. Once at the bottom of the stairs, however, he released her and went to open the door for the guests.

There were approximately twenty-five people attending, not including Kelley, Rod, and herself. Within the next two and a half hours, Cassie learned exactly what was happening and how they were going to solve the problem. The problem had been Clawson asking the landowners to relocate to the other side of town as he would buy them out and agreed to help them all move. People knew, however, that he wouldn't keep his word. In return, they refused his offers, and Clawson retaliated.

No one had been able to prove that Clawson was behind the many accidents, three of which had resulted in fatalities that were plaguing their town until now. Now, Kelley and Roderick had located witnesses to the crimes—witnesses who were willing to risk their lives to testify against Clawson. Even though a lawsuit could take months to achieve, they would wait it out.

After the meeting, everyone adjourned to the family room where a buffet had been set up. While everyone ate the tiny sandwiches and other treats, Cassie noticed Kelley pull a husky, white-haired gentleman aside. She walked over to the table of food but kept her eyes on the two gentlemen deep in conversation.

She was so lost in thought she nearly tripped over the man in front of her. "I'm sorry, I didn't mean . . . ," her words trailed off as she recognized the older man from the airport. He had been the one warning her to be careful. He apparently remembered her too.

"I see you're still here," he winked at her. "Weaver's the name. Lived here all my life, and not about to leave now. I didn't mean to scare you that day at the airport, but I thought you should be made aware that you could be on dangerous ground." He piled a huge portion of pasta salad on a plate and then turned back to her.

"Thank you for the consideration. But I don't think I am in any immediate danger," she tried to sound confident.

"You're welcome, but don't underestimate Clawson. You are working with his rival, and he could charm the rattle off of a rattlesnake. Well, nice seeing you again, and best wishes with your boss. You stick with him, missy, and I guarantee you will be well-looked after." Winking again, he left her openmouthed, ready to deny it, but she closed it again and accepted a drink from the waiter.

It was getting close to eleven o'clock when the last person left, and as Kelley ushered the gentleman to the door, he shook his hand and said, "Let's just pray our plan works. It will be a bumpy road, but I believe we will beat him." The man nodded in agreement and then walked out the opened door. Once Kelley had shut the door, he turned around and captured Cassie's tired expression. Smiling weakly, he noticed the strain in her face, "It has been a long day, and I know that you are not used to all of this yet. Maybe we should sleep on it before I attempt to fill you in completely. Would that be all right with you?"

"Actually, I was hoping you would fill me in now." She was bluffing, because she didn't want him to think she couldn't handle the pressure, but he wasn't going to be bluffed. The look in her eyes told him the truth.

He slowly walked over to her and tilted her face up, so he could gaze into her warm hazel eyes. The longer his gaze brushed over her face, the more Cassie wished he would kiss her again. But he was enjoying her discomfort and prolonged the torture. "No, I think we will wait until tomorrow. Go upstairs and get some rest. We have a busy day tomorrow."

"Before I go, will you please show me around the grounds tomorrow also? It would be nice if I could step out and not get lost." Her plea gained her a disarming smile that caused her heart to miss a beat and her knees to go limp. She could have sworn that if he had moved his hands from her arms she would have fallen on the floor.

"I guess I have been neglecting my duties as host, even though you work for me. Of course, I would be honored to show you around. First thing tomorrow, we will walk around

CANADIAN DESIRES | 133

the house and grounds. But now, bed." Without allowing her time to argue, his lips brushed lightly across hers. "Good night, Cassie." Breaking the spell that surrounded them, he turned her toward the stairs and turned himself toward the study doors, leaving her speechless and staring after him. Deflated and humiliated, Cassie ran up the steps and into her room.

"The nerve of that man!" she thought out loud. "He has the power to make me go weak in the knees, and he knows it. Damn! I wish he didn't get to me so much." Cassie sat on the edge of the bed and caught her reflection in the vanity mirror. "Well, my girl, you are just going to have to get over him, because you can't afford to make the same mistake twice. It doesn't matter how attractive and charismatic he is, you will just have to become immune to it." Closing her eyes, she knew it would take all of her willpower not to fall for him. She couldn't risk being humiliated again.

CHAPTER XII

Cassie woke in the middle of the night to a loud thump. She sat straight up in her bed and looked into complete darkness, trying to scan the room for an intruder. "Who's there?" she whispered hoarsely. But no one answered. She was sure someone was in the room with her, and the only lamp in the room was on the vanity table. Fighting the wave of nausea that attacked her, she crawled out of bed and made her way to the nightstand. On the way, her foot became entangled in something she couldn't tell what, but she winced in pain as she headed toward the floor, bumping her head on the table in her ascent. With horrid thoughts whirling around inside her throbbing head, she succumbed to the darkness enveloping her.

As flashes of light mixed with blurred shadows surrounded her, Cassie fought to reach consciousness. With a loud scream, she awoke to find Kelley holding her. Without any forethought, Cassie wrapped her arms around his neck, holding him close, which seemed to ease her frightened mind. It didn't matter that she had scolded herself into keeping her distance; she had been attacked or thought she had been. So much happened in a matter of just a few seconds that Cassie could not figure out exactly what did happen. The only thing she could remember was that someone had been in her room, ruffling through her drawers, looking for God knows what. If she had stayed asleep, she could have been killed. The person had not wanted to be disturbed, or else he would have confronted her. It didn't matter now because she was safe. Allowing him to comfort her, she missed the looks of surprise on the servants' faces, not to mention Rod's face when he entered the room.

Pulling her away from him and pushing her gently back against the pillows, Kelley scanned her face. "You are all right now. You appear to have tripped on something and hit your head on the vanity table. You are going to have one nasty goose egg for a while, not to mention a headache." She touched her forehead and winced at the pain. Holding her hand, he said, "When you didn't come down for breakfast, I got nervous because you are usually an early riser. Or at least, that is what I took you for. Anyway, I came in and found you lying on the floor, and there was blood around your head. I called for a doctor, and now here you are." He smiled at her. "I think we will hold off on the business for a few days until you have recovered, and then we can start our next phase. Before that, however, why don't you tell me what happened last night?" She didn't know what to say. There were too many people in the room, and Rod was eyeing them both a little sheepishly, as if he had caught them holding hands in the classroom.

"I . . . can't really say for sure." She looked around the room at everyone and then back at Kelley. The anxious look in her eyes must have conveyed her inner thoughts, because Kelley smiled and turned around to Rod.

"I think there are too many people in the room, don't you?" His icy glare at Rod caused him to jump into action.

"Of course. Let's all go downstairs, and I will make some tea. I will be back in a little bit." He nodded to Kelley and ushered everyone outside the room. As he closed the door, he winked at Cassie, which caused a vein to tighten in Kelley's neck.

"You don't have to be jealous of Rod, you know. He's not my type." The look of surprise turned to amusement as he sat back to study her petite frame, wrapped in a filmy blue negligee with white lace around the edges. "Last night, or rather this morning, I woke to the sound of bureau drawers being opened. I asked who was in the room and got out of bed to turn the light on. But I tripped on something in the middle of the floor." Looking around, she realized there was nothing between her and the table. "Was there anything around my feet when you found me?"

"No." His look of concern had her stomach turning in knots.

"You do believe me, don't you?"

"I don't know. Why would anyone want to rummage around in those drawers? They have been empty for years, except for a few blankets and such. Are you sure someone was in here?" His hands grasped her firmly as he continued to examine the situation.

A thought occurred to Cassie that she hadn't wanted to think about since the night she got there. It was going to irritate him, but she felt compelled to tell him. "There is something you should know." She could feel a shiver run up her spine as his eyes narrowed on hers. "The day of the funeral I found something, and I didn't know how it got here. Do you remember the necklace that Janelle showed me down in the basement?"

"Yes, I remember the one. It was an heirloom from Mother to Janelle. Why?"

"Well, it turned up in a silver box on top of the bureau. I don't know how it got there, but it disappeared later. I can't help feeling somebody was looking for it or was putting it back in the drawer." Watching his eyes, she continued, "I know you think it's crazy, but I swear on my life that I was going to ask you about it that night after the funeral, but your friend Charisse showed up, so I dropped the matter. I placed the box back on top of the drawers and forgot about it. But the next morning, it was gone. Now, I can't decide if I should be frightened or not. You do believe me, don't you?"

Her eyes were getting misty as she pleaded with him. Without any hesitation, he pulled her to him.

"Yes, although I can't understand why he or she would hide it in here. I do believe you. I think I had better get Janelle to open up the trunk, because if it is missing, we have a thief running around the house. And that, my dear, is something I won't tolerate." He gently stroked her hair as his mind raced for an answer to the problem. Someone was endangering her life by playing hide-and-seek with the necklace. In which case, he insisted that she keep the bathroom light on all night to prevent any further accidents. Also, he would attempt to keep his ears open for any intruders. "Now, you get some rest, and I will find Janelle and check this out for myself." He laid her back against the pillows gently. Before he moved away, he caught the sweet scent of her, and his gaze lingered on the perfect small mouth that was only inches away from his. Without a second thought, he lowered his lips to hers.

What he thought would be a slow, sensual teasing turned into a heated, passionate kiss. His arms pulled her closer to him, wrapping her in total ecstasy. As one of his hands moved to the small of her back, the other one wrapped itself in her hair. The passionate longing in his kiss burned a path all the way through her as she succumbed to the tantalizing feel of his mouth on hers. The pressure of his mouth increased slightly as he provoked a response from her. Willingly, she gave in to the feel of his hard body against hers and the feel of his warm tongue as it probed her mouth, searching out her passions and desires. As she wrapped her arms around him, Cassie could feel her head beginning to throb, and wincing slightly, she raised her lips from his, long enough to look into his fiery green eyes. His passion, heightened by her response to him, clouded his mind momentarily, because it took him several moments to regain his composure. He looked into her hazel eyes and thought he saw rejection when in fact she really wanted him. But her head had begun to spin due to the bump on her forehead. Thankfully, he backed away, but not, she thought, without some regret.

"I am sorry. We agreed that wouldn't happen again, didn't we?" He had definitely mistaken her actions, but she was actually grateful, because she had been trying to avoid the physical attraction she felt for him. And it was getting harder the longer he stayed.

"Yes, we did," she replied weakly. She wanted him, but not here and not like this. If she ever gave herself to him, it would be on both their terms, and when she was physically ready. "It's all right. I just have a really bad headache. Is there any aspirin?"

"I'll get it. And then, I want you to get some rest. I am going to find Janelle, and then I have another meeting this afternoon, so I will be late getting home. If you need anything while I am gone, have one of the servants get it for you. Rod is going with me, and we are meeting Kirk in town. Here you go." He handed her a glass of water out of the bathroom, along with a couple of pills. As he watched her swallow the pills, his gut wrenched at the thought of having to leave her. She was having an oddly unsettling effect on him, but he knew he had business to finish. Bending over her, he kissed her forehead lightly and said, "See you later." And without another word, he left the room, closing the door behind him.

Alone at last, Cassie wondered if Janelle really knew what was happening, or if someone had really intended to steal the necklace. What if Kelley hadn't really believed her? "He would have said something, surely," she thought to herself. "On the other hand, he could have agreed with me just to keep me calm." Cassie pulled herself up in bed, frowning as the pain in her head continued to throb. She had to prove herself, but she didn't know how. Then the thought struck her. "Maybe I should open the trunk myself to make sure that I hadn't imagined it. I know the necklace had been on top of the dresser, but it had disappeared like it appeared, mysteriously. I have to find out."

She reached for her robe and sat up on the side of her bed. Fighting off the wave of nausea that threatened to consume her, Cassie stood up. She closed her eyes until the dizziness subsided and then headed for the door. She turned the handle and cracked the door open wide enough to make sure the hallway was clear, because she didn't want anyone to catch her out of bed, especially Kelley. When all appeared clear, she opened and closed the door behind her. She stood very still on the threshold due to another wave of nausea, and then she padded softly down the hallway to the top of the steps. Before starting downstairs, she heard voices and backed up into the darkness of the hallway. Kelley and Janelle appeared at the bottom of the steps, and Rod joined them. Kelley was infuriated, she could tell, but she listened intently to what he said in shocked horror.

"How could you have been so stupid, Janelle? That necklace should still be in the trunk. So help me, if you have taken it out, I'll . . ." He was threatening her with his hand when Rod interceded.

"Hold on, big brother. Let's not forget, the necklace belongs to Janelle now. When Father died, he left it to her. So she can do whatever she wants with it. I just hope she has the good sense to realize what she has." He looked from one to the other and then asked her, "Is the necklace still in the trunk?"

It was a simple question, but one that caused Janelle to hesitate, "No. I took it up to my room," she watched the horror in both men's eyes as she finished, "because I had planned on wearing it on my husband's birthday party. But it disappeared. I have no idea what happened to it. Besides, how do we know Cassie hasn't stowed it somewhere to take it home with her? After all, she is just a secretary; it's doubtful she could afford to buy one." Without warning, the slap could be heard vibrating through the foyer.

"Whoa!" Rod held Kelley at bay as Janelle's hand moved to her inflamed red cheek. "I realize you care for Cassie, and she is your secretary, but there is no cause for violence. Besides, I don't believe she is a thief. She is too sensible for that. No, Cassie didn't take the necklace, but we need to find out who did and why before we tell her."

"That's easy for you to say. Look, I didn't want to believe it either, and maybe it's not true, but Kelley, she was the last one to see the necklace. Maybe you should check her room again. Maybe it's still there. I doubt it, but it wouldn't hurt to look. It's possible someone left it there for someone else to find. Of course, we would have to look when she isn't in the room. Wouldn't you agree?" Janelle asked, rubbing her cheek.

His composure restrained, Kelley rubbed his eyes. "I just want you to think about whom you are accusing. But yes, we should look in the dresser again. Whoever wanted it more than likely found it, because he or she had plenty of time, especially after Cassie lost consciousness. Once she has recovered, we will search the entire room." Catching the gleam in Janelle's eyes, he added, "To prove she didn't steal it."

"Okay?" Rod looked from one to the other as they agreed.

Standing there weak and dumbfounded, Cassie slowly retreated back to her bedroom. As she sat on the edge of her bed, she couldn't believe the words she heard from Janelle. It was as if she intended to use Cassie to avoid suspicion herself. Just because she was the odd man, or in this case, odd woman, Janelle expected them to believe her. It was comforting to know that Kelley was supporting her instead of his sister. Eventually, however, they would have to confront Janelle about the necklace, and Cassie doubted she would have a plausible explanation for the disappearance. She was already laying the blame on someone else—her. Neither Rod nor Kelley, however, were going to believe the accusations made against Cassie. Still, it did little to answer the all-important question. Where is the necklace?

Feeling dizzy, Cassie lay back against the pillows, closing her eyes against the throbbing pain in her head. She knew she had to find out for herself, because eventually they would speculate that she had taken it and made up the story of the intruder to cover her tracks. If only she knew where to start . . . Somehow, Cassie realized she would have to find a way to examine Janelle's trunk in the basement, without arousing suspicions. Also, she would have to search her own room thoroughly to make sure the intruder didn't place it somewhere else. Whoever it was, he was determined to place her in the middle of the problem. The fact that Janelle herself had accused Cassie made her believe that Janelle was covering up something and laying the blame on her to avoid suspicion. But what would she use the necklace for? Surely, even Clawson wouldn't ask for that high a price for uncovering Janelle's paternity. Opening her eyes, Cassie knew she was going to have to confront Janelle, but she didn't know how.

In the course of her deliberations, there was a knock at her door. Peering around the door as it opened, Janelle poked her head in. Upon seeing her awake, she entered the room with a silver tray loaded with a teapot and two cups, along with two fruited cakes. "I hope you feel like having some tea. Kelley thought it would be a good idea if I brought you some. He had to run an errand, but he said he would be back shortly to discuss something with you." Setting the tea on the overnight table, she poured herself and Cassie a cup while glancing around the room. Cassie noticed her examination of the room but declined to mention it. "Are you feeling better?"

"Other than a throbbing headache, I'm fine. How are you doing? Have you found the answers you were looking for?" It wasn't quite the way she had wanted to approach the subject, but she couldn't back out now. Hopefully, she would tell her about the necklace on her own.

Smiling demurely, Janelle sat down on the vanity chair, "As a matter of fact, I am on the verge of receiving a big payoff, which is the reason why I am here talking to you. I need your support."

"What for?" Cassie sounded startled.

"Well, it appears the necklace that I showed you in the basement has disappeared, and it shouldn't have. I was going to use it to pay a debt, but someone apparently didn't want me to. I know you wouldn't take it, but it was hidden here because I felt my room wasn't safe." Watching the growing comprehension on Cassie's face, she continued frantically, "Oh, don't worry. I wouldn't have left it here for anyone to find it, but I hadn't counted on you finding it either. But for the life of me, I can't imagine who else would have taken it. I need you to back whatever story I tell them. Could you do that for me?" Janelle's eyes started to tear up, which caused a knot in Cassie's stomach.

"I hope I don't regret this, because I have a feeling that suspicion is already directed toward me. You don't think that Clawson had someone else take it for you? I know it's a long shot, and you shouldn't be involved with him, but you need to find out if he already has it. In the meantime, I will hold my tongue. You know, however, that I can't keep lying to Kelley, because eventually he will find out. I will give you the next week to find out. By then our business should be almost finished." She didn't like it, but she had to play along until Janelle could locate the necklace. Otherwise, Kelley would never forgive her, and she didn't want anything to destroy her relationship with him—even if it was just business.

*   *   *

In a cramped, dusty little pawnshop clear across town, a clerk sat examining his new merchandise. "Pull up a chair, my friend, we have a deal." The well-dressed visitor sat down in the chair across from the shopkeeper. "I have not seen a necklace like this in ages. It's worth a fortune." Eyeing the rubies, diamonds, and sapphires appreciatively, he turned the necklace over in his hand as if he were handling a newborn baby. "I believe I can find a buyer for, say, forty-five percent." In response, the cold stare and the drawn revolver told him it was not acceptable. "Okay, no need to get nasty about it. I will take thirty percent, but no less." After mulling it over briefly, the stranger stood up, nodded his head at the clerk, placed the revolver back in his pocket, and left. Clawson would be well paid.

*   *   *

After Janelle had left, Cassie settled back against the pillows and dozed off. When she opened her eyes, it was to find the room in total darkness. Sitting up straight, Cassie looked out the window and was shocked to discover how late it was. She had been more exhausted than she had first felt. But she was wide awake and hungry. She must have slept through both lunch and dinner, and she wondered if she could still get something to eat. Very slowly, she dressed in a light blue cotton dress and pumps and found her way to the door in the dark. As she peered out her door, she saw Kirk and Johann arguing at the top of the stairs. She didn't even know when Johann had returned from home.

They were not yelling, but they were definitely arguing over something. Kirk appeared to be furious at Johann, and Johann was shaking his finger at Kirk. When they realized Cassie had opened the door, they both turned to look at her at the same time, and their expressions changed abruptly, from aggravation to concern—at least Johann's did. Kirk immediately turned and stormed off down the stairs. Johann's eyes followed him briefly before returning to her. He walked slowly over to her and said, "I hope we didn't disturb you."

"No, you didn't. "Cassie looked anxiously down the hall, expecting Kelley to appear. Looking back at Johann, she smiled, "Actually, I was getting hungry. It appears I have slept the day away, and I feel much better. Where is everyone?" She waved down the hall.

"Well," he smiled mechanically, "Rod and Kelley had business to take care of, Kirk just left, and Janelle went home to her husband. She did say she would check in on you tomorrow. I daresay that she has taken a liking to you, which is a rarity. Janelle is not one for opening up to strangers, but then you are almost part of the family." As Cassie started to say something, he added, "Now, don't try to deny it. We have all seen how you react to Kelley, and I believe that he is falling under your spell. When I heard you got hurt, I returned home to help Kelley. I am sorry you had to hear Kirk and me arguing. It was nothing. You know, brotherly love, we do it constantly. By now you probably know about Kirk's gambling. Don't worry about it. I think you can still get something to eat if you want." With a gleam in his eyes, he walked away, leaving her speechless.

Taking a swift glance down the hall, she turned toward the stairs and made her way down. Once on the landing, she looked around for the door to the kitchen when her eyes caught the cellar door. Suddenly the thought struck her, "This would be the perfect time to look. No one is around, and I could be down and up without anyone suspecting anything. Also, it could prove if Janelle was being honest with me or not."

Listening for any movement around her, she crept over to the cellar door. Slowly, she turned the handle until it clicked, and she opened the door to total blackness. Remembering there was no light switch at the top of the steps, she clung to the wall as she made her way down the steep stairway. By the time she reached the bottom, she felt as if she were going to faint from claustrophobia, not to mention the pungent smell of dampness and mustiness. The combination made her nauseous, but she kept moving as her hand brushed against the wall to find the light switch.

Flipping the light on, Cassie adjusted her eyes to the fluorescent lighting. Once she had her bearings, she turned her attention immediately to the trunks. "Now, which one is it?" She examined each one of them carefully, trying to remember the markings on the lids. Her attention was drawn to the one with a flower carved in the middle of the lid. That was it. Cassie stood in stunned silence as she observed the scratch marks all around the lock. She knew Janelle had a key, so why would she have broken into her own trunk? Cassie bent over to examine it more closely. "Maybe," she thought, alarmingly, "someone else was looking for it and didn't know Janelle had already removed it." But that wouldn't explain how they knew it was in her room. She would have to talk to Janelle and ask her if she had told anyone else where she had hidden it. With her conscience satisfied, she stood up and retraced her steps to the light switch.

As her hand moved up to the light switch, she brushed against something sharp. Wincing, she pulled her hand back and watched as the blood dripped off the palm of her hand. Quick as thought, she picked up a dust rag that had been lying on a washboard just a few feet away. As she wrapped her hand in the rag, she returned to the light switch. Her fingers moved along the wall surrounding the switch, careful not to cut herself again. Almost snagging herself, her eyes narrowed on a small piece of metal hanging out of the wall.

Very gently, she tugged on the jagged metal fragment, and after a few curses and a couple of oaths, she managed to free it. She rolled it over gingerly in her hand, examining it closely, and realized to her horror that it was a knife blade. But who and why would anyone have used a knife in the wall around the outlet? She began to search along the floor and around the outlet for any further signs of tampering when something shiny caught her attention out of the corner of her eye.

Turning, she caught sight of a small bench with several tools lying on top. Cautiously, she moved across the room and let her eyes roam over the instruments that lay across the table. It appeared someone had been down here assembling something, but she couldn't tell what. There were fragments of colored glass and coils of metal wire, but nothing appeared to be missing. It was as if someone had been working on a project and attempted to hide his or her work. Moving her hand along the table, Cassie stepped over the shell of a utility knife, which was missing its blade. The next question was how it ended up in the wall.

Taking the blade with her, Cassie returned to the outlet and moved her other hand along the outer edges. Within minutes, she noticed a small groove that outlined the switch. As she went to pry it open, she suddenly heard voices upstairs in the hall. Quickly, she switched off the light, leaving herself in total darkness. She knew there would be hell to pay if she were discovered down there. So braving the darkness and swearing to return later, she made her way up the steps, keeping the blade hidden in her hand.

Once she reached the top of the steps, she cracked the door slightly to see if anyone was there before she emerged. Sensing no one around, she opened the door and closed it behind her and headed toward the kitchen. By the time she reached the kitchen, her forehead was beaded with perspiration and her mouth was dry. Very quickly and efficiently, she wrapped the knife blade in a paper towel and placed it in the bottom of the wastebasket. She then removed the rag from her hand. She was in the process of washing the blood off when she heard footsteps behind her. With blood draining from her wet hand, she turned around catching Kelley's horrified glare.

"What the hell happened to you?"

CHAPTER XIII

For a brief moment, Cassie was dumbfounded. Stuttering as she turned back to wash the blood off her hand, she said, "Oh . . . it's nothing . . . really. I just . . ." Taking a quick glance across the countertop, she caught sight of an empty can. "Cut myself on a can lid. Clumsy me, huh."

Grimacing, he approached her from behind to examine the superficial wound. "That doesn't look like a cut from a can lid. Are you sure there isn't something you would like to tell me?" He looked down at her questioningly.

"Well, that's what happened." Turning off the water, she placed a paper towel over the cut and turned around. "Do you have any gauze bandages, because I don't think a Band-Aid will do?" The glib hit home as a smile creased his forehead. He walked into the pantry, giving her a little breather and then returned with a first-aid kit.

"Let me see." He held out his hand, and she gave him hers. Still applying pressure, he used his other hand to remove a tube of antibiotic cream from the box and removed the towel long enough to place the cream over the wound, which seemed to slow the bleeding down. Picking up a roll of gauze, he began to wrap it around her hand, allowing just enough pressure to stop the bleeding. Then he took a pair of surgical scissors and cut the rest of the gauze off and applied a little bandage tape to hold it in place. "There." He surveyed his work and then her face. "That should do, but you know, you are going to have a hard time typing with this." He smiled again, which caused her heart to flutter. He had the power to make her weak in the knees and wondered if he knew. Placing his hand under her elbow, he began to stroke her arm, creating tiny shivers up and down her spine.

"Oh, I will manage somehow. Is there something you needed tonight?" She smiled sweetly, causing his grin to widen.

"As luck would have it, no. You are off the hook, mostly because you are still recovering from the bump on your head, and because I am too tired. Rod and I made a huge discovery tonight." Catching the anxious look in her eyes, he added, "We will discuss it tomorrow, but right now, we need to get you back to bed."

"If you don't mind," she said, "I would like a little something to eat first." Her statement brought a confused smile from him as he countered.

"What was in the can?"

Just as quick, she responded, "That can was here when I came in. I went to move it, the can slipped, and I cut myself. That's the whole story."

Still smiling, he replaced the gauze pads and the scissors into the first-aid kit and gathered up the used pieces and threw them into the trash can. In doing so, he noticed a knife blade that had unknowingly fallen out of the towel Cassie had wrapped it in. With a slight frown on his face, he straightened up and looked at her squarely in the face. "Are you sure there isn't something you would like to tell me about this evening?"

Willing herself to remain strong, she answered, "No, should there be?" By the expression on his face, she couldn't tell if he believed her or not, but he obviously was not going to press the issue. It would have been too humiliating for her to have to explain what she was doing in the basement when he had warned her how dangerous those steps were. Changing the subject, she asked, "What's on the agenda for tomorrow? Are we heading back to your informant's house?"

"Actually, no. He will be away for the next couple of days. As for tomorrow, I am going to give you a guided tour of the grounds, and then we will be meeting Johann in town around three o'clock." As he informed her of their plans, he leaned casually against the countertop and gazed methodically over her face as if studying every detail of her well-defined face—the oval-shaped eyes with the long black lashes, the small nose with a slightly pointed tip, the high cheekbones which enhanced her whole face, and those lips that were perfectly rounded and needed to be kissed. Catching himself, he smiled and said, "Come on. I will fix you something to eat, and then I will walk you to your room. We have a busy day tomorrow." As he moved away from the counter, he picked up the first-aid kit and replaced it in the cupboard. Then he rejoined Cassie, and they scoured through the refrigerator for leftovers from dinner. As they ate, Cassie plied him for information on his meeting.

"I thought I said we would discuss it tomorrow," he said as he poured them both a glass of red wine. "But I can see that you're not going to wait. Well, we found several stolen artifacts in a few pawnshops. Someone has been selling priceless jewels on the black market."

"Do they have any suspects?"

"No, at least none that we are aware of. They are not willing to believe Clawson is involved. A lot of the higher officials are friends of his." As he took a sip of wine, his gaze followed his glass back to the table. "We do have someone to watch, however. He has been hanging around Charisse, asking all kinds of personal questions about my family. One question in particular pertained to Janelle's necklace." Pausing briefly, he lifted his eyes to look into hers. "All I can say is we are on the right track, and eventually someone is going to make a mistake." He watched her finish eating and then asked, "Are you done? If you are, I will walk you to your room." Placing the dirty dishes in the sink, he led her out of the kitchen.

Halfway across the hall, he stopped. Before she realized he had stopped, Cassie was about two steps ahead of him and was about to ask him what was wrong when she noticed what he was looking at. Cursing inwardly, Cassie realized she had left the basement door slightly ajar, causing Kelley to become suspicious. She slowly moved over, closing the gap between them, and turning her head in the same direction, she inquired cautiously, "Is something wrong?"

Giving her a brief cursory nod, he strode over to the basement door and opened it. After a few brief moments, as if listening for any sounds from below, he shut the door and faced Cassie. "You wouldn't have any idea why this door was open, or did you hear anyone go downstairs while you were in the kitchen?"

Dumbfounded, she stumbled over the answer, "N . . . no. There is no reason for me to be wandering around down there. And no, I didn't hear anyone either. What makes you think anyone was down there anyway?" Cassie had recovered enough to sound thoroughly confused to him.

"Because," he took a deep breath, "I was the last person down there, and I know that I closed the door. So that gives me a reason to be a little suspicious, doesn't it?" He was watching her face for a sign, of what she wasn't sure. "But I suppose I didn't get it latched good enough." Turning around, he took Cassie's good hand and guided her up the stairs. Pausing just outside her door, he gently took both of her hands in his and said, "Well, this is turning out to be quite a trip for you, but I hope to have things well in order in the next couple of weeks. Then, we can enjoy the festival before heading back to Indiana. Good night, Cassie. Pleasant dreams." Brushing his lips lightly across her knuckles as his eyes held hers, he secretly longed to carry her into the room and share his passionate need for her. He was almost sure that she felt the same way but knew the timing wasn't right yet. Without another word, he reached around and opened the door for her. Turning around, he headed down the hall to his own room, closing the door behind him.

Once inside her own room, she silently breathed a sigh of relief that he hadn't followed her inside. She wasn't sure anymore if she could hold her feelings back. Deep down inside her she was aching to feel him touching her, but her mind was telling her to back off. That course could only end in pain for both of them, and she couldn't withstand another loss. The only course she knew she should take was to keep it professional. Besides, her involvement with Janelle's problem was making it more difficult to confide in Kelley. If he found out what she knew, he would be furious and more than likely send her packing back to the States. And regardless of how she felt about him, she didn't want to be separated from him.

With a long, low grumble, she crossed the room and opened the pinewood closet where all of her dresses and nightwear were hanging. Instead of picking her usual, sensible nightgown, Cassie picked out the lacy, practically see-through black camisole and matching sheer silk robe. She had brought it along on a whim. Kent had told her she needed to express herself a little more. "Well, Kent," she whispered to herself, "you were right about not expressing myself more clearly, but you won't be seeing me in this." She grinned to herself as she held the seductive nightwear in front of her. As she carried them toward the bathroom, she picked up her night bag.

After soaking for what seemed an hour, Cassie finally emerged from the bathroom all freshly cleaned and invigorated. Feeling alive and in better spirits, her brightness was short-lived as she stepped out of the bathroom. All of a sudden, her lungs felt like they were caving in on her, because sitting on the side of the bed was Kelley, looking weary and bemused.

Stunned by her attire, but noting the anxious look on her face, Kelley slowly stood up and even more slowly ran his green eyes over her slim, petite figure. "I thought you were never going to come out. But I am glad I waited." His expression mirrored his thoughts exactly, which caused Cassie to blush and wrap her robe tightly around her. "Forgive my staring, but if I had known how beautiful you would look, I would have been prepared." Shaking his head and cursing himself for behaving like a naive schoolboy, he slowly walked over to her and placed his hands on her arms, so that she could not move. Not that she would have wanted to, but he made sure she looked straight at him.

"Business first, sweetheart, and then," his eyes held hers with a deep, passionate longing, "well . . . we'll see." Removing his hands, he moved over in front of the windows, willing himself not to look at her for fear of losing his train of thought. In a very low voice, he asked, "Would you like to tell me how you really hurt your hand, or should I take a stab at it?" When she failed to answer him, continuing to look out the window, he very softly asked, "Do you trust me?"

The question threw Cassie completely off guard, but in a somewhat even tone, she replied meekly, "Yes."

Turning his questioning eyes on her, he countered, "Then why would you lie to me?" Cassie was feeling a little panicky but remained silent as she gazed back into those hypnotic green eyes. "I realize that I have put you in an awkward situation, and you have done a beautiful job of handling it, but you need to confide in me a little more. Otherwise, you could be endangering yourself without realizing it." He looked into her confused face and sighed in exasperation. "I know you didn't cut your hand on a can in the kitchen, because I found a knife blade in the trash. After I left you, I became suspicious and went back down to the kitchen. When I found the blade, I wondered where it came from and concluded that you had been in the basement before we got home tonight. You became excited when I noticed the door was slightly open." His searching gaze was making Cassie more and more uneasy. If he kept up this line of questioning, she was afraid that she would cave in. But he refused to give up.

"Please tell me what you were doing down there? And what Clawson wanted with Janelle? He was seen leaving the garden area just before you and Janelle were locked in a heated discussion." He sighed. "Cassie, I have to know. Things could get extremely ugly in the next few days, and I wouldn't want to see you get hurt, and I mean that literally."

All Cassie could do was stand there. She had promised to give Janelle a little bit of time, but her confidence was weakening as she looked into his pleading eyes. In the back of her mind, she reminded herself that she had made a promise, and she had never broken a promise before. In her heart, she knew she should trust him and confide in him. Still, she hesitated. "D . . . d . . . do you really think Clawson would hurt her—or me?"

"I think he would do anything to keep his control over the situation, and that includes taking advantage of innocent people like you. For that reason, I must know why you are protecting her, or else I will have to confront Clawson myself, and I am not yet ready to let him know how much I know. Do you understand?"

"Yes," she replied, more calmly than she felt. Inside, her nerves were making her nauseous. "I just don't understand why it's so hard for you to understand Janelle. She needs your help, not your admonishments. After all, she does have the right to know where she comes from, doesn't she?" Cassie's pleading eyes melted into his, which caused him to cave slightly.

"Please don't look at me like that. You don't realize the effect it has on me." As he moved over to the side of the bed, he pulled her over to him. Holding her in front of him, he studied her face, as if he wanted to know everything inside of her. After careful scrutiny, he answered, "All right, I will give her one week to come forward, if things haven't boiled over by then. But until then, promise me you will stay away from Clawson, okay?" Her nod was enough, and he continued to hold her. "You do look magnificent tonight. With the full moon outside and the candles lit around the room, it would appear to be magical."

Very slowly his left hand rose to her cheek to gently stroke the side of her face. Closing her eyes to the feel of his fingers on her warm skin, she could sense the passion rising in her but refused to listen to the warning signs in her brain. She wanted this as much as he did, maybe even more. When she opened her eyes again, his green eyes were darker and more hypnotic. She was drowning in a sea of enchantment and couldn't stop herself from falling. As she continued to gaze into his eyes, the hand on her other arm slowly moved around her waist, drawing her closer. Once she was molded to him, he allowed his hand to move from her face to stroke her fine, soft hair back from her face and rest easily on the back of her neck. Moving his fingers into her hair, he gently tilted her head back so that she had to look up into his eyes. Briefly, his eyes roamed over her face and rested on her parted, moist lips. Without any further hesitation, he slid his lips sensually over hers, drawing her deep desires to the surface, prolonging the inevitable.

While he teased her mouth relentlessly with hungry kisses, Cassie lifted her arms willingly to caress his muscular frame. With each kiss he gave her, she would respond even more aggressively, as if she had been holding back all her passion from her past. It was as if time had stood still for her, and she wanted him to feel it too.

As their passion ignited, Kelley sensed her relinquishing and started a new assault on her. Aroused beyond belief, she allowed him to slip the filmy negligee off of her shoulders into a pile on the floor at her feet. His glance took in the slim rounded beauty of her body, causing a jolt inside of him. His imagination had not prepared him for how stunning she really was. With a low, throaty voice full of passion, he mumbled against her lips, "I never knew how beautiful you were until now, not to mention enticing." Picking her up, he gently laid her on the bed as he removed his own shirt.

Cassie was not content to let him have his way, so she raised up on her knees, and as she feathered his chest with light kisses, causing deep sighs of pleasure from him, she tugged at his belt until it withdrew, and she slowly, methodically unzipped his pants. When his pants and underwear hit the floor, her breath drew in sharply at the sheer size of him. The muscular frame with his clothes on was nothing compared to the actual sight of him without them. He was lean, tan, and muscular all over. She would swear there wasn't an ounce of fat on him. But the sight of him standing there in front of her, wanting her, was overwhelming. With passion rising in both their eyes, Kelley reached out for her and, pulling her into his arms, could feel the heat in her body responding to his throbbing manhood.

Every touch, every caress, was bringing new sensations that caused Cassie's mind to go blank to everything around her except him. She was his, if only for one night, but still her kisses became more heightened and insistent. Kelley's movements became more erotic as wave upon wave of passion unleashed itself, until finally neither one of them could deny themselves. Without any hesitation, Kelley lowered her to the bed, taking her passionately, but gently, not forgetting he wanted her to enjoy the feeling as much as he was. Within moments, they were soaring higher than any mountain could ever reach, and once they reached the pinnacle of their passion, Kelley gently brought them back to earth, murmuring sweet nothings in her ear. Once the heated feelings had subsided, they lay in each other's arms and slept.

CHAPTER XIV

Exhausted, but relishing his warm body next to hers, Cassie refused to sleep for fear of waking and finding him gone. With only a few more hours before daylight, she lay quietly in his arms, listening to his steady breathing and vibrant heart. She had never felt so wanted or satisfied with anyone else, not even Kent. It was funny to think of him at that precise moment, but compared to Kent, Kelley was a master at the art of seduction. He had moved his hands and lips expertly over her, provoking responses from her that she had never allowed herself to feel. She was completely powerless against him as his tantalizing kisses and sensitive and sensual touch were swallowing her very being. He had led her on an erotic journey that just when she thought they were coming to the end, he would lead her down another path. But when the end had come, he lowered her gently, easing her back into the real world without any complications. She had been cradled in his arms when the heat had died, and the only thing left was the glowing ember of their lovemaking. Now, he kept her close to him, wrapped in his arms in order to keep her from leaving. What he didn't know, and what she had to keep hidden, was the truth of her feelings for him. No matter what, she had to maintain some distance between her heart and him.

"Aren't you tired?" came the low, husky voice.

Smiling broadly, Cassie softly murmured, "I was afraid to sleep. I thought I might wake up and find it was all a dream.

I'm still not sure exactly what happened last night." As her hand continued to play with the few scatterings of chest hair, his right hand came up under her chin, forcing her to look him straight in the eyes.

"We did what we have been fighting not to do since we met. But that isn't what you are asking, is it?" His eyes softened as they looked into hers. "Cassie, I really need to know what you were doing in the basement. If you think you know where Janelle's necklace is, please tell me. I can't protect you forever."

In the darkness, Cassie could feel her anger rising. He was protecting her when she heard them all conspiring against her. She couldn't believe her ears, that he was actually accusing her of stealing after the passionate lovemaking they had shared just moments ago. Removing herself from his embrace, Cassie got up and retrieved her robe that had been discarded onto the floor. After wrapping it around her slim shoulders, she turned around to face him. In the moonlight, Cassie looked like a glowing ghost with her white skin and shiny hair. The only thing making her appear human was the color of the negligee. Looking at her made Kelley want to reach for her and draw her back to his throbbing manhood, but he left her standing there.

"How can you say that after what just happened? The fact that you can accuse me of taking something that means so much to your sister and then turn around and have sex with me is repulsive. Why should I take the damn thing in the first place?" Unable to look at him anymore and feeling the tears welling up in her eyes, she turned around to face the vanity.

"Is that all we had—sex? I don't believe that was all it felt like." She could hear the bed creak as he pushed the covers aside and rose up on his feet. Within a few steps, he was standing behind her, surveying her luscious curves in the vanity mirror. He ran his fingers gently through her long hair and then brushed it aside to reveal the whiteness of her neck. He lowered his lips to taste the sweetness of her skin, but sensing her change of mood, he raised his head and looked at her reflection in the mirror. The look on her face was pleading, so he dropped his hands and moved over to the window. "I'm sorry, I seemed to have picked the wrong time for this discussion, but if you were in the basement, I would have to assume that it had to do with the necklace. Or were you looking for something else?" Suddenly he turned his questioning eyes on her, which caused her to back up into the shadows where he couldn't read her expression.

Sitting on the side of the bed for support, she replied, "I was in the basement, but only to make sure that it was gone. I thought it might have fallen out of the case. Maybe Janelle removed it herself but forgot where she put it. It could happen." She didn't want Kelley to find out that Janelle had asked her to hide the truth, but then she hadn't expected Janelle to turn on her either. Still, she had given her word, and she would keep it.

"Not likely. Janelle keeps track of everything that belongs to her. She knows how much her inheritance is right down to the last penny. No, she wouldn't have misplaced it. But I can't believe that you would have taken it either. So I guess we will just have to inform the police."

The cottonmouth Cassie was feeling made it hard for her to ask, "Why don't we wait a few days and see if it turns up? Maybe one of your brothers borrowed it to have it appraised or something. Can't we wait a few days, please? It might turn up on its own." She waited for his answer with goose bumps growing on her arms.

The look of astonishment on Kelley's face made her even more anxious, but after a few moments, his face lightened. "I guess Janelle has her reasons for hiding it, if she does know where it is. All right, we will wait until Friday, that's two days from now. After that, I'll call the Mounties, agreed?"

"Agreed."

"Now, I—" Before he could say anything, a flash of light caught the corner of the window. In one large step, the heavy fabric of the curtain shielded Kelley. Peering out the side of the window, he could make out movement in the garden below.

Without hesitation, Cassie jumped to her feet and whispered, "What is it? Is someone out there?" Quietly and quickly, she moved beside him, but he held her back away from the window.

He stole a quick glance at her before turning his full attention back to the patio below. "There appears to be a couple of intruders on the property. One is apparently moving away from the house, and the other is coming back." Cassie's hand had moved over to his chest and could feel the rapid beat of his heart racing as if he had just run a marathon. "Damn, it's too dark; I can't see who it is. I better get dressed and head down there." Holding her hand in his, he lightly kissed her fingertips before muttering, "I'm sorry, but we'll have to finish this later." Stealing one long look at her frozen form, he reached for his pants and pulled them on. As he zipped them, he stated, "For your information, we will find out what happened to the necklace together, or I will be forced to search you." And with a mischievous grin, he left the room, leaving Cassie stunned into silence.

With one quick movement, however, she was by the window peering out, searching for what or who had been the object in question. When she was sure nothing was there, she returned to the side of the bed and sat down. She picked up the alarm clock and read, "Five thirty; by the time I take a shower and get dressed, breakfast will be ready."

It only took her a few moments to gather her outfit and her toilet supplies and head into the bathroom. As the water ran over her slim figure and massaged her neck, Cassie began to collect herself. She allowed herself to reflect on the past week and the night she spent in Kelley's arms. He had been the perfect lover, gentle but demanding, playful but mindful. Every touch had awakened new senses in her she didn't know she possessed. The only problem was he was her boss, and she had sworn that it wouldn't happen twice. But that didn't stop her from wanting him, and by the intensity of his kisses, he apparently felt the same.

Cassie closed her eyes and let the water run over her face. The gentle spray relaxed her, and she finally came to a decision. She didn't like the choices, but in the end she knew she would be getting hurt. So she would take the lesser of the two evils. When they returned to Indiana, she would turn in her two weeks' notice and hope that Kelley would understand her position.

She turned off the shower, dried herself off, and dressed. After applying fresh makeup and examining herself in the full-length mirror on the door, she opened the door and stepped into the bedroom, stopping just inside the room. Kelley was seated on the side of the bed holding the little box that Cassie knew had contained the necklace.

Stammering, she asked, "Wh . . . What's that?"

He stood up without taking his eyes off of hers. "This is the box that Janelle swears her necklace was in. I found it on top of your dresser." The confused look in his eyes made her stomach turn over. "I don't suppose you have an explanation as to why the box would be here but the necklace isn't."

Cassie looked at the box and prayed that she could keep her wits. Slowly she looked up into his face and decided she had better explain everything, but first she had to be sure he would trust her. "Would you believe me if I said that I found it here?" The look of disbelief on his face made Cassie fear that anything she said wouldn't be enough, but she was going to have to try to make him believe her, because she wanted him to trust her completely. "I found it here the day of the funeral. I thought I had been dreaming, but I wasn't. I took it down to dinner that night, intending to ask Janelle about it, but Charisse showed up, so I forgot about it. Then, after I was attacked in my room, the necklace disappeared.

And that's all of it, or so I thought, until I heard all of you downstairs discussing the matter and more or less accusing me of taking it. I didn't know what to do, so I kept quiet, hoping it would turn up." She didn't add the fact that Janelle had asked her to keep quiet, but then she hadn't expected her to turn on her. Meanwhile she kept her gaze steady as she faced him. She prayed that he wouldn't ask for anything else, because she didn't want him to know she had found a secret compartment in the basement wall. "There is nothing else I can say, so I guess you are just going to have to trust me." She watched his expression change to one of concern.

"Well, I guess I could talk to Janelle about it. I just wish you had confided in me, and then I could have been up front with my brothers. That necklace is worth thousands, and Janelle isn't about to let it go so easily. For your sake, I hope it turns up soon, or you will be facing more than just your boss." Standing up, he approached her, and taking her in his arms, he whispered, "I'm sorry. I didn't believe you were capable of stealing." For a moment, Cassie thought he might kiss her, but to her astonishment, he only gazed into her eyes and added, "In case you're wondering, whoever was outside appears to have vanished. So you are safe for the time being . . . and I intend to show you the grounds this morning. I feel that I have been very distracted lately and not a very good host. Therefore, first thing after breakfast, we will walk around the grounds, and I can tell you a little of the history of our home and country. Would you like that?"

Smiling, she quickly said, "I would love it. I was wondering if you would ever ask." Motioning her forward, Kelley allowed her to walk out the door first and then proceeded to follow her down the steps and into the dining room, where the maid was placing the food on the sideboard for everyone to fend for himself or herself.

"You will find that the evening meal is the only one that we dress for and insist on being served. Everything else is a la carte." He held the chair for Cassie as she sat down with her coffee, eggs, ham, and toast, and then he sat down across from her. While enjoying their food and each other's company, they heard the front door open.

A few seconds later, dressed in a very chic, very expensive designer dress, cut to perfection, Charisse walked in, bathed in some exotic perfume that made Cassie almost choke on her eggs. "Well, I guess I am not too late for breakfast after all." As the maid took her coat and small handbag, she waved her off with a well-manicured hand and prophetic sigh. "I hope you are going to allow me the privilege of your company today, sweetheart." Her dark green eyes seemed to glow with malice. If she had been a cat, she would have been rubbing against his leg purring. The sickeningly sweet plea was not lost on the man she sat beside with.

"Actually, Charisse, I was about to show Cassie the grounds. I have not been the proper host and intend to correct my error. Unless you would like to join us, I suggest you come back later." His caustic attitude, although not lost on either woman, did not perturb her. She would not give up so easily.

"I would love to join you." She grinned maliciously. "I do hope you have your walking shoes on because the grounds are quite extensive and rugged at that."

"I will be fine. I had planned on walking this morning anyway. I usually walk home from work every night. It calms my nerves." Cassie knew she was baiting her, but she wasn't about to let that baby-doll face win over her. "If you are ready, Kelley, I would love to get going." The fact that she had used his Christian name made him smile wickedly but put the edge on Charisse's already dark green eyes.

*   *   *

In an early-morning ritual of coffee and wheat toast with peanut butter and butter, a solitary gentleman sits under a large canopy. As he sips his coffee and reads the morning paper, a small Indian servant delivers a note and quietly waits for a reply.

The gentleman grimaces at the writing on the paper, sets his cup down on the table, and gets up. Nodding to the servant, he says, "Thank you, Abdul. If you would, please get my briefcase out of my study, bring it here, and start preparing the guesthouse. One of my associates will be arriving soon." With just a curt little nod, the servant was off on his errand, and the gentleman picked up the phone.

"Ah yes, we need to talk. I will be sending my jet to pick you up; it should be there in three hours. Someone is going to pay quite handsomely for the information I have just received."

CHAPTER XV

Surrounded in greenery and multicolored flowers, Cassie was in complete awe of the different variety and extensiveness of the gardens. From her window they had looked long and scraggy. But now that she was walking through them, she could tell it had taken a lot of time and preparation on the landscaper's part. He would have had to start each plant separately in a greenhouse and then transplant them here in a set pattern. It probably took several hours, maybe even days, to come up with the arrangements that would complement each one of them. The wild orchids in six different shades next to the greens of hanging vines and wild strawberry plants all blended together to form a rainbow of color. Then, on the backside of the gardens were the enormous fir and pine trees. The trees themselves seemed to reach heaven.

As they rounded a bend in the pathway, a large Roman goddess appeared as a water fountain. At this point, Kelley turned to her and said, "This is the high point of the gardens. We light this area up for birthday parties and other special occasions and place tables and chairs around the fountain. It's the perfect centerpiece for celebrations, don't you think?" He glanced down at the smiling face of the girl holding his arm.

"Absolutely. It's breathtaking out here. Whoever designed this garden should be commended." She blushed as Kelley winked at her. On his other arm, Charisse was not amused.

"Thank you, the gardens were my father's idea and my creation. It took quite a long time to get it just right," he said, beaming, proud of his achievement.

"Oh, let's not forget who else had a hand in this. If memory serves, Janelle was instrumental in getting the project off to a profitable start. Or have you forgotten what her contribution was, darling?" The cattiness of her voice put the edge on Cassie and seemed to irritate Kelley as well.

"No, I haven't forgotten, Charisse. In fact, I am constantly reminded by Janelle what she has done for this family, and that she feels we owe her more. But until I feel it is safe to do so, she will just have to wait like everyone else." The heated glance told Charisse that she had overstepped herself, and she had the nerve to look shocked.

"I don't understand you people. It's her money. You really have no right to decide when or where or what she does with it. Besides, I suspect she will be coming into better circumstances soon." Ignoring the controlled look on Kelley's face, she continued, "There is a rumor that she is involved with someone of means, which means that her husband's sorry little ass will be ousted from her life permanently this time." Her remarks left a cold, dark feeling crawling up Cassie's back. "If I were you, Cassie dear, I would hop on the next plane home before you're the next victim."

Cassie could feel the anger vibrating off of Kelley as she turned to see cold, vacant eyes. He was seething with unbridled anger at Charisse's last remarks. "Why would I be a victim, and why is it not safe for Janelle to inherit her fortune now? Wasn't her father dying enough?"

Charisse was apparently not finished with her tirade. "Oh, you didn't know. I would have thought Kelley would have told you, but you are only his secretary." The last remark hit Kelley like a slap in the face.

Very slowly, he began to explain. "It's not quite so easy for Janelle to inherit. Being the only girl in the family and the fact that Father was not very close to her made things difficult. She had to prove over and over again that she was just as confident and capable as the rest of us. Father accused our mother of infidelity with our neighbor, Clawson, and that's one side of the feud that's been building, because unknown to Father and everyone else was her affection toward another man. Someone who was always right there when she needed him. But Mother's family was proud of her and their union into society, and she wasn't willing to destroy that union. Now, Janelle has to prove to the family that she is in fact a McGillis."

"Mr. Jamison. The man I met at the funeral. He said that he had helped your mother when she needed it." The expression on his face confirmed it. There had been a lost feeling in Jamison's face, and Cassie could not have known then about the love shared between Kelley's mother and himself. "So what did Charisse mean by it wasn't safe?" Cassie had to sit down on the side of the fountain to steady herself.

Without allowing him a chance to respond, Charisse interjected, "It's not really a matter of safety. It's more like a question of family associations. You see, Cassie, Janelle has to prove herself worthy or capable of inheriting, which is ridiculous if you ask me." She looked at Kelley disparagingly.

"My father ensured that Janelle would inherit only if she proved herself. That meant through public and private associations. She had to stay married to the same man, and she had to promote some kind of environmental project. Father was to choose both. The conservatory where we met is her handiwork, and her current husband is the man. On the outside, it doesn't seem like a whole lot. But the man she married was Clawson's brother. Father had caught them in one of the guesthouses when she was sixteen, and the next year they were married."

"My God, does that mean that Clawson could inherit some of Janelle's estate if anything happened to her?" she asked, astounded.

"Yes, it does. But that isn't stopping Janelle from wanting it or doing everything she can to provoke a fight. She doesn't want Clawson to gain from her husband's good fortune, but her husband is too good-natured, especially when he is too drunk to know what he is doing. He has already signed over his rights to some of her property. My guess is that Clawson will use his leverage to gain the rest of her estate, which fences off the last two-thirds of this property here. The largest mineral deposits and the largest wood population on the estate." He sighed heavily before adding, "Charisse knows better than to discuss these matters openly. You will have to excuse her thoughtlessness." He eyed her angrily.

Stammering, Charisse defended herself, "Well, you have said more than I have, so if anyone should be excused, it's you. I am sure Cassie really doesn't want or need to know everything. After all, she won't be around long enough to witness the outcome. Now! If you will excuse me, I have had enough fresh air. I will show myself out of here." The click of her heels on the cobblestone path was deafening as she made her way back up to the house, leaving them in silence.

Suddenly, a dark cloud seemed to pass over Kelley's face as he walked over to her. Taking her in his arms, he held her head against his chest, cradling her as if protecting her from unseen demons. The rhythm of his heart picked up as his breathing became heavier. Then, moving her slightly away from him, he lifted her chin up, so he could look into her hazel eyes. "We had reason to believe that Father was in the process of changing his will." When she started to pull away, he forced her to remain where she was. "What we didn't know was the will had been changed the night before he died. It's already been signed, and the lawyer has confided in me that it will be read in a fortnight. No one else has been informed, and I am hoping that you can continue the silence until then. You see, if Clawson finds out, he will use any means possible to keep from losing that land. He will lash out at anyone in his path, and you, my sweet, are going to be a prime target, mostly because you are linked to me." He released her then, allowing breathing space.

Looking up with tears in her eyes, she asked, "What are you going to do? Is it possible he had something to do with my being attacked in my room and the intruder outside my window?" The memory caused her body to turn cold and shiver. She rubbed her arms up and down as if trying to warm herself from a cold draft.

Kelley pulled her back into his arms and said, "There is no way in hell anyone is going to get to you. I won't allow it." As if to prove his feelings for her, he gently tilted her head back and allowed himself a few moments to gaze into her already darkening hazel eyes. Before he could kiss her, however, a figure emerging caught in the corner of Kelley's eyes caused him to release her abruptly and caused Cassie to stumble slightly while gathering her composure. Recognizing Rod, Kelley let out a small grimace as he moved toward him.

Discreetly, Rod cleared his throat, avoiding the embarrassment of catching them in a brief moment of passion. "I am sorry to interrupt your morning walk, but we have a problem. Janelle has been taken to the emergency room." His excited look made Cassie uneasy as Kelley's face became dark with anger.

"What happened?" Kelley asked, suppressing his anger.

"I will tell you on the way. There isn't enough time to tell you here. Cassie, I am sorry for intruding, but family comes first." Kelley shot him a menacing look as he responded to Rod's last statement.

"I am sure Cassie knows how important our family closeness is, so you don't have to tell her."

"I'm sorry, Cassie. I didn't mean to berate you," Rod excused himself.

"That's all right. But you two had better get going, and don't worry about the work here. I will use the time to get myself organized. Now go!" Cassie more or less shoved Kelley in order to get them to move. Without any more hesitation, they were gone.

*   *   *

After three solid hours of flying time, Kent Wallace Jr. was ready for a hot shower and a good meal. As he stood in front of the airport waiting, he kept glancing at his watch nervously. Clawson had said it was urgent. He hoped that whatever the problem was, it could be taken care of without too much attention, because his dealings with Clawson were becoming increasingly dangerous and was coloring his reputation in the business world. The fact that he had married Clawson's only daughter didn't help much either. But this time, Cassie was involved, and that made his position even more precarious. He didn't know if Clawson knew about his association with her or not, but he prayed Clawson wouldn't find out.

Taking another glance at his watch, he had been informed someone would be here to meet him. Obviously, the driver had been detained. He was on the verge of reentering the airport when a black limousine pulled up to the curb. The chauffeur got out of the car and opened the door. "I am truly sorry, Mr. Wallace, but there was an accident on the highway. Please get in. I will be taking you to Mr. Clawson's hacienda." The driver took the bags on the sidewalk and proceeded to pack them in the trunk before returning to his own seat behind the steering wheel. Once on the road, Kent poured himself a scotch out of the liquor cabinet in the small bar beside his seat. The plush interior of the limo did little to comfort his already shot nerves. He loosened his tie a little, sat back, and closed his eyes briefly.

It was another hour before they drove through a huge wrought-iron gate and wound around several small ponds and clusters of green shrubbery. Straightening his tie and finishing off his drink, he took a deep breath as they pulled up to the porch of one of the most posh estates in the region. It was a close second to the McGillis estate, which lay on the southern border of the Clawson property. There had been several attempts by Clawson to claim a part of the McGillis land, but they all failed. Survey after survey agreed that the old McGillis patriarch knew exactly where his land started and stopped. And he wasn't about to sell, especially to Clawson. The feud had started when the old man married Bethany. She had been the daughter of the wealthiest family in the region, and she had fallen in love with Patrick, and no one believed he would ever hurt her.

Little had anyone known that Clawson was in love with her too. He would have given anything to marry her, but because of bad blood between families and bad financial ties, Bethany's family had shunned Clawson's. He had instead married beneath his station but kept a firm watch on old Patrick. Patrick was a land lover. He would sacrifice his own family to protect the land, and although Bethany had known that, she had agreed to marry him. After the children were born, Patrick began to avoid her. He spent more and more time away from home, embedded in environmental issues, and she became more and more despondent. She had begun to seek solace in any man that showed her compassion. Even though Clawson was a bitter rival, she played him as well. But there was one man no one counted on, and no one knew his name. It was this unknown lover that supposedly fathered Janelle, the youngest child, but that was never proven. Not long after she was born, Bethany died, leaving Patrick questioning the baby's true heritage and inflicting his own form of revenge—the will.

Clawson, however, had married and had one daughter that he doted on despite the fact that his wife was leaving him for safer pastures. The daughter was brought up with no expense spared and shared her father's keen business sense. It was the deal between Clawson and Kent that evolved into a torrid romance with Jaclyn and then the well-publicized wedding. He hadn't expected to come home and find Cassie gone, but he couldn't blame her. Anyway, she had landed on her feet quite well, for the time being. She was going to be in for a rude wakening.

As the door to the limousine opened, the front door of the house opened, and a uniformed butler stepped out. Behind him, Clawson made his way down the front steps. "Ah, I see you have made it in one piece. I was beginning to worry you weren't coming." His delight at seeing Kent was causing Kent's skin to crawl. In the back of his mind, he knew that whenever Mick was nice to him, he was about to become involved in something illegal or something suspicious. "We have to make plans, and fast, my boy. We have gotten some bad news, and I will not lose this fight, even if someone has to go down. Understand?" Feeling the increasing clouds of doom, he was ushered into the house, and the front door shut behind him.

*   *   *

During the last three hours of Kelley and Rod's absence, Cassie made a huge dent in the workload Kelley had assigned her. He had obviously stayed up after their interlude and revised their priority list. As she was just finishing the bulk of the caseload, she was hunting through the desk drawer looking for the box of staples when the brown envelope caught her attention. It was sticking partially out of the folder that Kelley had tucked back into the drawer after reprimanding her for trying to open it. Ever since he had accosted her about it, the file had loomed in the back of her mind. And since Kelley was nowhere around to catch her, she figured this would be the perfect opportunity to solve one of the many secrets.

Very carefully, Cassie removed the folder, making sure nothing else moved out of place. Gingerly, she opened the folder and began to read its contents. Within just a few seconds, she realized the folder contained background information on herself. But it hadn't come from the personnel department, she was sure of that. What was Kelley doing having her checked out? In a state of utter confusion, Cassie removed the contents of the manila envelope. Shock and horror caused her to freeze in her chair. She had spread in front of her a series of photographs, all containing herself. As the tears came to her eyes, Cassie began to examine each one of the photos. The first one was at the conservatory, the day she ran into Kelley. There was even a picture of her dining with him that first night. The next few were on her lunches and errand runs and the night she thought someone had followed her. She had been right to glance around her, and she knew that someone had followed her into the dress shop. Now more than ever, she was paranoid. Was Kelley having her watched? Didn't he trust her by now? After all, they had been intimate, or maybe he was just playing games. Either way, her heart began to ache. She had dared to believe in him, but now there was only speculation. She would have to confront him. In the back of her mind, however, alarms were ringing. What if she was in danger from Kelley?

"No," she told herself flatly. "He hasn't even attempted to hurt me." So there had to be another set of circumstances. Too confused and too upset to think about it any longer, she stacked up the pictures and replaced them on top of the envelope in the file folder and returned the folder to the drawer. Feeling depressed and humiliated, Cassie gathered her purse off the top of the desk and headed toward the study doors. As she came out of the room, she ran right into Kirk.

CHAPTER XVI

"Kirk!"

At the sound of his name, Kirk turned from the door and frowned. He hadn't expected Cassie to talk to him, since he had been less than polite with her. Although he had ulterior motives for avoiding her, he had been given strict instructions to keep an eye on her. His gruff expression went unnoticed by Cassie, who was very intent on getting out of the house. If he played his cards right, his debt would be paid in full. A menacing smile crossed his face as he replied, "What can I do for you?"

Stopping a few feet from him, she looked up into those cynical doe brown eyes. After a brief hesitation, she asked, "Are you heading into town, because I need to mail some letters and get some stamps? I thought if you were going, it would save time, and Kelley wouldn't have to take me later. After all, he will probably be at the hospital all day, and these letters have to be mailed today. So will you please run me in?"

"Why would Kelley be at the hospital?" An anxious expression, replaced by a dawning suspicion, crossed his face as he interrogated her. "Is someone sick, or has there been an accident?"

"Well," she responded, "Janelle has been rushed to the hospital. I had no time to find out why as Kelley and Rod left as quickly as possible."

"I probably should say no, but what the hell, you can't stay cooped up here with nothing to do. I'll complete my business and go straight to the hospital. You will have to catch a cab home. Deal?"

"Deal. Thanks, I will go get the letters." With a lift in her step, Cassie returned to the den, grabbed the letters, and closed the door to the den on her way out. When she had reentered the huge front hall, Kirk was talking on the phone with his back on her.

"Don't worry, I will take care of everything. I will deliver the package within the next hour. We will be done with the matter, right? No. This is it, take it or leave it. Bye." Turning around, he stopped. Without giving her a chance to ask about the phone call, he said, "Ready?" With a mock smile and a brief nod, they were off.

Once outside, Cassie inhaled deeply, enjoying the fresh air and the smell of the fall season. The mountains in the distance were magnificent. From where she was standing, she had a perfect view of the Three Sisters, or the Three Nuns, unofficially called Faith, Hope, and Charity. They are the signature landmarks of Canmore, and one of the most popular sights for tourists. They're so green and lush tourists would often stop and take pictures, or take hikes along the outskirts of the mountains, pausing only for a short picnic lunch at the base. Stretching her arms up and then around her, hugging herself, she took another gulp of air and let it out slowly. Kirk held the door of his sleek black Lamborghini open for her as she crawled in.

Within minutes, they were pulling out of the driveway and running along Highway 1A. They rode in silence until suddenly Kirk took an off ramp to Highway 1. Cassie sat, confused for a few moments before she asked, "I thought you were heading into town. Where are we going?" She was trying desperately to control the panic in her throat.

"We are going to town, but the town I am meeting friends in is Banff. I'm afraid you are going along for the ride. You should be all right though. If you have any problems at all, call the limousine service. Just tell them Kelley McGillis will pick up the tab." He sounded impatient, as if he were tired of her already.

"Great. I was hoping I could take care of all of this before he knew I was gone. But it looks like he will find out now. Thanks," Cassie returned just as annoyed.

"That's the best I can offer you. Sorry." The rest of the trip was made in complete silence, each one fuming over the miscommunications. After at least a forty-five-minute drive, Kirk pulled up outside the Banff post office. After depositing her safely, he said, "If I were you, I would call the house and let someone know where you are. At least then, they won't be so inclined to worry about you." Cassie shut the door and watched him drive away and felt a cold shiver run down her spine. Suddenly, she felt alone and vulnerable. She began to wonder if her idea of leaving the house was worth the isolation.

Oblivious to the black sedan with tinted windows parked parallel a few feet behind her, Cassie made her way into the post office. Once inside, she sorted her mail by priority. Ordinary correspondence—follow-up reports to brokers and stockholders, second class—letters of intent to clients in the States, and first class—letters of recommendation to landowners in the surrounding area were all stacked separately. After paying the necessary postage and meters, Cassie left the mail with the clerk and breathed a sigh of relief. As she turned to leave, she bumped into a firm but soft male suit.

Embarrassed and slightly flushed, Cassie stammered, "Excuse me. I'm terribly sorry. I didn't realize anyone was back there." As she spoke, she looked up into the darkest brown, almost black, eyes she had ever seen. They seemed to engulf her in an endless black hole. Taking a deep breath, she took a small step backward but would have tripped over her own feet if the stranger had not grabbed her arm. Wincing at the pressure of his hand on her, she mumbled, "Thank you, but you are hurting me."

Easing his grip on her, but not releasing her, he smiled menacingly. "Sorry, I just didn't want you to fall and hurt yourself. But then women have often told me that I take their breath away. Although I don't think that was it." He was being flippant, but Cassie couldn't stop herself from concentrating on the hand on her elbow.

"I'm sorry. But I really don't have time to discuss your personal life. Would you please excuse me, Mr. . . . ?" She tried to release his hold on her arm.

"Verant, Douglas Verant."

"Mr. Verant, now excuse me."

He followed her gaze to the hand on her elbow, which he casually dropped. Then he allowed her to pass by, never taking his eyes off of her. Once she was out of the door, Cassie headed straight for the nearest store. She needed to gather her senses before she called for a car. After browsing aimlessly for a few minutes, she returned to the street. Moving with the other patrons, she crossed the street and continued to walk down the sidewalk on Main Street. Banff was not a large town, but it was one of the biggest tourist attractions in Alberta, Canada. She remembered reading a little bit about the town while on the plane.

Banff was the first National Park in Canada—third in the world after Yellowstone in the United States and the Royal in Australia. Starting as a land reserve in November of 1885, after appointed land surveyor George Stewart mapped out the entire boundaries of the Banff Hot Springs Reservation, by June of 1887 the Rocky Mountains Park was established. In 1892, Lake Louise was added as a forest reserve and then added to the Rocky Mountains Park in 1902. Once this area was joined, the park had reached its maximum size. In 1930, the area was officially declared Banff National Park. With its elevation at 1,371 meters and the maximum population at 8,500 people by January 1, 1990, Banff became the only self-governing town in the Canadian national parks when it was declared Alberta's 109th town.

Cassie was amazed at the way the mountains seemed to spike above the town as if guarding it from the outside world. Including the town and four mountain blocks surrounding it, the area measured at exactly 20,160 square kilometers. Between Banff and Canmore was Mount Rundle. Named after the missionary Robert T. Rundle of the Stoney Indians, it formed the western wall of the Bow Valley and spanned twelve kilometers with the town itself sitting in the heart of the valley where the Spray River and the Bow River met. Where these two rivers merge lines up on the lower slopes of the Tunnel Mountain—where the Canadian Pacific Railroad went through it—and the Sulphur Mountain. Guidebooks suggested taking a gondola ride down the side of Sulphur Mountain overlooking the town. The view was said to be breathtaking. Inhaling deeply, Cassie considered asking Kelley to take her up there before they left.

Walking down Main Street, Cassie's nerves began to subside. The fresh air and exercise brought a new sense of perception and euphoria. In her mind, it was just what the doctor would have ordered, because despite Kelley's warnings, she didn't believe she would be in any danger. She had nothing to hide. The problem with Janelle would be worked out soon. On the other hand, if Clawson was the type of man she was warned about, he could be a serious threat. But she wasn't going to dwell on the matter today. She was going to have a nice afternoon, and no one was going to stop her. Or so she thought.

Slowing down, she looked in one of the shop windows and considered going inside for a brief look around. There appeared to be a little mall within the building, so she decided to browse. Within the next hour, she had walked through six different shops and bought several new outfits and little trinkets for her mother and father. She knew it was the least she could do for them, since she was thousands of miles away. As soon as she could, she would wrap them up and ship them to her parents. When she came up to another store, the hairs on the back of her neck started to stand up. She had the worst feeling that she wasn't alone anymore. While she stood looking through the window of a gift shop, she noticed a reflection in the window of the man in the post office. With a growing sense of fear, Cassie made a fast decision to enter the store, hoping that he would leave her alone.

After a few moments of checking out the merchandise in the back of the store, Cassie finally relaxed and forgot about her unwelcome guest. She became so engrossed in her looking that she lost track of time as well. The one shop led into a mall that she browsed from one store to the other, skipping the most expensive ones. Unaware of her companion, she began to fall backward. If it hadn't been for the quick thinking of the gentleman behind her, she would have fallen to the floor.

With the grace and composure of a schoolgirl being caught looking at a boy, she muttered a quick "Thank you." But the hand that held her refused to move. The anxious look in her face turned to absolute fear when she realized who held her. "You can let go now. I am fine," she stated matter-of-factly, pulling herself free of his iron grasp.

"I can see that. Perhaps it is hunger that consumed you. After all, it is close to one o'clock, and you have been in town since . . . well, I don't remember when we met. I could remedy that if you would permit me." She couldn't believe her ears. She hardly knew the man, and he was inviting her to lunch. On second thought, she hadn't realized how late it was, and she didn't feel like walking any further. Sensing his eagerness, her curiosity peaked.

"I suppose it wouldn't hurt to have a salad somewhere. Do you know a good place?" she asked as casually as she could.

"As a matter of fact, I know a little Italian place just down the walk. Allow me?" Taking her parcels, he led her out the door and down the street to a bright red door. Balancing her parcels, he opened the door for her.

CANADIAN DESIRES | 179

Once seated, the waiter took their drink orders and left them to glance over the menu. Keeping her eyes on the menu in her hands, Cassie was aware of those dark eyes studying her. As the waiter returned with their drinks, they proceeded to give him their orders. Against her wishes, he ordered a bottle of wine and then turned his dark eyes on her. "I hope you feel better. You looked extremely pale in the store." It was an attempt at casual conversation but did little to appease the knots forming in her already upset stomach.

"Yes, I do feel a little better. But I fail to see why I should interest you, Mr. Verant. Perhaps you could enlighten me." She eyed him speculatively over the rim of her wineglass.

"Well, I thought you were a tourist, but the postal worker said you were delivering mail for the McGillises. I guess that piqued my curiosity. You see, I know Kirk and Johann from our childhood. Although they never actually spent time in my neck of the woods, Kirk and I have remained fairly close. In fact, I have been in touch with him recently and have just finished finalizing some business arrangements. So I guess I wondered where you fit into all of this. I saw you getting out of his car and decided I should check things out. I hope you can forgive me for causing you any distress." His smile was anything but pleasant, but she felt a little better knowing he was close to a member of the family. Still, she thought she should remain cautious.

"I see. Well, that explains most of it. What kind of business are you in, Mr. Verant?" she queried, hoping he would open up to her.

"Douglas, please. And the business . . . well, you might say, it's the finest of art circles. We travel around collecting priceless pieces and selling them to prospective buyers. There is good money in collectibles. Don't you agree?" he asked carelessly.

"I suppose so." She didn't quite know how to answer him. The thought struck her that "priceless pieces" could mean necklaces. She fought for the right phrase to ask. "But what exactly does the 'priceless pieces' mean? Is it like paintings or anything of value?" Her question caught him slightly off guard, but his smirk hit home.

"Anything the seller wishes to sell. No matter how big or how small, the price depends on the age, make, and name of the piece in question. It's actually a very diverse and broad field. However, I wouldn't let just anyone get involved in this business. It can be quite overwhelming at times." On the verge of making her argument, she noticed his face had gone red and his eyes began to smolder, and from behind her came a voice she remembered all too well.

"Well, isn't this cozy. I would think that Kelley would keep you on a shorter leash, my dear." The dig hit home as Mick Clawson took the seat to the right of her and looked straight into her wary eyes. She realized she was in a lot of trouble.

CHAPTER XVII

Cassie was so surprised and shocked by their unexpected visitor that she wasn't sure she answered him. But whatever she said caused a large grin to cover his face. She had barely heard herself say anything but was relieved that he was amused rather than annoyed. The last thing she wanted to do was get involved with Clawson, and now that he had caught her out of the house and with a complete stranger, it made things ten times worse. She was not going to be able to avoid the fury Kelley was going to unleash on her tonight. In the back of her mind, Cassie's thoughts were in complete senselessness. Should she try and call the house, beg their pardon, and get up and leave or ask Kirk's friend for a ride home? Before she could find the answer to her problem, Clawson repeated his question, only this time he was a little more serious.

"I'm sorry, but I don't understand your question. I initially had business to take care of in town, so a family member dropped me off. Mr. Verant has agreed to take me back. The rest is none of your business, Mr. Clawson, and please do not discuss business around me. If you have anything to say, say it to Mr. McGillis. I am sure he would give you better answers than I could." She had noticed the grim frown on Mr. Verant's face soften at her binding him down to take her back.

Allowing her the privilege, Douglas sat up and responded, "I can vouch for the little lady. We ran into each other at the post office, and since I have an urgent business with the youngest brother, what more can I say? I'm a generous man." Cassie missed the gleam in his eyes as he looked at Clawson.

Eyeing Douglas speculatively, Clawson inquired, "I would have thought Kelley would have accompanied you. After all, he wouldn't want you slipping up and spilling something by accident, now would he?" Before she could answer, the waiter returned with her pasta salad and then departed again.

"I have already told you, I refuse to discuss business outside the office. After I finished mailing my correspondence, I decided to do some shopping. It was very generous of Mr. Verant to buy my lunch, but what I do outside the business has nothing to do with you or Kelley." She took a bite of her salad as the use of Kelley's name brought smiles to both men's faces but was left unnoticed by her. "Is something funny, Mr. Clawson?" she returned just as sternly.

"None, dear. I believe you have put me in my place, but I wish you would consider me a friend—outside of work, of course. You might find we have a lot in common." His eyes lazily roamed over her, making her stomach turn on the salad she was eating. She put her fork down, picked up her wineglass, and took a long, slow drink, trying to still the queasiness under his probing gaze.

Under offense, Douglas intervened, "I think you had better stick to fighting battles with the real pros and leave Miss Garrett alone. She has told you twice to back off; now I think you had better before one of us says or does something we will regret later." The menacing look in his deep black eyes caused Clawson to sit up and stutter.

"My apologies, Miss Garrett. I did not mean to offend you, but I was merely pointing out that Kelley has taken a shine to you, and if he could see you out here with myself and this stranger . . . well, I think you get my meaning. Anyway, I should be going. My son-in-law is visiting, and we have a lot of work to do before the hearing." As he started to get up, he added, "Oh, incidentally, Miss Garrett," he stood up straight and turned halfway around to include the approaching man, "I believe you know my son-in-law personally." Cassie sat there in shock as Kent Jr. approached the table.

"Hello, sweetheart. If I had known you were going to be here, I would have brought flowers, but then that wouldn't be proper, would it?" He nodded toward the other man, and then he and Clawson turned and walked out of the restaurant.

"What was that?" Douglas asked in a whisper.

"That," she sighed heavily, "was a mistake. One that should never have happened." Looking up at his concerned features, uncertain what he was concerned about, she explained, "He was my old boss, before Kelley. He had proposed to me before his business deal with Clawson took on personal overtones. I didn't know anything until I saw the wedding pictures. He had gotten married over here, so no one knew until the paparazzi got the scoop. While he was on his honeymoon, I interviewed a couple of people, hired one, and left. End of story." She took a big drink and let it burn down her throat, wishing it would calm her nerves. She hardly noticed how quiet Mr. Verant had become, until she looked up into his face. His dark eyes were hollow voids, and his mouth had turned grim. If one could imagine it, he looked like hell itself. He appeared so cold and hard but had the charms of a gentleman. It was hard to tell what he was thinking, but it didn't appear to be pleasant.

Before she could ask, he leaned against the table, causing his suit coat to open up, exposing the shininess of black steel. The barest glimpse of the gun under his coat caused alarms to go off in her head. Why would he have a gun? Why was he following her? And how had he known her name? She was sure she hadn't told him. If she wasn't afraid before, she now feared for her life. She had more or less forced herself to be taken home by him, but would she make it back alive?

Sitting upright and too quiet, Douglas scanned her face and then followed her gaze. Buttoning his coat, he confided in her, "It's for protection, nothing more. I have a dangerous job taking care of all of those valuables. Sometimes you have to go to extremes, and this is my way of insuring myself. Don't worry. I won't hurt you. I think we could find a better use for you. Don't you?" His smile was quick and a little too unsettling for her. She didn't know why, but she felt as if she were walking into a whirlwind and being sucked into oblivion.

"Well," she tried finding her voice, "if you are done with your drink, I think we can go now. I'm not really that hungry anymore." Standing up, he paid the bill and, leaving a tip on the table, followed her out the door. Before moving two steps, she heard a voice behind her.

"What the hell is going on here?" he demanded loudly. He stood there, hands on hips, looking from one to the other.

"Kelley!" she started but never finished because Douglas interrupted her.

"Hey, look, it wasn't her fault. My name is Douglas Verant, I work with Kirk." Not breaking the deathly stare that Kelley had on him, he continued to stammer, "I ran into her in the post office, and she turned me down for coffee. But a little later, I ran into her in a music shop, and she about collapsed and would have if I hadn't caught her." Suddenly Kelley's anxious gaze turned to her with concern. "I bought her something to eat because she said she hadn't eaten since breakfast. I hope I didn't intrude on the two of you."

Looking slightly embarrassed and exhausted, Kelley muttered quickly, "Thank you. That was very thoughtful of you, Mr. Verant. Is there anything I can do for you in return?" His eyes never left her face as her eyes melted into his.

"No, I don't think so. I got everything I wanted already." Kelley turned questioning eyes on him at his words. "I meant the pleasure of a lady's company, that's all. Well, look at the time. I have another meeting this afternoon. It was a pleasure,

Miss Garrett, now you go back and get some rest." Without another word, he left them standing there.

Breathing a little heavily, he wrapped his arm around her and led her to the limousine. "Get in. We'll talk on the way home." Once inside the car, Kelley took a bottle of scotch out of the little refrigerator and poured them both a tumbler. Handing her one, he ordered, "Drink and then explain to me what happened after I left this morning. Kirk was not home when we got there, and neither were you. I got nervous since you weren't home by one o'clock, and here it is nearly three. Tell me everything and don't leave anything out." He took her empty glass and moved into the seat directly across from her, so she was forced to look him in the eyes.

"I'm sorry, Kelley. I was going to wait until you had time to take me around town, but it never seems to work out. This problem with Clawson is taking all of your time. I guess I decided to take things into my own hands." Her eyes never left his, and she could not read his thoughts under the stern set of his already tired features. "I finished the correspondence to the clients and decided to mail them myself. Kirk was heading out, and I just happened to catch him at a good point. Although it took a little finagling, I talked him into taking me to town. We agreed that I wouldn't tell that he took me, because he didn't want to incur your wrath and I didn't think it was necessary for you to know. I had planned to be back before you, but unfortunately things didn't work out that way. I got to the post office, mailed the correspondence, and when I turned to leave, boom. He was right behind me. The funny thing about today is that I could have sworn he was following me on purpose. But I don't know why." She wasn't going to add anything else, but the thought of Clawson's underhandedness and the look on Kent's face as he approached the table kept coming back. She closed her eyes briefly before adding, "He was right about my fainting, but the worst part of all of this is when Clawson showed up unexpectedly and assumed the worst."

A terrible and maleficent silence infiltrated the vehicle, and Cassie's eyes opened again to see the fury in his face, but before he could say anything, she finished her story, "That's not the only thing. Kent Jr. is his son-in-law, and he is here for some kind of hearing." Slowly taking a breath, she didn't comprehend the meaning of her words as she repeated Clawson's statement.

"Is that everything?" he questioned, mulling over everything, as if reorganizing his train of thought. "What else did Clawson say to you?"

"Not much. He accused you of keeping me on a leash, and then he implied we were an item, but I refused to be baited. I also informed him twice that I would not discuss business with him. Then Kent showed up, and I couldn't say two words. There, you have it. Can we forget this now?" She sat back against the seat and closed her eyes.

"Did he say what kind of hearing?" His voice was so low it was barely audible. She looked at him exasperatingly and muttered a "no." Cassie didn't see the nervous twitch at the side of Kelley's mouth as he reviewed the entire event, frame by frame. So Clawson was filing a petition of land rites. Now more than ever, Kelley needed to find something on Clawson to stop him from gaining control of McGillis property. Janelle's family rights were being questioned, and the truth was going to come out.

CHAPTER XVIII

Very slowly, Kelley leaned over in his seat and reached for her hands. When her eyes opened and caught his expression, she sensed the tension in the air. In a low, almost inaudible voice, he asked, "Did he say anything about Janelle's necklace?" The look on Cassie's pale face mirrored her surprise, so Kelley explained, "Janelle was apparently beaten, and there appears to be a connection between the beating and the disappearance of the necklace. I gather by your expression that he never mentioned the necklace." Releasing her, he sat up into the seat beside her as a thought struck him. "What were you doing in Banff instead of Canmore? You could have done your mailing in town."

Cassie was embarrassed and a little annoyed. It hadn't occurred to him that she needed a break from all the excitement of the past week. In addition, she had to rat on Kirk for taking her when she had promised not to. So now she had to set the record straight and apologize to Kirk later. "Honestly, I didn't know Kirk was coming to Banff. I thought he was running into Canmore. Only when he turned onto the main highway and passed the Canmore exit did I realize what was happening. I am sorry, but I thought I would be able to call for a car and return home before you got there. It appears that I was mistaken. Please do not blame Kirk for this, because if I hadn't begged him to bring me, I would have found another way. I was tired of waiting around, and the letters had to get out. There was no way of knowing when you would be home, so I took matters into my own hands, and then I got caught up in the shopping and didn't realize how late it was, and that's it. You pretty much know the rest."

Turning her head slightly, she couldn't tell by his eyes if he bought all of that or not, but she wasn't willing to change her story. He would just have to live with it. Then another thought struck her; one she hadn't realized until now. "You don't think Clawson has the necklace, do you? Or do you think this Verant has it?"

As he gripped her hand in his and leaned back against the seat with an exasperated sigh, he muttered, "I don't know. Verant seems to be the charming sort, but even Kirk is leery of him. I vaguely remember Kirk telling us a long time ago that Verant has a history of questionable dealings, but I have no proof of him being involved. If he does have it, how did he get it out of the house? With all the security we have, there would have been no way he could escape undetected."

"Then who, and why would anyone want to steal it? What does it have to do with all of this? I was under the impression it was just an heirloom from Janelle's mother. What's going on, Kelley? If Clawson is pumping me for something, I think I deserve to know the whole story." Cassie released her hand from his grasp and folded her arms across her chest.

Kelley looked at her crossly for a moment, but his expression softened at the sight of her sternness. He had to admire her tenacity in the face of their current situation. She was trying to be brave, all the while showing concern for his family. God, how he wished he could take her right then and there. She was so small, fragile, and beautiful, sitting there beside him. He could feel his stomach turning at the thought of someone hurting her, but he wanted to confide in her. On the other hand, the less she knew the better. He had to protect her at all costs. "The only thing I can tell you is the necklace was made from stones found on our property.

Clawson thinks the piece of land Janelle will inherit contains more precious minerals. We believe he is using Janelle as leverage to gain possession of that land. The only thing is Janelle would have to sign over the rights to it, but it's not even hers yet. Paternity has to be decided before she can inherit now. The test was done this morning. If the results are what we think, Janelle may not inherit the land."

"I don't understand. You don't believe she is your true sister. Why would you think that?" After a brief hesitation, she answered herself, "You think Clawson is her father?"

Kelley looked at her as if she had injured him deeply, but the thought had struck them all more than once. Mick Clawson seemed to favor Janelle, because she was married to Mick's brother. He would go out of his way to help Janelle even when she was arguing with her brothers. Although there was a definite resemblance between Janelle and her brothers, her attitude or brashness seemed to resemble Clawson. Up until now, no one had ever questioned the paternity, and Cassie hadn't realized how crucial the answer was. By all appearances, if Janelle was Clawson's daughter, she would have to annul her marriage to his brother, but because of her mother being McGillis, she could still inherit the land. The will said nothing about paternity; it simply stated "she had to remain married and provide a suitable environmental project," which she had done. However, the circumstances at present could only cause more frustration and trouble for themselves. If Clawson were declared her father, he would use his parental rights to acquire the land. The only problem is Janelle is old enough to permit whomever she wants to use it, and the question is, would she allow anyone to take it from her?

"Kelley, what will happen if Clawson is determined to be her father? Are you sure there was no one else involved?" Cassie's expression became anxious.

"We all thought Clawson was her father for a while, but we have reason to believe otherwise now. It appears that one man befriended Mother when everyone else turned their heads." The absent look on her face forced him to spell it out, "You pegged it before—Jamison. When we were growing up, Father would take off on one of his crusades and Mother would be left holding the fort. There were so many problems with the upkeep of the grounds and the house that she became overwhelmed. Jamison was the closest neighbor, and Mother used to rely on them for comfort and help. When his wife would visit her family in the country, he would spend a lot of time here. We just never paid any attention to him. Oh, there were the looks and the walks along the gardens, and periodically, we would see them coming from the cabins, but we never questioned her, even when Janelle was born. There was a heated argument the night before she was born, and Father left the house. After he left, Mother threw herself down the stairs, forcing a premature labor. Yes, she is our sister, but Father made it known that she wasn't his, or maybe he refused to believe she was. As time went on, we all began to question it. But Jamison rarely showed his face after she was born, and Clawson showed up at the hospital the same time Father did. It was all they could do to keep them apart. Clawson accused Father of pushing her down the stairs and injuring his child, which incensed Father further. Clawson wanted the paternity test done then, but Father wouldn't hear of it. He would see Mick dammed first.

"A few months later, Father found her dead in her room. She suffered a massive hemorrhage and died instantly. Out of respect for her, Father put the matter behind him and always kept Clawson dangling on a hook. Now, we can only hope for a miracle. Despite the cruelty of my father, I still loved him—and my mother. Believe me, Clawson will pay, even if I have to kill him myself." Turning his angry eyes on her, he softened. "I'm sorry. It looks as if we have a long road ahead of us. But I do intend to take you out tonight. You deserve a break, and I intend to be the perfect escort."

"Are you sure you want to be away tonight? Janelle might need you."

"She will be fine. The doctors have sedated her, and she should sleep easily tonight. Her husband is behind bars, which is where he belongs."

"What provoked him?" she queried.

"Janelle was only able to tell us a little bit. Apparently, he thought he saw her alone with someone else, and she was handing him some money. He accused her of infidelity and went on a drunken rampage. That's all we know." He looked disturbed.

"You don't believe it. What do you think happened?"

"He was definitely drunk, because the police confirmed it. When we asked Janelle if she had been with anyone else at that time, she refused to talk about it, almost as if she were hiding something. I intend to question her about it after she returns home." Leaning back on the seat, he slid his arm around her shoulders and drew her head down to his chest where she could hear the hard rhythm of his heart. She closed her eyes and prayed that Janelle wasn't Clawson's next victim. She had a funny feeling that the future was about to deliver a fatal explosion.

* * *

As he placed the revolver on the nightstand, Verant picked up his half-filled glass of scotch and took a long swig of the fiery brown liquid. It burned as it went down his throat. His expression mirrored his thoughts about the previous encounter with a beautiful, brown-haired, hazel-eyed nymph. It was a shame they had to be enemies. He was sure she was the key to the whole affair. In all of his travels, he had learned to read people and know what it would take to knock them off balance. This girl appeared to be easy, but there was definitely an underlying layer of ice he would have to chip through. He decided one week would do it, and then he would make his move.

Another problem, however, had reared its ugly head. Clawson and his son-in-law were two of a kind, but he would have to figure a new game plan if he was to gain the ultimate prize. As he downed the last of the whiskey, he turned toward the table in the corner of the room. He picked up the top photo of the woman who would unknowingly provide everything he needed to succeed. She would bring McGillis to his knees and destroy Clawson at the same time. The thought of total annihilation brought a sinister smile to those almost fathomless eyes. Dropping the photo, he picked up the little black box and held it firmly in his hand. "Kirk, my boy, you should have played by my rules. But I guess you'll learn. Too bad." He set the box and his glass on the table and turned toward the bathroom. "Shower and get plenty of rest, because you have a lot to do in the next few weeks, and don't worry, Miss Garrett. If everything goes as planned, you won't be hurt." Before entering the bathroom, he glanced once more at the gun on the stand and grinned again.

CHAPTER XIX

The dining room was set with meticulous care. Each place setting had to be in its exact spot and the silverware polished to a high shine and distributed in correct order. A single starched white napkin was folded with precision and placed in the center of the plate. The wine and water glasses were placed in the proper spots and displayed no water spots or dust anywhere. An assortment of flowers and green foliage graced the center of the table in a large Ming vase. It added an Oriental touch to the room, which was otherwise done for the staunch Frenchman.

Kent Wallace Jr. entered the room in his most elegant black evening attire, and his gold Rolex watch glowed from the lighting in the room. He was a model for the perfect gentleman, but underneath that exterior lay a dark secret that no one was expected to see. Now, his true nature was to be tested. He smiled across the room at his host as he walked over to his chair to sit down for dinner.

Smiling in return was his charming host. The smile that greeted him, however, masked the malicious and malevolent presence underneath a cool and confident outer shell. The host of this shell could laugh with you one moment and tear you apart the next. As Kent had found out when first dealing with him, you don't back him into a corner, because once cornered, he would turn on you, and the victory would be his. Although Kent had allowed him to take control, he couldn't stop Clawson from controlling all of him. He had initiated the meeting between Kent and his daughter, which in turn had drawn him deeper into Clawson's dark world. Only now was he beginning to understand this marvel of a man that sat there smiling at him as if he were every bit the gentleman, when in fact, he was the devil incarnate.

"Please," that fiendish voice purred, "sit down, Kent. We have new tactics to discuss. I trust you had a productive afternoon, despite the surprise of seeing Miss Garrett."

Relaxing into the chair to the right of Clawson, he allowed himself to smile forlornly, "Yes, it was a surprise, but . . . it's ancient history." He didn't wish to discuss his past and Cassie, especially since he still wanted an explanation from her, but he would wait until the right moment to approach her. That moment, he knew, was not far away. In fact, if everything went as he planned, she would be at his mercy, and her new boss and his father-in-law would be ruined. A wicked smile played at the corners of his mouth as he addressed his host, "As a matter of fact, I had a very informing afternoon. But before we get into that, you need to know that Patrick's lawyer filed a paternity suit. Janelle has already given her blood over for the test, and Patrick's blood type was retrieved from the coroner's office. I have been informed to relay the message to you, because you were named one of the three possibilities." He watched as the comprehension of his words formed on Clawson's face.

"Three . . ."

"Yes. Apparently Matt Jamison was involved with her, which means any one of you could have fathered her. You are the last to be tested. Jamison showed up first thing this morning and was told by the attorney that there was a gag order on the suit until paternity could be proved. I assured them that you would be willing to come down for the test first chance you got. I hope that was satisfactory."

"Yes, that is satisfactory, but it's such a shock. She must have hidden it very well, or no one paid enough attention.

This should prove very interesting. I will drive to the hospital in the morning and donate. Did they say how long before the results would be given?"

"At least two to four days, considering that it is DNA testing." Kent leaned back slightly as the maid served their dinner. Classic French cuisine with herb and butter snails in accompaniment and a fine, expensive Bordeaux made Kent smile appreciatively. "Now, on to other matters." He sounded elated as he poured their wine into their glasses.

"Yes, other matters. Do you have all the information on the mining rights? Once the suit goes through and Janelle is declared my legal daughter, we will need all the necessary papers and equipment to start this excavation. I am sure we will have no problem obtaining the necessary permits. You did contact the people from CEPA, CANMET, and the Mining and Mineral Science Labs? That's just for starters."

"Have you forgotten a couple of things? For instance, Janelle hasn't been declared yours yet, and she hasn't given you the rights to the property either. Maybe we should hold off for a few weeks until we know the outcome of the DNA test. I told you there were three of you, and how do you know that she isn't Patrick's?" he asked, already knowing the answer.

"Because Patrick was rarely at home, and when he was, he was disinterested in his beautiful young wife. Sometimes I think that man had no sense at all. She had given him sons, so he considered his duty done, and he left her alone. Bethany was a wonderful young woman with a lot of promise, but she settled for something she didn't really want. She bore his children, and anything else was just the icing on the cake. Alas, she died before she could make a different choice. Now her sons are left hanging on to the property and don't realize its potential. That is where we are coming in, my boy. We are about to show the McGillis family just where the power is coming from, and Janelle and your Miss Garrett are the keys to the whole situation."

"I don't see how Miss Garrett would be of any help. She is only an executive secretary." He was becoming nervous. In the back of his mind, he had other arrangements for Cassie, but Mick was not supposed to find out about them until the time was right. Playing it cool, he said, "I think we should leave her out for the time being. I mean, if Janelle is the primary source of the controversy, maybe we should concentrate on getting her to waive her rights as heiress to the property. As it happens, I found out today that Patrick had made a new will, and it's to be read within a week after his death. Well, that will be tomorrow afternoon, and unless I missed my guess, we should see some hefty fireworks. There was a right of persuasion clause in the will that he had, this new one amended it."

"Is there some way you can find out before it's read?"

"No. It has been sealed, and not even the lawyer knows what's in it. My source tells me that he changed the will before he died. We shall see what happens tomorrow. The first thing you need to do is take your test at the hospital, and then we'll have a meeting with Ben Callis." He took one of the snails, dipped it into the butter, and placed it in his mouth, savoring the flavor as it slid down the back of his throat, and then smiled widely as his host looked on.

"I hope Ben took care of some unpleasant business and has some good news for us. Otherwise, I am going to have to pull some strings that I really don't want to pull. I do hate to start family feuds, but if it's necessary to win this thing, I guess we'll have to." He picked up his wineglass and toasted to their success and the destruction of the McGillis Empire— no matter what the cost.

*   *   *

As they pulled into the driveway, a metallic blue convertible was parked in front of the house. It only took a moment for Kelley to realize whom the car belonged to. He was not willing to listen to Charisse's endless tirades this afternoon. He had promised some time out with Cassie, and he was going to make sure she got it.

As the long black limousine pulled up to the front steps, the front door opened, and Rod walked out. When the car stopped, Rod opened the door to help Cassie out and wrapped his arms around her, hugging her as if she had been kidnapped and just returned home. After the hug, he smiled childishly, "Thank God you are all right, cherie. We were afraid someone had taken you away from us. Can I offer you something to drink?"

Allowing herself a quick glance behind her to make sure Kelley was still there and grinning when she saw him, she answered, "I would love one." He led her into the salon, but her relief was short-lived as they entered the room and Charisse slowly stood up and gave Kelley a caustic stare.

"Well," she stated rudely, "isn't this a sight. My lord, Cassie! You look like you have been run through the ringer. Maybe you should lie down for a little while. After all, you just recovered from a blow to the head, didn't you? You really shouldn't have gone out without a chaperone." Cassie could sense her irritation but was too tired to fight with her.

Pretending not to notice her attack, she answered, "I will be fine after I sit down for a little while. Besides, Kelley and I have some work to do. I believe we have a meeting to attend tomorrow, and I know that you will want those briefs done before we go. Am I right?"

It only took a moment for Kelley to catch the light in her eyes. "Yes, we do need to finish them." Pausing briefly, he looked at Charisse and apologized, "I'm sorry, Charisse, but now is not a good time for a visit. Or do you have an emergency of some kind that we are not aware of?"

"No. Well, maybe. I just thought that you would like to know that Ben Callis was seen driving up to Clawson's estate. Rumor has it they have formed an alliance, and some sort of deal has emerged involving your whole family. I suggest you watch your back, Kelley dear, because they are trying to pin the murder on you."

At the sound of the word "murder," Kelley became rigid and his eyes an icy glare. "What do you mean murder? No one has been murdered, or has something happened that I haven't heard yet? Charisse?"

Looking for the entire world like a little girl who snuck the cookies out of the jar, she very coolly and calmly stated, "Janelle's husband had bonded himself out of jail and was found two hours ago. Apparently shot with a .45 caliber, and there were no witnesses, or so they say, and they believe it was the same gun that killed your father."

"Charisse! Shut up!" Rod's voice sounded angrily.

"What I don't understand is that if he loved her and was so softhearted, why would he beat her up?" Becoming aware of Rod's desperate voice, Charisse realized her folly. She closed her eyes and then looked up at Kelley. "Kelley . . . I . . ."

"What do you mean by the same one that killed my father? He wasn't shot. He died of a heart attack." Kelley turned an angry glance at Rod, who stood erect with a frown on his face. "I don't understand, Rod. What are you not telling me?" he demanded as he leaped at his brother, pinning him to the salon door.

"Please, Kelley! I'm sorry. I thought it would be best to hide it from you. You were out of the country, and there were no witnesses and no suspects. It appeared that he had taken his own life, but the problem was he never owned a .45-caliber gun. Father was declared dead, and we told the police to investigate the matter quietly, and they agreed. The gun was never actually found, and everyone was told he had suffered a nervous breakdown because he couldn't handle it anymore. I know we should have told you, but there was never enough time, and now it appears the same person is stalking Janelle. There is no reason except for this drunken brawl that anyone would want to hurt Alexander. He was not a bad person; he was just a little too softhearted and weak. He could never say no to anyone. The police are beginning to suspect someone else of the beating, but Janelle won't talk about it." Kelley released his brother and very limply moved back against the edge of the small loveseat in the middle of the room. He looked as if his whole world was collapsing and there was nothing he could do to stop it. Cassie could actually feel his pain, and it brought tears to her eyes.

She stood up shakily and placed her hand on his shoulder comfortingly, ignoring the jealous rage in Charisse's eyes, but he refused to be comforted. He gave her a sideways glance and shrugged off her hand and then stood up straight. "I want to talk to the police. If Father was murdered the same way Alexander was, we need to warn Janelle and talk to the Mounties about protection for her. I am not going to let anyone destroy her life. I have always believed deep down she was Father's, and someone is trying to take her inheritance from her. It will be up to us to find out who and why. Cassie, I want you to stay here, please. I need to take care of some business and talk to the Mounties. We'll talk when I get back. Charisse, I need you to get a message to someone for me. I'll be right back, it's in the study." He disappeared into the hallway, leaving Rod and the two women looking at each other uncomfortably.

Kelley moved around the big mahogany desk, and opening the bottom drawer, he retrieved the letter he had been saving for the past year. As he went to shut the drawer, he realized that it had been unlocked. He was sure he hadn't unlocked it, and upon further inspection, he noticed the green file had been moved into a different slot and the photos were sticking out. He gingerly picked up the folder and opened it, glancing over the pictures with anger in his eyes and then, concern. He knew she had seen them. They had been inside the manila envelope when he put the file away, and now they were lying on top. Unconsciously, he sat down staring at the photos. What was she thinking? Why hadn't he told her about them? There was no time now, he would have to confront her later, because his primary concern was for his sister. Closing the folder, he returned it to its proper slot and closed the drawer—this time locking it. Then, he picked up the letter and left the room.

By the time he returned to the salon, Rod had poured himself and Cassie a scotch, and Charisse had disappeared. "Where's Charisse?" His tone was harsh and provoked the desired response.

"She went out to her car to wait. She said the air was too stuffy in here for her." His gaze encompassed Cassie, and Kelley was even more incensed by Charisse's actions. "Rod, get the car, I need to speak to Cassie a moment." His fiery eyes were glued on hers, and it made her shudder. She wondered what she had done now.

"I'll be outside. Please, excuse me, my dear. I am glad you are home safely." Without another word, Rod exited the room, leaving Kelley looking utterly defensive.

"There are some things we need to discuss when I get home, but now is not the time. Janelle needs help right now, and that's all that matters. Do you understand?" Cassie shook her head, bewildered at his words. She had done something to irritate him but couldn't figure out what. "Good. I promise you everything will be explained later." Before letting her go, he lowered his mouth to hers, catching her slightly off guard; he pulled her close as his mouth ravaged hers. Giving into the feel of his lips on hers, Cassie let out a small moan, wishing he didn't have to stop and cursing herself inwardly for wanting more. Regretfully he pulled away, smiled charmingly, and walked away, leaving her breathless.

She stared at the empty doorway for a few moments before she came to her senses and slowly walked to the couch. She dropped down onto the sofa and lay back with her eyes closed. Opening them, she sat up. He had gone to the study to get the message. She remembered the photos and remembered she hadn't locked the drawer back. He knew she saw them. Suddenly, she had a sick feeling all over and prayed that he would forget about them, but she doubted he would.

CHAPTER XX

As Kelley and Rod left the grounds, the black Geo Prism that was parked just beyond a group of trees, hidden from their view, stood watch as they pulled out of the driveway. Lowering the light green notebook, the occupant laid the papers in the seat beside him and started the engine. He slowly maneuvered the car around the trees and entered the estate gates. Somewhere between the main house and the gates was a dirt road leading around to the back where all the gardens and underground mines were located. These mines had been closed years ago for safety reasons, but there was something left behind that needed to be recovered before anyone noticed it. It was not likely, however, that anyone would find the object in question, because hardly anyone ever wandered through the caves, but just to be on the safe side, the uninvited guest decided to take a last look around. It looked like everyone was gone, so there was no problem with searching. He wouldn't be noticed.

*   *   *

Cassie was in the process of eating her snack and redoing her itinerary. They had several meetings tomorrow, one of which was the reading of Patrick's will. Cassie hoped for everyone's sake, especially Janelle's, that she was declared legally a McGillis. Then, Clawson would drop his pursuit of the land, and Janelle would be at peace with herself. She couldn't imagine the pain and heartbreak of never knowing where you actually belong and then turn around and have your husband killed for no good reason. This matter was definitely getting out of hand, and someone was going to have to be stopped.

She picked up her letterhead and began to make notes and arrange their day. The first thing that needed to be done was check in with the hospital. Cassie was sure they would have an armed guard on her by tonight, and tomorrow, Clawson would probably show up for his DNA test. In the back of her mind, she thought Clawson really believed Janelle was his. What would he do if she weren't? Cassie couldn't imagine the outcome of the test and feared the effects it would have on certain individuals.

The next item on her list was the meeting with lawyers about the Special Places program. If this law was put into effect to protect Janelle's property, no one, not even a member of the family, could mine or develop the land for any reason. Cassie was sure that no one knew about the program being initiated, but after looking over the land surveys and the government documents that Kelley had left for her to go over, she feared Clawson might try using illegal tactics to undermine the program. In his mind, money was all he needed, and no one was above being bought.

So intent on arranging the papers for Janelle to fill out and sign, Cassie was unaware of the visitor standing just inside the doorway. "Boy, you never worked that hard for me." Cassie jumped in surprise and shock to see Kent standing there, absorbing her petite figure.

"What are you doing here? I didn't hear anyone knocking." She tried to calm the nerves in her stomach. She wasn't prepared to confront him.

"It's nice to see you too. Me, I am doing quite well, as you can see. I ran into Johann as I was coming up the steps. I promised him that I wouldn't be long." He didn't move, and she didn't want him to stay, but out of courtesy, she offered him a chair. "Thank you," he said as he casually planted himself in a straight-backed chair.

"Would you like a drink?"

"No, thank you. As I said, I wouldn't be staying long, but I had to talk to you, and I think you know what about." His eyes were a captivating blue but held a malicious gleam as they burned into hers. "How could you desert me like that, Cassie? I gave you everything. A damn good job and the lifestyle to go with it. I left on a business trip and came back to find you packed up and gone. You could have at least waited for me to come back to the office. I could have given you a shining reference." Looking around, he added, "But I see now that you landed on your feet quite well. Tell me, is he a better lover than I am? I've heard he's quite the romantic."

"How dare you! You have no idea, do you, of the scrutiny I was under? Even your father started questioning me, and that was humiliating enough. As for my working for Kel . . . Mr. McGillis, that was pure luck or chance—take your pick. I ran into him by accident, and he offered me a job. Seeing how I had just left you and there were no other prospects, I couldn't very well turn him down. Besides, I needed to work, not that it means anything to you. If you remember, you had promised your love to me, and then I found your wedding picture in the paper. What do you think went through my mind at that moment? Anyway, it doesn't matter now. I am over it, and I am enjoying my work. As for Mr. McGillis, he is my boss, and that's all he is or will be, for that matter. Now, if you are through, I suggest you leave before I call Kirk."

"Kirk left with Johann. I am afraid you are alone, sweetheart." As he informed her, he stood up, continuing to stare into her eyes. "However, I could remedy that." He moved with surprising speed and was around the huge desk before Cassie could refuse. Pulling her close to him, he wanted her to feel his anger and frustration at her leaving him. Yes, he was married, but she was still heavily on his mind.

She had refused his advances over and over again, but if she expected him to believe she hadn't been with Kelley, she was mistaken. "I think you owe me a little something, since you didn't even leave me a note. My wife isn't the faithful little homemaker, Cassie, and we don't exactly see eye to eye. However, we both believe in affairs. It just adds a little spice to the marriage. You would be surprised how much I have learned being close to Clawson." Cassie struggled to back away from him, but his strength was amazing. He managed to pin her to him in a position that didn't allow her any room to move. He raised a hand to the back of her head, pulling her hair back. "Ah, honey, come on. Just give in a little. You know, if you play your cards right, you could help put Clawson and McGillis in their places, and we could be on the road to Eden. Think about it, sweetheart. You and me and millions of dollars. We could go anywhere. What do you say? Kiss me, I have missed you." Cassie couldn't pull far enough away to avoid the kiss. It was brutal, punishing, and was meant to subdue her. Fighting with every ounce of strength she could get, she finally managed to push back.

Placing her hand on her bruised lips, she cried, "You bastard! You're crazy, and I want you to leave. Now!" She screamed at the same time as she fell back against the desk, knocking all the papers off the top of the desk.

Unperturbed, he grinned wickedly. "I know you still want me, Cassie. I will be in touch, because you don't realize how important you are. I will show myself out." He turned and left, leaving Cassie burning with disgust and crying from the pain he had inflicted on her lips. Trembling, she slowly looked down at the papers scattered everywhere. Her hands shook so badly; she could barely pick them up. She had picked up one full stack when she heard the door open again. With tear-filled eyes, she could hardly make out the form of Rod standing in the doorway. He took one look at her and asked what happened. Unable to speak, Cassie ran from the room and out the veranda doors. She didn't even stop when she heard Rod yell after her. As she neared the fountain, she slowed her pace.

Coming to a halt right by the fountain, Cassie looked into the clear water flowing around the statue. With all its beauty, it couldn't erase the pain and anguish she was feeling. How could he expect her to go running back to him or even forgive him? He was crazy if he thought for one minute that she would want him now and still married to the enemy's daughter. The memory of his lips on hers made her feel nauseous and lightheaded. Weakness forced her to sit on the side of the fountain and gather her wits, but she could still feel his arms tightening around her. Closing her eyes, she willed herself to forget the scene, but no matter what had happened, she would always feel repulsed by him.

On the other hand, who was she to talk? He was right. She had landed on her feet quite nicely, and she had slept with her boss too. All the times she had spurned Kent, telling him that she wanted it to be right between them before they got married. Now, it seemed futile to argue. She had succumbed to her hidden desires. Kelley had sought out and provoked the needs in her that had lain dormant for years. All she wanted from him was his love, and she was sure she wasn't going to receive it. She was his secretary and nothing more. Once they returned to Indiana, the romance would end, and they would be back to business.

"Well," she thought aloud, "I guess I should enjoy his closeness as much as I can, because once we get home, that's it. I'll just have to eat my heart out and live with the mess I have made." She walked over to the steps that led down to the guest cabins. In the distance, she could just make out the first cabin. "I just need to clear my mind. Maybe if I look around a little while, I will feel better." Taking the first step on the cobblestone path, Cassie made her way down the slight incline. Before too long, the path went from stone to dirt.

When she reached the end of the path, she came to the first guesthouse. The sheer size of it suggested that it would be elegant inside. She climbed the steps and peered into the window. "Good lord," she thought, "they could live here, and no one would guess that it was just a guesthouse." Cassie shook her head in astonishment. The floors were wooden in the living room and tiled in the dining room and entryway. There was an iron staircase leading up to what she guessed were the bedrooms. The tapestries and draperies were elegantly made in handwoven material and no doubt cost a fortune. There was what appeared to be a mahogany dinner table in the dining room, and she could just make out the sideboard and the china cabinet. At one end of the living room was a huge fireplace for those cold winter nights and cozy little interludes. She wondered if anyone had ever been seduced in front of that fireplace, and then she caught herself wishing for the impossible. "Forget it, kid." She continued to scan the room and saw a small rectangular desk in one corner and tons of books aligning the shelves behind it. The sofa and chairs were matching in a crushed mauve color. The entire room was breathtaking. With a deep sigh, Cassie straightened up and began to walk down the steps of the old cottage and began her trail again.

She was just about halfway down to the next cabin when she caught sight of the vehicle. It was a black sedan with tinted windows and a Canadian license plate. But what struck her as odd was the fact that it was parked beside a metal work shed. There was no one around by the looks of it, so she crept up to it to inspect it further. She leaned over, trying to get a better look at the interior. There were several folders on the seat and, to her surprise, a revolver. Why would anyone leave a revolver in the car and in plain sight? Then she thought of Janelle's husband. "Oh my God, whoever killed Patrick and Janelle's husband must be here somewhere. But where and why?" Looking around anxiously, Cassie caught a glimpse of an old sign off to her left. Instinct told her she should go for help, but by the time she returned with help, whoever was here would be gone. She would just have to see for herself.

Cautiously she moved closer to study the sign. It read, "Danger. Closed Mine. Do Not Enter." Just beyond the sign was the entrance to an old mine. Taking a deep breath, Cassie continued her pursuit. She wished she had brought her flashlight, but she hadn't planned on stalking anyone out. She was just inside the entrance when she noticed the torches aligning the walls. She carefully picked one up and looked around for something to light it with. She believed that no one would leave a lighter around, but she did find a set of matches on the ground. Apparently someone had dropped them by accident. After lighting the torch, she slowly walked toward the center of the mine. There were caverns leading in two different directions and an elevator right in front of her.

She was on the verge of taking the cavern on the right when she heard a noise coming from her left. Squinting slightly, she could just make out the faint glow of another torch. Quietly, she moved closer. She rounded one bend and found another turn to her left but kept her eyes on the firelight ahead of her. Blowing out her torch, Cassie felt her way along the dark corridor until she had reached the entrance to the next cavern. She was on the verge of rounding the corner and surprising the intruder when her foot hit something hard. She winced and let out a little yelp.

Clamping her hand to her mouth, she knew whoever was in the cavern heard her, and she tried to back out along the same path. Panic started rising in her chest as she watched the light coming closer. Just when she thought she had been found, she took a step back and landed on the ground, hitting her head hard on something, and before she succumbed to the darkness of unconsciousness, she could see the light dancing in front of her and then bouncing away. There was no more.

CHAPTER XXI

"Mr. Clawson, I assure you the test will be accurate. DNA is widely used nowadays." The doctor reassured him that there is no way it would fail. One way or the other, Janelle was going to learn her true identity.

"Thank you. I would hate for a mistake to happen, because this young lady has been through so much this week. Please call me as soon as you receive the results." Clawson handed him his business card and left the room. Outside in the waiting area was Kent, sulking after his meeting with Cassie.

"I thought you were going to wait until tomorrow to give the blood." His attitude seemed abrupt, but Clawson just let it pass.

"The sooner we know, the sooner we can take care of business. I know Janelle will want nothing to do with the family once she finds out she doesn't belong there. It's just a matter of time before I have my heiress and my property to do whatever I want. Come on; let's go see Ben. I am sure he will have some good news for us, and I suspect he has taken care of a little matter of disposal." Grinning, he led Kent out into the bright sunshine that would remain until at least ten o'clock. The nights were so bright in Canada.

"What disposal are we talking about? You're not doing something I am not aware of, are you? You agreed no secrets in this deal." He was suddenly on edge, as if he should have been informed of every move Clawson made. But Clawson had other ideas.

"It's nothing you need to worry about. Ben had some cleaning up he had to do, and I trust nothing will ever be discovered. Don't worry! As long as we stick together, they can't pin anything on us. Now, we have to meet Ben at the La France restaurant. Please do try to be civil. I don't know why you are all fired up, but you need to concentrate on the business at hand. Let's go." Clawson's chauffeur opened the door for him and closed it after Kent deposited himself on the seat directly in front of him.

"Okay, no questions this time. But please, do not shut me out again. Things are going fairly smooth right now, but I have a distinct feeling things are going to get out of control and fast." He looked at Clawson with earnest eyes as Clawson agreed.

*　　*　　*

"How long has she been gone?" Kelley was pacing the study floor, drilling Rod for more information. "You said she didn't say anything to you, but she was crying when you came in. What the hell happened, Rod? She wouldn't take off like that without good reason. Was there anyone else here when you returned?"

"No. But there was a car leaving the driveway just before I entered. It was one I hadn't seen before, a black Geo Prism with tinted windows. I couldn't tell who was driving, but whoever it was obviously upset her. She headed out the veranda doors toward the gardens, and that was the last I saw of her. That was four hours ago. I can't imagine she would have stayed out there. It's getting late and getting colder." Rod was getting nervous too but nothing compared to the effect it had on Kelley. He was almost despondent. Where could she have disappeared?

Rod had picked up the rest of the papers from the floor, and Kelley had gone through them to make sure nothing was missing. As luck would have it, nothing had been taken. But where was Cassie? Kelley stood in the veranda doorway and looked out toward the garden. Maybe she was sitting by the fountain. She had been in awe of its size and grandeur. Taking the initiative, Kelley started walking toward the pathway that led to the fountain and hollered over his shoulder, "Contact Mitchell and tell him that I will be a little late." Without hesitating, he headed down the winding path to where the fountain stood.

By the time he reached the fountain, storm clouds had moved in, and there was thunder and lightning in the distance. There was no sign of her anywhere. As he made a complete circle of the area, he thought to himself, "What happened to make you run off crying? Who was in that car, Cassie? If anything has happened to you . . ." He didn't dare think of what could happen, so he just kept his thoughts on finding her, hopefully alive. She was not familiar with the lower grounds, and she could have gotten lost. His eyes fixed on the ivy wall that led to the steps. He quickly traced a path down to the first cottage. In the dirt in front of the house, he noticed the footprints, and his mouth twitched with hope. He continued to follow the prints and stopped at the second cottage.

The footprints detoured around the house and, to his horror, were scattered by tire prints. No one had been down here since their father was found in the cavern. He told himself that she wouldn't go into the mine by herself, especially if there was a killer stalking her. But then, she would only think of protecting Janelle.

Upon entering the cavern, he noticed that two of the wall torches had been displaced. They were lying on the ground and had apparently been lit. He called out just as a bolt of lightning hit somewhere close. The ominous crack of thunder said it was going to be a bad storm. He knew he had to find her before it got too dark to see. Taking a lighter out of his shirt pocket, he reached down and picked up one of the torches. Lighting it, he moved forward slowly, calling out her name as he inched his way along. He watched the ground and followed two sets of prints. As he reached a halfway point between caves, one set of prints stopped, the others were coming and going from deeper into the tunnel. He followed those first.

As he rounded a bend, he could see where someone had been digging in the middle of the cavern. He bent down to examine the area further when he noticed something shiny sticking out of the dirt. As he reached for the object, he heard a sound coming from behind him. He quickly backtracked and stopped with the path that led further into the mine where the other prints stopped. He lifted the torch to get a better look when the light focused on her small oval face. He let out an oath and crawled over the huge rocks that she had fallen over.

Propping the torch up, so he could check her out, he gently rubbed his thumb across her lips and down her cheek and called her name, "Cassie? Can you hear me?"

Sluggishly, she began to move. As her eyes became focused, she realized it was Kelley holding her hand. "God, my head feels like a hammer hit it. What happened? Is he gone?"

"If you mean our visitor, yes. But don't worry about that now. We need to get you out of here, because there is a storm coming, and it sounds bad out there. Can you stand?" He gradually helped her up, picking his torch up at the same time. When she tried to stand on her own, she began to reel backward but landed in his arms, instead of on the ground. "It doesn't look like it. I'm getting you out of here." He put out the torch, picked her up in his arms, and carried her through the length of the cavern until they reached the opening. The wind had picked up quite a bit, which made it impossible for him to get very far, and the lightning was vivid with streaks that seemed to come within a few miles of them. Not willing to risk them both getting hit, he ran up to the first cottage and threw open the door.

He entered the living room, deposited her on the couch, and went back to shut the door. After he made sure everything was in order, he picked up some newspapers and matches and proceeded to build a fire. Once that was done, he picked up the phone on the desk and dialed the house. "Rod, it's me. I am in the first guesthouse with Cassie. She was injured in one of the old mining caverns. She was following someone. As soon as the weather breaks, you and I need to do some searching in the tunnel. There is something buried there, and we need to find it before our intruder comes back." He paused briefly to listen to Rod's answer and was cut off when lightning hit. "Damn! Power just went out. Well, it looks like we are going to be here a while." He looked at her lying there and started toward the bedroom. When he returned, he had the first-aid kit and a blanket and pillow. "Let me look at your head. I will be checking periodically for a concussion, so don't plan on sleeping for a while."

He reached for a candle and lit it, holding it just behind her head. Taking a cotton swab and some cleansing solution, he cleaned the wound and examined it carefully, making sure that he didn't hurt her any more than necessary. When he finished applying a light dressing to the gash on her head, he sat beside her on the couch and placed the pillow on his other side. He then took the blanket and began to wrap her up inside it.

Cassie was getting a warm feeling all over and not just from the events of the day. Just the nearness of him made her crazy, but she was living the fantasy she had earlier, and she wasn't willing to let it die. She looked up into his eyes as he encircled the blanket around her. Both their breaths caught as they gazed into each other's eyes. Without a word, their lips met in a slow, sensual kiss that left both of them hungry for more. His mouth covered hers in a more possessive and passionate kiss that seemed to drain the rest of her strength, but she was unwilling to stop now. That was his job. "No," he said regretfully, "I don't want to hurt you. When we make love, I want you to be able to share the pleasure. You are in no condition to feel anything except a headache." Gently, he positioned her against his chest, avoiding the wound on her head, and then he lay back against the pillow with her small form molded to his—wishing the circumstances were different.

*   *   *

Standing in the window watching the lightning play out, Verant held tightly to the whiskey bottle. His temper had flared. His meeting with Clawson had not gone very well, and that no good son-in-law was a waste of his time. Truth be told, he could screw them both and walk away with everything, but he had to bide his time until the deals were finished. His malevolent grin returned to his face as he thought of the double cross. Playing the two of them against each other was going to be entertaining and rewarding in more ways than one. If plans proceeded the way they were, he would be wealthier than in his wildest dreams, and Clawson would be history. As for Kent Wallace Jr., he would be disposed of neatly and quietly.

There had always been the family feud between Clawson and McGillis, but if the results of the paternity fell through, Clawson was prepared to sacrifice anyone or anything to acquire that land. Once it was his, Jr. would be history, or as Mick put it, "a missing person." Little had Mick known that Kent had struck another deal of his own that would ensure his survival and let daddy dear disappear without a trace. With the business in his pocket, Jr. would be set for life. Either way, he was there to destroy one or the other. He couldn't lose, and the money was still his. The only question was, "Who offered the most?"

The one thing that plagued him was Miss Garrett. "Why is she so important? She was just a secretary, or maybe Clawson was using her to get to McGillis." Verant wondered just how much McGillis has told his new secretary, and if she had her own price. It would be very exciting to find out what lay beneath that cool exterior. He was sure she would surprise and please him at the same time. Feeling a little bit more relaxed after his earlier confrontation, he took another long swallow of the fiery liquid. There would be a new game plan, and Miss Garrett would be his prize, not to mention his pawn to win the game. She would ensure his success at beating both Clawson and Kent in their own game, because only she could get the information he needed to hang Clawson, and once Clawson was ruined, Kent would be out of the picture. On top of that, McGillis would never trust her again, and she would be left out in the cold. Such a simple little plan. "Just play along a little while longer, and you will have it all." He set the bottle down, picked up the black box that was sitting on the table, and opened it. In the center of the box lay the most priceless gift of all. He wondered just how much McGillis would pay to have it returned. It was a good thing that brother of Janelle's was an easy mark, or things could have turned ugly. The necklace Kirk had passed off to him as Janelle's had turned out to be glass, and the shop owner had not looked it over close enough to tell the difference. It was too bad the storeowner hadn't survived the mugging. He was still a good man.

Kirk, on the other hand, still owed him for his mistake, and Verant was going to make sure he got restitution. Once things blew over, he would take care of his wayward partner, and the youngest McGillis wouldn't have to worry about needing protection, because he wouldn't be around. If there was one thing Verant couldn't stand, it was a double-crosser; although he didn't count himself as one, he wouldn't let a little gambler/hustler steal his thunder. All that was left was to approach the prospective buyers and negotiate a fair price that would benefit everyone.

He took the necklace out of the box and held it up in the light. The lightning danced across the room and caught the necklace in its path, leaving a broad multicolored spectrum on the wall, and flashing it on and off like a strobe in the middle of a dance hall. Its brilliance and sheer size was magnificent. Verant was sure he could retain a large profit from it, and in the end no one would be able to trace it to him. Laughing to himself, he replaced the necklace in the box, "God, I love wealthy people. They are so easy to please. All you have to do is wave something nice and expensive in their face, and they fall like dominoes. I wonder what Miss Garrett would fall for." He set the box down, retrieved his bathrobe from the closet, and headed for the bathroom.

CHAPTER XXII

The distant thunderclap heralded the passing storm. It was several miles in the distance now, and the light rain tapped against the windowpane. As Kelley lay there on the couch with Cassie breathing easily in his arms, his thoughts were miles away from the weather and kept whirling around in his mind. The thought of Cassie being swept up in the middle of all the chaos made him sick to his stomach. He should never have brought her here, but he knew she was safer around him. His other secretary, Marguerite, had been gunned down in his sister's conservatory. He had found her leaking information to an outsider, and he wasn't sure who it was until now. He had proof that the younger Wallace was playing games with his father-in-law and placed his business and family in the middle of the game. It was only a matter of time before things would come to a head, because the reading of the will was today, and the test results from the DNA would be sent to the lab. Clawson really believed he was Janelle's father, but Kelley wasn't sure at all. He wanted to believe she was his true sister, but the circumstances said otherwise, and Jamison was always a little too close to the family. His father had actually at one point accused his mother of the affair, which she denied. Then when she got pregnant, their father rejected her altogether, swearing the child wasn't his. However, he never sought to disprove it, which made people believe he was either the real father, or he just wanted to protect his family name. So the question always remained unanswered.

Now, things would be put right, and Clawson would be furious if he learns he isn't the father. Kelley could see the vengeance in his mind. His mother had never been unkind to him. In fact, when their affair ended, she sought out Jamison, and he never refused her anything. He couldn't because he had been in love with her since childhood. The only problem was that his family didn't have the financial standing and social status to support her. His mother did her duty as wife and mother but never discouraged the other men from hanging around, and his father didn't seem to care until she came up pregnant. She had humiliated and shamed him, and this was his way of getting even with her even in death.

Kelley stared at the ceiling and prayed that Janelle was Patrick's. Deep in his mind, he started to wonder why his father had redone the will without telling anyone. There must have been a moment of doubt in his mind, or he knew that she was his and decided it was time to admit it. Either way, he had made his peace. It all came down to truth or consequence.

Truth would give her the inheritance she deserved. Consequence would be allowing an outsider to claim the land that had been theirs for ages. In addition, it would cause a rift to grow between Janelle and her brothers. She had always felt alienated by them even though they would have done anything to protect her. Time would provide the answers they were all looking for. As for Cassie, she had walked into something that hadn't really concerned her, but Clawson's and Wallace's hatred of the McGillis family put her in the middle. To what extent, Kelley was unsure, but he knew they would stop at nothing to destroy him, everything he had worked for, and anyone associated with him.

Listening to her light breathing and watching her hair glow in the firelight, Kelley felt an overwhelming need deep within him. "Whatever happens, I am not going to let anyone hurt you . . . ever." He wrapped his arms around her, holding her closer, as if protecting her from the outside world.

Lying there, Cassie listened to his rhythmic heartbeat. She wished in her heart they could stay like this forever but knew it was impossible. She worked for him, and he was tied up with all of this family business right now. There never seemed to be a break for them, and she doubted that would ever change, even when they returned home. She would savor every moment with him and would always think of this moment to keep her from dying inside. The feel of his arms around her, his heart beating beneath her ear, the passionate warmth they shared. It all made her want to cry, but she held it in. If he knew what she was thinking, he would let her go the minute they got back, and that was something she didn't want at all costs.

As his hand brushed lightly around the wound on her head, she winced slightly and raised sleepy eyes toward his. When their eyes locked, hers with contentment and his with passionate longing, it took only a brief moment before his lips touched hers in a kiss that exuded a wanton desire for her but kept her on the edge begging for more. As the kiss deepened, she turned in closer to him, brushing her small breasts next to his chest. He had discarded his wet shirt on the floor before he had lain down and had removed her wet clothing before wrapping her up in the blanket. With the feel of her skin next to him, he became even more aroused by her. With a teasing motion, she placed her arm around his shoulder, drawing him closer, and in the meantime, her lips never left his. When her lips did move over his, and into the crook of his neck, he groaned aloud and buried his face in her hair.

So lost in each other, they didn't notice the shadow in the window—the angry, incensed shadow, with clenched fists ready to break the window out. He stood there watching as Kelley moved over her little by little, drawing himself into her. As they consummated their passion for one another in wave upon wave of seductive caresses, the stranger watched in jealousy and envy. She was his prize, and no one would stop him until he had her body and soul. Backing away from the window, he ran through the trees and out to the road where his vehicle was sitting. He placed himself in the driver's seat and turned on the engine to warm himself and the car. His gaze shifted to the gun in the passenger seat, and as his hand skimmed over its shiny surface, he whispered to himself, "It won't be long now." In the next moment, he put the car in drive and headed down the road.

*   *   *

As morning broke with brilliant sunshine after a night of stormy weather, it brought with it a sense of renewal. This was going to be one of the days he had been waiting for. The will would be read, and his right to challenge the family would be his. Although a new will had been found, dated just before Patrick died, her inheritance was as good as his, and he wasn't going to let anyone or anything spoil it. She was his, and he knew it. Bethany had confessed her love to him so many times that it couldn't be any other way. Everything he wanted was now within his grasp; it would only be a few more days.

As for Kent, he would be easy to dismiss. His daughter had had enough of him and wanted out of the marriage. With the right payoff, he was sure Kent would oblige. After all, he didn't really love his daughter, and his escapades were beginning to be too expensive for papa. He was starting to show a careless disregard for Clawson and his business. Now he would get rid of him for good and leave him without any hope of a future.

It wasn't long before a whistling, bright-eyed young man approached the breakfast table out on the veranda. "Well, it's going to be a beautiful day. Don't you think so?" Kent was in a strangely good mood, despite the disagreements they voiced the previous day. Their meetings with Verant and Ben Callis hadn't gone very well, and Kent was beginning to feel out in the cold.

Clawson had made some decisions without consulting him first, and now Kent had no idea where they were heading. Originally, they were supposed to file a petition for the rights to one-quarter of the McGillis land, Janelle's inheritance, and then split the proceeds of the sale to the mining company. That was the first deal.

Now, in the instance that Janelle was not confirmed his, Clawson had schemed to get Kelley out of the picture. Without the oldest brother, the rest of the family would crumble. Clawson had hired some people to do his bidding secretly and dispose of any evidence linking him to it. Kent had no clue as to who was doing what and/or to whom. Kent had lost all control over Clawson; not that he ever really felt that he had any, but that wasn't the point. Clawson was dealing in secrecy, and that frightened him more than anything, because once the deals have been established, someone ends up hurt or dead. He just prayed it wasn't him and continued to smile.

"Yes, I believe it will be a beautiful day. Would you care for some breakfast before we leave for the hospital? I believe Janelle is being released today, and I would like to wish her well. I know once she goes home, they won't let me within a hundred yards of her." He held out a coffee cup for him, and Kent accepted it graciously.

"I can't imagine why. You are only possibly her father and possibly in a prime position to inherit some prime land.

Do you really think that land is worth that much? That mine has been closed for years." Kent sat down opposite his father-in-law and shot him a curious look.

"I am positive there is something down there. Patrick was careful not to let things slip, but he had one weakness. Booze. If you could get him to drink, he was more than willing to let his guard down. He swore there were precious metals down there, and he was making good money off of it. Of course, to begin with, no one believes him." Clawson picked up his orange juice, took a long swallow, and then continued, "Only when he showed up with that necklace of Janelle's did anyone start believing him. We still have our doubts, but somehow he was making a fortune out of the mine. The minors were sworn to secrecy, but it wasn't coal coming out of those mines, and little by little, Patrick was coming up rich in jewels. Some of the house servants said it was coming from the mines, and he was having the stones set by a foreign broker. When the mines closed, Patrick started selling the jewelry, but the most priceless pieces he kept for his wife, and now it's Janelle's." He became silent for a moment as he pondered his ex-rival's dealings all those years ago. "I find it hard to believe that no one would have seen the jewels being transported, unless it was done at night under careful guard. If he lied to everyone, his credibility would be ruined. But that is a question that should be asked, because when the government started poking around on their land, they immediately shut it down and considered it a health hazard, and no one ever questioned it. Supposedly, it was petered out, but I intend to open it up and start digging again. I believe in my heart there is something down there that he didn't want anyone to find, other than what we hid down there."

"I think you are wasting your time. The mine has been closed for years, and no one has been down there. Even the road to the lower grounds has been fenced off with a no trespassing sign attached to the fence. Why would they hide anything down there when all of their assets are tied up elsewhere? Surely Kelley's not that irresponsible. That man wouldn't let anything or anyone out of his sight for two minutes if it meant something to him." Slightly irritated, Kent picked up his fork and plucked a strawberry from the fruit plate sitting in front of him. After swallowing the fresh and ripe little berry, he added, "Maybe you should talk to Janelle first thing this morning before anyone else gets there. She may be able to shed some light on the mines. Didn't you tell me she used to play in them when she was growing up? She may remember seeing something that would give credence to your way of thinking. If not, I think I would consider dropping the matter altogether . . . unless you have an ulterior motive that I am not aware of. Do you?" He looked sternly at Clawson, expecting him to be up front with him but should have known better.

"Oh no, my boy." He laughed at Kent's expression and innuendo. "There's no ulterior motive. But you are right, maybe I should talk to Janelle first thing." He dabbed the corner of his mouth with his napkin and called the butler. When the little man appeared, he ordered, "Please have my chauffeur meet me out front. I am going to the hospital this morning." The short man in the white uniform bowed slightly and proceeded to leave the patio. "You, son, have another meeting this afternoon, and make sure he knows what to do. I don't want to have to clean up your mess as well." Without giving Kent a chance to argue, he got up and walked off. Within the next few minutes, Clawson was being driven out the front gates, and Kent was seething as he leaned against his bedroom window, toying with the black box he had acquired last night. It wouldn't be long before he would confront Kelley about his father's scam and ruin his reputation as well. In no time at all, Mr. McGillis would be out on his rear, and Cassie would be back in his arms where she belonged. Seeing them together made him cringe, and he very nearly busted the box on the table. But it wasn't just the thought of ruining Kelley that made his mouth turn upward into an evil sneer; it was the thought of destroying his father-in-law that made it all worthwhile. "If he thinks he is getting rid of me that easily, he has another thought coming. Daddy dear will not be around much longer, and my darling wife and I will have everything we want."

*   *   *

As they lay in each other's arms, warm and contented, Kelley gently touched her face. "We need to get dressed and get you to a doctor, so he can look at your head. I didn't hurt you last night, did I?"

She was so tired from their lovemaking that she didn't raise her head to answer him. "No. You were the complete gentleman. I don't think I have the strength to walk, however. With all the excitement of last night and the gash on my head, I'm afraid my strength has left me. I don't think I can walk for a while. Would you mind if we stayed just a little longer?" She nuzzled closer to him and smiled to herself when his arm instinctively tightened around her.

"Hmmm, not at all. I usually get a little more sleep at night than this, but I had a good reason to stay awake. I had to make sure you didn't have a concussion. Right?" He grinned.

"That's right." Using her left hand, she made small circles on his flat stomach and laughed a little when he warned her not to get him started again, or they would never leave the cabin, which would not have bothered either of them a bit. In a low voice, almost a whisper, she asked, "How did you know where to find me last night?"

While his hand was stroking the back of her neck, he hesitated and took a deep breath before answering, "Rod told me you ran out back crying. He didn't know what was wrong or who had been here, but he did see a car driving away. I don't suppose you want to tell me who it was?"

"Kent." She said it so simply and matter-of-factly that he suddenly turned to stone. He wasn't sure if he wanted to hear the rest of the incident, but she continued, "He came over to find out why I left in such a hurry. He more or less accused me of being a coward for not staying and facing him, instead of turning in my resignation and leaving. I stayed long enough to hire and train someone else for an entire week. I didn't leave him totally impaired, but on top of that, he still wants me and thinks I want him. He's crazy, Kelley. He grabbed me and kissed me so hard it was like a punishment, but he hurt me." She stifled a sob, but Kelley could hear the pain in her voice.

He knew that it was time to answer a few questions before things got completely out of control. Very carefully, not wanting to hit the back of her head, where the gash had finally stopped bleeding, he moved her over and got up off the couch. Reaching for his pants, he pulled them up and zipped them as he moved over to the window behind the couch. Cassie had to turn slightly to watch his reflection in the window. She couldn't understand what she had said to make him move away from her, but he was about to surprise her.

"What's the matter?" she asked nervously.

He didn't look at her but continued to watch out the window as the sun started to move over the tops of the trees. "I know that you saw the photos in the desk drawer." He turned expressive eyes toward her as he began to explain the situation. "You have to know, Cassie, that I didn't take those pictures. I think I know who did, however, and that puts you right in the middle of all of this mess. It started right after you left Wallace Industries, and the night I ran into you was no accident." He continued to watch as a cascade of emotions cross her beautiful features. He knew she didn't understand now, but soon she would, and he wondered just how long it would take for her to leave him.

He was on the brink of explaining everything to her when the phone rang. He hesitated before picking up the receiver, because it may have been about Janelle. After a few moments, Cassie could see the anger in his eyes. Something was wrong. Janelle, dear God, what could have gone wrong? After he hung up, she asked anxiously, "What happened? Is Janelle all right?"

"Yea, she's fine. Clawson showed up, and he is visiting her right now. We have to go, and while we're at the hospital, they can check you out too. You'd better get dressed. I don't want to carry you up there in your birthday suit, because I don't have time to explain what happened last night." As quickly as she could with her head beginning to throb, she put her clothes back on and slowly stood up with his help. Kelley put the fire out, and before she could say anything, he picked her up like a small injured child and carried her out of the cabin and up the winding trail.

As they reached the edge of the veranda, Rod and Kirk met them. Rod spoke first, "Good lord, cherie, what happened to you? You had us so worried."

Kelley answered for her as he placed her on the little settee on the patio, "She was spying on someone in the mine down by the cabins. Someone has been digging for something down there, and I intend to find out who and why. Anyway, Cassie took a wrong step by the looks of it, and apparently the intruder left her for dead." He looked at her with pain in his eyes, which she couldn't imagine why, but then she had so many thoughts whirling around in her head that the headache from the wound just turned into a migraine.

Suddenly, Kirk sounded nervous, "Did she see who it was? Maybe we could catch him . . . whoever it was?" Kelley eyed him suspiciously when he stuttered his question.

"What would he be looking for, Kirk? You used to work with Verant. What would be down there of interest to him, or Clawson for that matter? If anything happens to Janelle or Cassie because of something you are mixed up in, you will regret it. Janelle is still our family, and Cassie is my friend as well as my employee. Neither one of them deserves to be harmed." He turned weary eyes to Rod and asked, "What did Mitchell say?"

"Only that you were right. There isn't much time, Kelley. Clawson knows more than he is willing to admit, and he could be pumping Janelle for answers right now."

Casting another angry glance at Kirk, Kelley turned softened eyes on Cassie. "Are you ready?" When she nodded her answer, Kelley picked her up again, and they all headed for the front of the house where a black limousine was waiting.

As they rode to the hospital, Cassie's thoughts whirled even faster. Kelley told her he knew who took the photos, and to make matters worse, he admitted he had intended to run into her that night. Closing her eyes, she laid the side of her head against the seat where the wound was not against the headrest. If he hadn't run into her by accident, then what had he been doing there? Who was he meeting besides her? She had to find out . . . soon.

CHAPTER XXIII

When they reached the hospital, Kelley helped Cassie out of the car while Kirk and Rod waited behind him. Cassie assured him she could walk into the emergency room, allowing him time to run up and check on Janelle. After making sure she would be taken care of, and the bill sent to him, he proceeded to the elevator with his brothers in tow. Cassie watched as the elevator doors closed on the three of them, and she wondered what they would find when they got upstairs.

*   *   *

As the elevator doors opened to the second floor, they could already hear the yelling coming from her room. Kelley bolted toward the door in a fit of rage, ready to strangle anyone that got in his way. Approaching the room, he could see the nurse restraining Janelle from getting out of bed. Her suitcase was on the chair, partially packed.

He stopped just inside the door and looked from the nurse to his irate sister, wondering just which one he should be mad at. "What the hell is going on here, Janelle?" Kelley's tone mirrored his confusion and irritation.

"I'm getting out of here, and don't you try to stop me! Let go of me!" She pulled her arm free of the aide's firm grasp. "Did you see him? He was here just a moment before you got here. Kelley, he thinks Dad was into smuggling. He was asking me all sorts of questions about the old mine we all used to play in. What is he talking about? I want some answers!" She was flushed and excited, and Kelley wasn't sure if he should check her out or not.

"Calm down, or I won't tell you a damn thing!" His tone defied argument, even though if looks could kill, he would have been dead at her feet. He gave the aide a calming glance, and she proceeded to leave the room. Once she had left, he explained, "We know he's hired someone to dig in the mine, but we haven't found him yet. Cassie saw him, but she fell in the mine and gave herself a beautiful gash on the back of her head. She's down in the emergency room being looked at. I don't know if she can identify him or not. Janelle, I need to know about Verant and Ben Callis." He looked her straight in the eye when he said it and wasn't surprised at her shrinking back. "Please, Janelle, I have reason to believe he is going after Cassie. I won't let him hurt her. Ben, on the other hand, is a little weasel that we can deal with on our own terms. If he is the one digging, we can get him for trespassing on private property. You and Kirk are the only ones that really knew Verant when he lived here."

Janelle looked at his pleading eyes and realized that he was in love with Cassie. She had never known him to be so possessive over any woman. He was still her brother, and that was enough to convince her. Sensing her change of heart, Kelley motioned his brothers to close the door and sit down. Janelle gave Kirk a stony glance before she stated, "Be careful, Kelley. Douglas Verant is a shadow figure. He looms out of everyone's nightmares. Kirk and I didn't realize how twisted he was until he showed up after Father died. He was suspected of killing Dad, but no one could prove it. No weapon could be found that matched the bullet type. My brother-in-law hired him as a consultant on a present deal he is working on." She paused briefly. "There is something you should know about Verant, Kelley. Your secretary,

Marguerite, was his mother. She had remarried. I saw a picture of her in his wallet and asked him about it. He didn't want to talk about her, but he said someone had killed her for no reason. I didn't ask any more questions. You don't think there is a connection here, do you?" Janelle looked worried. "You said you thought she was divulging private information. Why would she do it? And who would want to kill her?"

"I have my suspicions but no proof." He turned toward Kirk and asked, "How close can you get to Verant? We need to find out exactly what kind of game he is playing."

"I can try, but I don't think he is going to trust me now."

Kelley's eyes turned cold as he queried, "Why not?"

"I tried to keep the necklace from him." Seeing the angry looks on their faces, he continued, "He wanted me to sneak it out of the house. I tried to make a copy of it, but he took it to an appraiser's office. He told me I had one more chance to fix the situation, or someone would get hurt. Cassie ended up with a bump on the head. I swear it wasn't me, Kelley, but I know who did it. Verant himself. He made sure I knew that everything had been corrected, and I was forgiven. But somehow, I feel he is just biding his time. Everyone he deals with, who doesn't follow his rules, ends up missing. So like I said, I will try."

"How did he get in and out without the security going off?"

"Me. I agreed to turn it off for one night, and Janelle had said she left the necklace in Cassie's room to feel safer." Kirk looked baffled, "Come to think of it, he kept the fake too. That means he intends to keep the original for himself or for someone else. Jeez, Kel, he plans on double-crossing Clawson and that no-good son-in-law."

Thinking back, Kelley remembered the night Cassie had cut her hand. He had seen the basement door open and had closed it. She hadn't offered an explanation, other than cutting herself on a can, but he knew otherwise. The razor blade had been in the trashcan. Now, he knew she had been in the basement and had seen the glass that Kirk had been working with. "Lord, she doesn't even know what she saw and probably thinks I am involved. No wonder she refused to comment on anything."

Interrupting his train of thought, Rod commented, "What a mess! Mitchell said that Father and Clawson had a falling out just about the time the mine started paying off. Clawson wasn't allowed in or around the mine at any time. That's when all the talk about the smuggling started, because one of the minors started talking. He mentioned something about jewels being buried in the cave, not having been found there. Clawson swore it was a scam from then on and swore he would confront our father." Rod looked around at his brothers and sister. "What if Clawson killed our father? He has a gun collection. We all know that."

"True, but he wouldn't be naive enough to leave a murder weapon in his own home. On another thought, he wants that land bad enough to kill for it. Sorry, Janelle," he apologized for being inconsiderate of her feelings. "We have another problem now. That's the paternity. What if she really is Father's? What would Clawson do then?"

"That's what bothers me. He really believes she belongs to him and is attempting to use that as leverage for control of her birthright. He is using any means of persuasion for the rights to the land. It looks like we will have to formulate a plan ourselves." He stopped for a moment, pulled out his wallet, extracted a business card, and asked for the phone. Within a few moments, he had called and asked for a meeting. "Now, we wait."

*　　*　　*

A black Geo Prism with tinted windows pulled into the public park and stopped behind one of the picnic shelters. With an envelope full of cash, the occupant of the vehicle waited impatiently for someone who should have completed his assignment and disposed of all the evidence. This person, however, was late. As nervous fingers tapped the minutes by, anxious eyes scanned the park for any signs of his employee. The scowl that crossed his forehead marked his frustration and anger at being stood up. He hated to be the one waiting when he was the one giving the orders.

The job should have been done quickly and quietly, and no one would trace the accident to them. It had all seemed so simple to begin with, but because of some unforeseen events, the time for revenge had come sooner than expected. Once his well-laid plans had come to fruition, he could dispose of all of his problems at once, and no one would suspect him. The evidence would all point to McGillis. The thought of seeing McGillis pay for his father's dealings was enough to turn his scowl into a wicked grin and an evil glare in his sinister eyes.

Holding his gaze steadily, he watched as the old Ford pickup truck rattled across the parking lot. He watched as it rounded the park and stopped short of his waiting car. The driver of the truck got out and approached the car. Lowering the windows, the man asked, "Well, is everything where it's supposed to be?"

"Yes, sir. It will only take a phone call to make the authorities aware of the body. No one will even miss the man. He was one of the best informants I have ever worked with. The forged mining records should be found with the body. There should be quite a scandal. Is that satisfactory?" The man looked around himself nervously, half expecting to see Mounties behind him. Turning his gaze back to the man in the car, he waited for his answer.

"Perfect. I believe the price we agreed on was $50,000. Enjoy it. You have done well, and I hope we can do business again someday." He smiled devilishly as he handed the envelope to the scruffy-looking man and added, "Have you seen Verant, Mr. Callis?"

"No. Come to think of it, he didn't show up this morning to help me. I checked on his room at the hotel, but there was no answer." He looked perplexed, but the man in the car said nothing to ease his tension.

"Thank you, I'm sure he will show up for his money eventually. He was supposed to deliver something valuable to me this afternoon. I will see him then. Go home now, we are finished, Mr. Callis." He watched with stony eyes as the old codger returned to his truck and drove out of the park. Once the vehicle had disappeared, the man in the car picked up his cell phone and dialed emergency services. "Yes, I would like to report a truck on fire outside the Angle Ball Park." As he hung up, the blast was heard throughout the neighborhood, and the Geo Prism disappeared out the rear entrance to the park.

*　　*　　*

Cassie had just finished up with the emergency room and was in the process of having her prescription filled at the hospital pharmacy when someone walked up behind her. She turned, smiling, expecting to see Kelley behind her, but to her shock and horror, it was Kent. Stuttering, she exclaimed, "What do you want? I thought I made myself clear yesterday."

"Yes, you did. I just wanted to apologize. My behavior was inexcusable, and I would like to make it up to you. I also need to talk to you. Can I buy you a cup of coffee?" His sincerity stunned her into a momentary silence.

"I guess so. There is a coffee shop in the hospital."

"Actually, we need to talk privately. I have information about my father-in-law that is important to you and your boss. There is a coffee shop a little ways down the street. Can we go there?" His tone was a little agitated and caused Cassie to hesitate.

"I don't know. Kelley will be coming down for me shortly. I would hate to be gone when he gets here. I am under orders not to go anywhere." Still, Kent seemed to be genuine in his request. Maybe she owed him a few moments. She looked over her shoulders, hoping to see Kelley come through the doors to rescue her, but no such luck.

Following her gaze to the doors behind her, he added, "I don't think he will be looking for you for a while. Mick upset Janelle badly this time. It might interest you to know that Mick and I don't always approve of the same methods. However, that will not be the case for very long. Things will change soon." His comment and blank stare went unnoticed by Cassie as she pondered her options.

"Well, maybe it will be all right if we only take a few minutes." He nodded his answer, and she followed him out of the doors under the scrutiny of the security guard.

Kent helped her into his car and headed down the road. When they reached the first light, he commented, "You know, it's such a beautiful day; why don't we just drive around for a while? I could show you some of the sights while we talk. How's that?"

"No, Kent. I agreed to talk to you over coffee, so that's what we will do!" She was fast becoming agitated as they rode out of town. He was not stopping for coffee, and she felt like a heel for believing him. She was so willing to put things right she hadn't thought about what he might be up to. Now, she was at his mercy and prayed Kelley was missing her right now.

CHAPTER XXIV

Mr. Mitchell followed behind the McGillises as Janelle proceeded to check herself out of the hospital. Once the papers were signed, Kelley asked his younger brothers to escort her home. In the process of their leaving, however, an ambulance came screaming up to the emergency room entrance. The emergency personnel were in high gear as a burn victim was wheeled into the corridor.

Standing aside to let the EMTs by, Kelley accidentally brushed the cart, causing some things to fall out of the victim's pocket or what was left of it. Very carefully he picked the things up and turned them over in his hand. As his eyes rested on the charred license, his eyes shot up to the room the cart had disappeared into. "Mitchell, that was Ben Callis, and I am almost sure he didn't set himself on fire! Look at this, there has to be at least forty thousand dollars here. A payment for services rendered, you think?"

Mitchell took the singed papers from Kelley's hand and examined them. "I don't doubt it. But who would go to those lengths to keep him quiet and then kill him anyway? This is one sick person we are dealing with. We need to get a warrant and search Clawson's home and business. I have a feeling someone is getting antsy." Mitchell hurriedly approached a public phone and called the police station. Within a few moments, he hung the phone up and looked at Kelley. "We have a witness to the burning, but we are going to have to move fast. There are a couple of Mounties going to Clawson's home and office with search warrants. We should hopefully find something that will nail him. Let's go!"

"I will be with you shortly. I need to check on Cassie. She should have been out of there an hour ago. I have a terrible feeling that she isn't in the hospital." Kelley walked over to the receptionist and asked if she had seen a young woman of Cassie's description, but the brown-eyed girl didn't recall seeing her.

But when Mitchell asked the security guard about her, he responded, "Yes, sir. She left with some blonde-headed man about forty-five minutes ago. They left in a black Geo Prism with tinted windows. I believe they headed out of town."

"Thank you." Mitchell relayed the information to Kelley, who swore under his breath as he raced out the doors with Mitchell close behind. As they got into Mitchell's car, Kelley explained what had happened and began to fear for Cassie's life.

*   *   *

Cassie was getting more and more nervous as they proceeded out of Canmore. They drove along Highway 1A for quite some time before Cassie could attempt to ask where they were headed. "I thought you might like to take the scenic route home. I am taking you around the town of Banff to the Sulphur Mountain. I figured the gondola ride would provide enough privacy for us to talk. How does that sound?" His wicked smile did little to ease her shattered senses. "Don't worry. They won't miss you for a while, I promise.

"Did you know that commercial and industrial growth have practically taken over the town of Canmore? The mines have all primarily been shut down, but with Mick's money and Janelle's approval, I plan to open a new section of land and start my own mining empire. Once Mick is out of my way, I should have no problem." He turned the car off the highway and entered the Banff city limits.

Having no idea what he was talking about, Cassie asked, "Is Mr. Clawson leaving?"

"Oh, eventually."

"Really? That's quite an announcement. I would think he would stick around to start more trouble for Kel . . . Mr. McGillis." She knew he heard her mistake but avoided his eyes.

"Please, Cassie. I know you and McGillis are lovers. It shows on his face every time you two are together. He thinks he loves you, but I don't believe that will last much longer. He has plenty of skeletons in his closet, and I intend to bring them out." He looked over at her and sighed, "I really think you should come back to work for me, Cassie. We could make a big dent in the new mining business and take those McGillises to the cleaners in the process. You and me, we belong together, and my present wife is always taking trips. She already knows how I feel about you, and she has her lovers to keep her company. Once dear old Dad kicks the bucket, I can divorce her and take over the business. She has no interest in keeping it, so why not?"

"Do you really think I would want you back after all the hell you put me through? How can you be so brash? There isn't a chance in hell of me ever going back. I like it just fine where I am, or haven't I proved that already?" She sent him a quizzical look.

"He will never settle down, Cassie. He is strictly business, face it. I know he followed you to the conservatory that night. Did he tell you why?" All of a sudden, she got a terrible feeling she had walked into a nightmare and couldn't escape.

"How do you know he followed me? You were supposed to be on your honeymoon." She was completely terrified now. The only way he could have known about that chance meeting was if he had been there himself.

"Ah, well, my new wife had other plans, so we stayed there for a few weeks. While she tended to her other business, I settled some of my affairs. Little did I know that you would bolt on me in record time. You couldn't wait for me to explain things, could you?" When she failed to answer him, he repeated, "Could you?"

"No. I didn't think there was any need to argue the matter. I felt you had made your choice, but I wasn't going to be there for you to rub my nose in it. Could we please turn around and go back now? I think we have been gone long enough." She was sitting as far over in the seat as she could get, as if she expected him to lash out at her. He apparently noticed her distress.

"I told you not to worry. I can't manhandle you and drive at the same time. Besides, I have other arrangements for us." He winked at her and then concentrated on driving.

Cassie eased a little but still kept a safe distance from him. She wished now that she hadn't listened to him. Kelley was going to kill her himself for putting herself in this position. He had ordered her to stay put, and she had directly disobeyed him. How long, she wondered, would it take for him to realize she was gone? She laid her head back and closed her eyes, willing herself to remain calm.

*   *   *

Kelley watched out the window in turmoil as Mitchell swerved in and out of traffic, hoping to catch a glimpse of the Geo. If Wallace was as bad as Kelley had told him, Cassie could be in real danger and not even know it. As wild thoughts raced through both their minds, the CB radio blared, "Calling Ron Mitchell, code—" Mitchell picked up the mike and responded, "This is Mitchell, go ahead."

"The black Geo with tinted windows was seen approaching the Sulphur Mountain in Banff, over."

"That's a ten-four. Thank you very much." Mitchell looked across at Kelley and tried to make him relax. "We are going to find her, and she will be fine."

"I'd feel better if she were here now. She knew better. I can't understand why she would attempt to leave with him after what happened yesterday. Did the guard say if she was forced to leave?" He was hoping the guard had missed something, and she had been abducted.

"No. But there could be another reason. It's possible he's trying to convince her that you're the guilty party. He knew that you would be busy with Janelle, so he probably planned this ahead of time." Before Kelley could reply, the radio blared again. "Code . . . stolen necklace found on estate, address East Barely Drive, Canmore."

"Isn't that Clawson's address?" Mitchell asked quizzically.

"Yes, it is. But right now, we are looking for Cassie. Have my brothers contacted to pick up the necklace and arrest the son of a bitch!" He was so intent on finding Cassie that the necklace didn't seem all that important. She was the most important thing to him, and he wasn't about to lose her now.

"Dispatch, contact the McGillis family to pick up the necklace at the station, and hold Mick Clawson for questioning. I want to talk to him, over." He held the mike in his hand, waiting for confirmation. "Well, we now have the necklace, but somehow I don't think we have Clawson where we want him. As soon as we find Cassie and Wallace, we need to head back to the station and run Clawson through the ringer."

"Mitchell, respond . . . ," the radio dispatch interrupted, "the sergeant wants you back now. Clawson wants to negotiate." Kelley and Mitchell exchanged glances, and Mitchell picked up the mike, "Coming in. Please have a Mountie follow black Geo Prism, but do not have them approach subject until I am there, copy?"

"Copy . . . ten-four."

"Sorry, man. If Clawson wants to talk, there's nothing I can do."

"I am coming with you."

"That's not a good idea. You two are sworn enemies, and he might clam up if he knows you are there," he tried to thwart him.

"No way, I deserve some answers, and I want to hear them."

Sensing that arguing would be a lost cause, the detective caved. "All right. But stay behind the glass, and keep out of sight. I have a feeling we could blow the lid off this case once and for all." When Kelley agreed to stay out of sight, Mitchell turned the car around and headed back toward headquarters. He hoped that Cassie could hold out for just a little longer. If she played her cards right, Mitchell didn't think Wallace would hurt her, but he wasn't sure.

*　　*　　*

Before they had reached the mountain, police had stopped traffic due to a bear sighting. There were two black bears attempting to cross the road before the entrance to the ride. Cassie opened her eyes and watched as they held everyone back to allow the bears to proceed into the woods. Once the bears were gone, traffic was allowed to move. When they entered the Sulphur Mountain parking lot, Cassie was amazed to see hundreds of people crowding their way in and out of the terminal to the gondola. Kent parked the car, got out, and ran around to open the door for Cassie. Helping her out, he whispered in her ear, "Come on!" He sounded like a child who had just been awarded the first prize in a contest. Cassie, on the other hand, tried to remain detached. When he tried to take her arm, she flinched and pulled back a little. The face he shot her forced her to allow him the pleasure of touching her. All she could do was grin and bear it.

They entered the building and stood in line for what seemed an hour but was actually only a few minutes. As the gondola ascended the mountain, a Mountie on horseback radioed the tower on the top of the mountain and continued his surveillance on the ground below. Within the confines of the gondola, Kent sat next to Cassie, and three other people sat across from them. The other occupants seemed jubilant and wanting to talk, asking all kinds of questions. Keeping silent, Cassie allowed Kent to answer all their questions and cringed inwardly at his responses. He had the gall to tell them they were just married. Even though it was just a front, she couldn't help but feel sick at the thought of being this close to him.

The ride came to a slow halt at the top of the mountain, and the excited family exited first. Once out on the walkway, Cassie felt his hand on her elbow again as he guided her around the sturdy deck. "Do you believe we are standing over seven thousand feet above sea level? It's amazing." He shot her a guarded look, almost as if he were assessing her mood. "What I said earlier, Cassie, I meant it. We could be great together. All you have to do is come back with me. Once I take care of family business, we can start all over again."

Studying her surroundings, looking for the fastest exit, she asked, reminding him, "I thought you said you had something on Clawson."

Turning blank eyes on her, he answered, "Oh, I do, but let's not talk about that now. What I want to know is what Kelley told you the night you met."

"I don't know what you are talking about. He didn't say anything to me, except apologize for running into me. He invited me to dinner, offered me a job, and I accepted. Could you please tell me what this is all about, because I really should be getting back? I know he has to be looking for me now, and my head is throbbing." She tried to sound as if she were getting bored with the question-and-answer session.

"Yes, well, you should know better than to walk around dark caves. It can be hazardous." Through her drug-induced haze, the horror of his words sank in. The blurry shadow in the mine had been his, and she hadn't recognized him. She knew she had to get away from him, now.

"You're right. I will have to be more careful. Anyway, are you going to tell me what you really want, or are you going to keep me guessing? I hardly think you brought me up here just to tell me you want me back." She turned toward the railing around the deck and leaned against it to steady herself. She was feeling more and more woozy, and she didn't want to be left alone with him.

"I need your help, Cassie. Kelley has some files, incriminating files, which could destroy my business. He has been blackmailing me for a long time, and you are my only hope in getting them back. He would never suspect you of taking them, and I would make it worth your while. Please, it could save my neck—and yours." Cassie didn't want to save his neck, but she hadn't considered Kelley blackmailing anyone. Until now, she had never really questioned his business, but that was before she had found the photos of herself in his study. He had been on the verge of telling her about them when the phone had rung, and he had forgotten the matter. He had been hiding the file from her, and now, she had every right to question his motives. Still, she couldn't accuse him without hearing his explanation first.

"I can't believe he would blackmail you, Kent. He isn't the type to stoop to that level. Take me back! I want to go back!" Cassie started to walk in the direction of the gondola when he grabbed her arm.

He pulled her to him and held her there as he whispered, "Don't make a mistake, Cassie. It cost Marguerite her life, and now you are headed down the same path. I don't want to have to hurt you, but if you push me . . ." Cassie had grown stone cold at his words. He was threatening her and admitting to killing Marguerite. She had to escape before he said anything else.

Tearing herself away from him, she hurried through the crowd without looking where she was going. She could feel a tingling sensation along her spine, as if he were right behind her. She pushed herself through a group of tourists and headed down the steps, into the wooded area below the gondola station. There was a trail that led off to her left, and she proceeded to run down the steep slope, brushing past everyone that had chosen to walk.

Not even halfway down, she came to a breathless halt. There was a little shelter with a wooden seat in it. Cassie entered the building and sat down for a moment. Between the altitude, medicine, and sheer panic, she felt weak and tired but compelled herself to continue. She tried violently to convince herself she could make it down, but it was no use. She made it to the door of the small hut and dropped. Darkness enveloped her before she could escape.

CHAPTER XXV

Sitting behind the two-way mirror, Kelley listened intently to everything that Clawson said. He answered each question that his lawyer allowed and agreed to plead guilty to several charges in exchange for testimony against his son-in-law. He told about the smuggling and conspiracy to commit the murder of McGillis's father, but Verant was the one that did the actual killing. The artifacts and jewels had all been buried in the mines. Apparently, Patrick had found out what they were up to and tried to stop them, and Clawson hired Verant to dispose of the problem. Ben Callis was supposed to dig up the jewels and the artifacts for him and bring them in without anyone noticing. But Miss Garrett had interfered in the dig, and when she was injured, Ben panicked and fled. Everything was working perfectly. Callis and Verant were supposed to bring home the goods and were to be paid well. Clawson was hoping that Janelle was his, so he could pass the business on to her, but paternity hadn't been settled yet. Also, with her as his heiress, he could lay partial claim on her property. Clawson hadn't realized how greedy his son-in-law had become, until the necklace and the green folder with the plan to double-cross him was found in his room. He had apparently snapped under pressure and now could be considered dangerous.

As Kelley sat there in stunned silence listening to his confession, an armed officer entered the room and handed the sergeant a slip of paper. He looked at Kelley with blank eyes and said, "They found Verant with a bullet in his chest an hour ago. He is still alive in ICU. They don't expect him to survive. It appears that Mr. Wallace is getting rid of his connections. They matched the slug in Verant with the slug that killed your secretary." He turned his grim expression toward the waiting Mounty and issued a warrant for Wallace's arrest. "Consider him armed and dangerous, and there may be a possibility of a hostage. Proceed with caution." The Mounty nodded and proceeded to fill out the warrant. Once everything was done, a group of Mounties was dispatched to search for him. While they were leaving, another gentleman came through the door.

Jamison.

"Kelley, I called your house with some news but was told I would find you here. I just thought you would like to know my lawyer called me. The results of the blood test are in." He held Kelley's gaze with relief in his eyes. "She's Patrick's. I just thought you would like to know. They really hustled to get the results out, considering the predicament that she is in." He shook his hand and congratulated him.

"Thank you, Matt. I know Mother meant a lot to you. No one ever suspected her feelings for you, except Father, but you were still considered a friend of the family. You will always be welcome. Right now, however, we have to find Cassie. Mick's son-in-law has her, and he is considered dangerous."

"I just saw him following an ambulance."

Before Matt could say anything else, Kelley had disappeared out the station doors with Mitchell close behind. They sped through traffic as the plainclothes detective radioed the hospital and found that no one had been admitted. He forwarded the call to the Banff hospital, and no one was there either, but one of the Mounties that had been tailing them called back to say that the young lady had collapsed at the Sulphur Mountain. Instead of taking the ride down, she had started running down the steep slope and had fallen victim to the altitude and effects of medication. Emergency personnel had carried her down the mountain, and Mr. Wallace had told them he would take her to the hospital himself.

When they left the mountain, other Mounties had followed them back to Canmore, but instead of going to the hospital or the Clawson estate, he proceeded down the road, past the McGillis estate entrance. His car was parked along the side of the road, and he was seen carrying someone down a lane connecting the guesthouses with the main house.

Kelley didn't have to hear anymore, because he knew exactly where he was going and why. He told Mitchell how to approach the grounds without being spotted by Wallace. "It might be best if we park up by the house and walk down the dirt path. If we took the cobblestone path, he would hear us coming, depending on how deep he is in the mine."

"I agree." He radioed, "Everyone, hold your positions. We are going to attempt to enter the mine from the front. No one is to shoot until the woman is safely out of the mine . . . over. Do you think he would hurt Cassie? I thought Clawson said he was still in love with her."

"In his state of mind, anyone is a threat, and if she provokes him, I am not sure what his reaction will be. She could reject his advances, and then he would retaliate as if she were just like Marguerite." He thought about it for a moment and then asked, "If he was on his honeymoon, how did he kill Marguerite? They would have had to have been in town without anyone knowing."

Mitchell calmly supplied the answer, "There was rumor that they knew Mrs. Wallace had another engagement, and her wedding only delayed it. She was seen socializing in Calgary the day after the wedding. It's quite possible that he flew back that day and confronted Marguerite. According to a diary she kept, she refused to steal any more documents after you caught her copying them. He threatened her and continued to stalk her. The day she died, she was carrying some potentially damaging information."

"That's when she called me to meet her there. He got there before me and killed her. Damn! I wonder how many files he took before I located her. The Mounties found several files in Wallace's room at the estate, but they didn't say which ones." Mitchell turned off the highway and turned onto a side road until the main entrance to the estate came into view.

"There's a dirt path that starts halfway down the driveway. Right there. Park here, and we can walk down." The detective parked the car and killed the engine. Checking his revolver, he got out of the vehicle and followed Kelley down the path. When they were in sight of the mine, they saw Rod and Kirk approaching from the main walkway.

Kelley moved into their view and motioned for them to stay back. He snuck around the yard, watching for movement in the mine, as he maneuvered his way over to his brothers. "Stay here. Mitchell and I are going in after them. We want to get Cassie out of there before Wallace kills her. I know what he is after, but he is not going to make it out of there."

Rod and Kirk eyed each other and then smiled at Kelley. "Don't worry, dear brother. The treasure isn't down there." Kelley looked at them, confused. With a look of approval, Kirk explained, "After bringing Janelle home, we did some searching. We found where they had been digging, and boy, oh boy, did we hit pay dirt. We not only found smuggled artifacts, but we found documents that were designed to implicate you and Father in the smuggling operation. All the names have been forged, and there was a letter from Janelle's husband to the officials, telling them everything. He was on the verge of spilling the beans about the operation, but I guess Wallace wasn't ready to come clean. What I don't understand is why would he hurt Cassie? She didn't know any of this. She was completely innocent."

"He doesn't know it. He expects her to know as much as Marguerite did." They looked at him with questioning eyes. "Yes, he killed her, and he thinks I have given Cassie specific information, but this time I kept it to myself. I thought I was protecting her." He wished now he hadn't left her alone in the hospital. Silently, he prayed that he would still have the chance to explain everything to her and tell her he loved her.

*   *   *

Cassie stirred a little and opened her eyes to find darkness all around her. Panicking, she forced herself to sit up and realized she was sitting in the mineshaft. The throbbing in her head was blinding, but she willed herself to keep her eyes open. She could barely make out the light coming from the torch; shakily, she got to her feet. In the dimly lit area, a large shadow loomed in front of her.

"Well, I see you made it. You should know better than to push yourself like that, especially when you are not used to the altitude. It can play havoc on a person. As soon as I dig up the files and artifacts, we are set for life, dear. We will be able to go anywhere. Money will be no object." He kept digging and digging. When he dug far enough, he swore to himself, "Where the hell is it? It was here last night."

"Last night? You were here last night. What's going on, Kent? I don't understand what's gotten into you." She pleaded with him as her eyes focused finally on the gun that lay to the right of him—the .45 revolver. Wrapping her arms around herself, she had tears in her eyes as she lowered herself to the ground along the wall. She had to get the gun from him.

Keeping her voice as calm as she could, she kept his mind occupied by asking questions. "What are you planning on doing when you retrieve whatever you are looking for? What are you going to do with me?" Inch by inch, she scooted across the dirt floor, closer and closer to the revolver.

"Well, I am not quite sure yet. We have to find them first. I can't understand it. No one knew they were here."

He was getting frustrated and angry, so Cassie knew she had to act fast.

"Keep him talking," she thought to herself. "Is Marguerite the only one you killed? She wouldn't have turned you in, Kent. She was a good woman, from what I heard. And what about your father-in-law and your wife? If you killed them, the law would hunt you down. Please don't do this, Kent. I am begging you."

"Spare me. You have already proved whose bed you prefer . . . but that will change once we are out of the country." He looked up at her, and the wanton look in his eyes convinced her he was definitely close to the breaking point. "We were good together once, and we will be again. I have connections that will guarantee us a good life." She could feel the sweat running down her back as she moved closer to the gun. He had returned to his digging and wasn't paying attention to her. She was on the point of reaching for the gun when a hand snaked out and grabbed her wrist.

"Oh no, you don't. I am making sure I have a way out of here, and you are my perfect weapon against everyone. With you beside me, they won't touch me. Now, let's move back against the wall, shall we?" His grasp was hard and firm as he pushed her back down on the dirt floor. Scratching his head, he surmised, "Maybe you told someone it was down here. You knew we were digging here." He looked at her for a moment and then reached for her arm again. "You ratted me out, didn't you? I guess I was wrong about you. You are just like Marguerite. The richer the boss, the better the prize." His disgusted look was enough to make her fidgety.

"I don't know what you are talking about. I didn't know it was you down here until this afternoon when you told me. I swear it. I still don't want to believe all this time it was you. You had me followed, didn't you?"

"Yes and no. I had you followed once you got to Canmore, but I had to get rid of Verant, because he double-crossed me. He was supposed to deliver Janelle's necklace to me.

But instead, he tried to be coy and gave me cut glass. If I hadn't taken it to an inspector, I wouldn't have known the difference. But I think he paid for it. I can assure you, he won't be talking for the rest of his life." His laugh was startling and made her stomach churn inside.

Placing her hands over her ears, she yelled, "I don't want to hear anymore! You're crazy, Kent. This was never like you. You have become maniacal, and I want no part of you or this smuggling operation." Out of the corner of her eye, she caught sight of a small shadow growing larger in the torchlight. Knowing who was out there, she kept him diverted. "I'm getting out of here, Kent. I think you should do this alone, without me. I am in love with Kelley, not you." After she said it, she realized her mistake. Her matter-of-fact statement infuriated him. He became violent and slapped her across the cheek, which caused her to fall back against the tunnel wall.

Holding her cheek, she regained her footing and went to sidestep him, but he refused to let her go. His arms steeled around her, so she couldn't move, and she began to panic. Screaming, she pushed with all her might and in the process tripped over the shovel he had laid by the ditch. Landing with a hard thump, she raised her eyes to her horror in front of the barrel of the gun. "No, please, Kent. You don't know what you are doing."

He was on the verge of pulling the trigger when another light caught his attention. He raised his gun, but Cassie wasn't about to sit still. She bolted upright and lunged for the gun at the same time it went off. She barely heard the other shots as she fell to the floor. The last thing she remembered was hearing Kelley say, "Hold on, sweetheart. I love you." Then darkness.

CHAPTER XXVI

What seemed an eternity in sleep was only a few days. When Cassie awoke from the gunshot wound to her stomach, missing her lungs by a half inch, it was to find herself back in Indiana at the women's hospital. Stable after a long bout with infection, she was now able to sit up and drink liquids. She was told it would be a slow recovery, due to the severity of the injury. Her next question was how had she gotten there? And where was Kelley?

No one knew anything, but her parents showed up to help her recover. They waited on their only daughter, hand and foot. Whatever she wanted they got for her, but even they were at a loss when she asked where her boss was. As the days turned into a couple of weeks, there was no word from anyone, not even to check on her progress. Cassie felt deflated on the day she was released and her parents were the only ones that showed up.

After making sure she was comfortable and had the proper nourishment, they said their goodbyes and headed home. Cassie felt humiliated that the man she loved hadn't bothered to call her or at least call the hospital. She thought she had heard him say he loved her. But even that was fuzzy. She looked around the apartment and decided to get up for a little while. All the lying around was finally getting to her. She was going to go stir crazy if she had to stay in and look at the four walls for another minute. Fighting the wave of nausea, she lifted her coat slowly and wrapped it around her small frame. "The fresh air will do me some good." She turned her head and hoped the phone would ring before she left. Nothing. She opened the door then closed it gently behind her.

The pace was slow but soothing. She measured each step as a step to recovery. She wouldn't go far, maybe around the public park. Before she reached the park, however, she found herself changing her direction and heading toward the conservatory. Despite the events of the past few months, it was still her favorite place to be. The smell of peat moss, dirt, and flowers combined to soothe her shattered and scarred senses. She had lived through a nightmare, and she wished through heartfelt tears that the man she loved were there with her. As the tears flowed, her body stiffened at the sound of footsteps behind her.

Slowly, she turned around, half expecting to find herself in front of another gun. But through tear-filled lashes, she could make out the muscular frame of Kelley. He was standing four feet from her, holding a file folder in his hands. He laid the folder on the flower ledge and walked over to her. Raising his hand, he gently stroked her hair and the side of her moist cheek, brushing away the tears that had spilled out. Before either one of them said anything, they were in each other's arms. All the passion that had been suppressed over the last couple months had surfaced and refused to be quenched. The only thing that kept them from falling to the ground in each other's arms was the small whimper that Cassie made. Frowning a little, he stepped back.

"I'm sorry, Cassie. I wanted to be here for you, but Clawson's trial date was set. The lawyers needed depositions, and we had to stay until everyone's side was told. God, what they did to you! I hope Clawson rots in jail for this. Once he goes, he could be eligible for parole in twenty years, because of the plea bargain." Wanting to feel her close to him, he pulled her into his arms and laid her head gently against his shoulder. As he held her, he gently rocked her, wanting to erase the past few months from her memory but knew he couldn't. They would have to deal with it day by day.

Standing there, embraced by him, Cassie finally summoned up enough strength to ask, "What about . . . ," she faltered, "what about Kent?"

Releasing her slightly, he moved her back a little to look into her sad eyes. "Dead. Mitchell shot him after he fired on you. He died instantly. That is one man I don't think I will miss. He caused you a lot of pain, and for that I'm glad he's gone. The damage he's done is irreversible, but we will make it." He pulled her back to his chest, holding her as if he thought she would dissolve into thin air.

Cassie felt relief and security in his arms, but she had questions that remained unanswered. Now she wanted closure. Very weakly, her frail voice was almost inaudible as she questioned him, "Kent admitted to having me followed. What did you mean by 'our meeting was not accidental'? And where did those photos come from?" She eased herself out of his arms when she felt his frame become rigid and propped herself up against a trestle.

He dropped his arms down to his sides as he turned around to pick up the folder. Opening it, he looked down at the photos of them together and of her walking down the street. "I didn't take these, Cassie. Verant did. Apparently, Mr. Wallace hired him to follow you, and when things started to go bad, he, Verant, decided to use them as leverage to get to me. I wasn't giving in to any of their demands, so they sought to use you as a bargaining chip. They figured if you were working with me, you would have access to all the business files. Little did they know that I had sealed the files that Marguerite had been secretly stashing. Her only fault was that she needed the money, but your ex decided that she couldn't bow out. He knew that Verant wouldn't dispose of her, because as it turns out, she is Verant's mother. She remarried, so she had a different last name. No one knew, not even me. She was supposed to meet with me the night she was killed. By the time I had gotten here, she was already dead. I called 911 and waited, claiming that I was just enjoying the scenery. They couldn't prove otherwise.

"The files, I confiscated before anyone arrived. I knew then that Clawson and Mr. Wallace were in cahoots with each other, but I didn't realize how rocky their relationship was until just recently. I had notified the Canadian officials of my findings, and they were being monitored. Then came you.

"Word had it you were supposed to have been his mainstay, and then he turned and married Clawson's daughter. Well, when you left their employment, I hired Mitchell, a plainclothes detective, to follow you. It was for your own protection, as well as for my benefit. I knew you had gone to the conservatory frequently with Mr. Wallace, and when you had gone the night after the murder, I decided to make my move. Little did I know what chain of events would follow." He closed the folder and handed it to her.

She held the folder close to her chest as she digested everything. It was all so overwhelming. "All that time, Kent and his father-in-law had been smuggling jewels and artwork into the country and selling it on the black market. But why kill your father and Janelle's husband—his own brother?" She made a horrified face as she thought about his carelessness for his own family.

"My father found out what they were doing and confronted Clawson. He had been starting rumors that my father was the one smuggling years ago. When the mine closed, no one ever went down there, so that's where they hid all the stolen merchandise. When the smuggling had started, we were pretty well grown up and out on our own. We had stopped playing in the mines, because Father had declared them off limits and unsafe. It was free and clear for them to hide their contraband. So one day, Father came upon someone digging in the mine. They were burying some confidential documents. Verant is the one that shot him at point-blank range. I didn't know anything about it until Rod told me, well, you know when . . ."

"And Janelle's husband?"

"Kent had found a letter written by him, addressed to the Canadian Mounties. He couldn't let things blow up yet. He had to make sure he had enough dirt on Clawson to blackmail him. In the end, however, I think he would have tried to kill him too. He was killing them one by one, but he messed up twice. First, Verant is still alive with a hole in his chest but in a maximum-security prison. And second, Clawson decided to turn state witness. He was willing to take some of the rap but let his son-in-law take the fall. In the end, I think Clawson felt defeated, because of the paternity test." The look on her face mirrored her confusion. "As it turns out, Janelle is our sister. No one can argue that now. So everyone got what they wanted or deserved." His eyes penetrated hers as he ended, "Except you. You got the worst part of it. You were shot, and it was my fault."

"Your fault?" she sounded confused. "You couldn't have known this would happen. The one thing I don't understand, though, is what Janelle was looking for in the trunk that she couldn't find."

"Janelle claimed there was a letter from Mother in her trunk, but no one had found it until after Janelle got married. I came across it while we were moving her stuff out. I didn't think Father would keep it, so I hid it in the wall and marked it with the knife blade. You almost found it. I am only sorry that I couldn't be here with you when you woke up. I felt compelled to send you back home, so that your family could take care of you, until I could get there. I know now that I can't live without you."

As the tears welled up again, she queried, "What about Charisse? I thought you two were lovers."

"Never! I could never love Charisse, and I think she knows it. I believe that she has actually transferred her affections for me over to Rod. She hasn't left his side since the ordeal in the mine. The only person I could ever love is you."

Cassie's eyes stung with happy and sad tears at the same time. "Oh, Kelley, there would be no way I could blame anything on you. I love you too." The air between them seemed to crackle with electricity. The acknowledgment of their love for each other consumed both of them. They both held their breath, each afraid to move for fear of breaking the bond between them. Suddenly, she was in his arms, and he was kissing her wildly. The photos scattered in the dirt at their feet.

Holding her steady, trying not to hurt her stomach, Kelley cuddled her to him in a possessive embrace. As their lips briefly parted, he whispered, "I'm not letting you go anymore. From now on you will always be by my side."

Smiling into his eyes, she said, "I wouldn't want to be anywhere else."

Edwards Brothers Malloy
Oxnard, CA USA
December 23, 2014